QUITTING THE HERO BIZ
Neighborlee Book 6

Michelle L. Levigne

Two Olde
Dragons
Writing
Wynd
Stories

Ye Olde Dragon Books

www.YeOldeDragonBooks.com

Previously released as *Hero Blues*, 2016
Revised

Ye Olde Dragon Books
P.O. Box 30802
Middleburg Hts., OH 44130

www.YeOldeDragonBooks.com

2OldeDragons@gmail.com

Copyright © 2020 by Michelle L. Levigne
ISBN 13: 978-1-952345-12-8

Published in the United States of America
Publication Date: March 1, 2021

Cover Art Copyright by Ye Olde Dragon Books 2020

Welcome to Neighborlee, Ohio.

Where? Somewhere on the North Coast of Ohio, south of Cleveland, right off I-71, north of Medina, in the heart of Cuyahoga County.

What is it? That's a little harder to explain.

Neighborlee is a place you need to experience.

The most important thing you need to understand: Neighborlee is *magic*. Some people say the town is alive. It exists to protect the weird and wonderful (and sometimes a little bit scary) from the cold, practical, material world.

More important, Neighborlee protects the outside world from the weird and wonderful that come to visit ... and sometimes come to stay.

First stop: Divine's Emporium, a four-story Victorian house sitting on a hill overlooking the Metroparks. Whatever you really need, you can find at Divine's. Even if you don't know what you're looking for when you walk in the door. The shop is often bigger inside than it is outside. Angela is the proprietor. Please stay on the first floor. You don't want to find out what is hidden and locked safely away upstairs. Like Aslan, Angela is good, but that doesn't mean she's safe. And neither are the secrets and wonders and doorways to other worlds that she protects ... and keeps securely locked.

Come in and explore. Meet the people who help Angela guard Neighborlee. Share their adventures of magic and wonder, danger and sacrifice. You never know who or what you'll run into as you walk the streets and listen to the stories of their lives.

Chapter One

"Talk about returning to the scene of the crime." Jane paused on the sidewalk in front of the Sipping Post, a friendly-looking café on the main street running through the shopping/business district of Neighborlee. She looked up and down the street, waiting for that sense of recognition and memory she had expected to haunt her.

Nothing. No shiver. No sense of two images snapping into place, reality versus hazy memories. No sense of guilty anticipation. After all these years, Jane had the task of the twice-yearly check of Neighborlee to make sure the Rivals hadn't shaken off their bruises from the last stifled attempt to plant roots in the mysterious, magical town, and begun another foray.

All these years, Jane had suspected Demetrius and Beauregard, her teachers, were keeping secrets from the children snatched away from Neighborlee before the Rivals could get hold of them. She had entertained the awful suspicion they were forbidden to return to the town where they had appeared as toddlers, seemingly out of nowhere. It had taken several years in Fendersburg, playing her role in the ongoing battle with the Rivals, to realize that staying *away* from Neighborlee was a crucial step in protecting the town.

Today, she had returned. Somewhat disappointing, she had to admit. The town felt so utterly normal and ordinary. She had expected something like a subliminal gong when she crossed the border into Neighborlee. A sense of coming home? Passing from the ordinary world into Faerie, maybe?

"What better way to hide from the outside world than to appear to be part of it?" she whispered.

It was now past noon and she had been walking around Neighborlee since nine that morning. Besides good exercise on a gloriously bright, warm, sweet-scented summer day, nothing had really happened. Everyone was friendly, no one looked at her as if she had grown an extra head or they considered her a threat. More important, she got no sense of danger or threat from anyone she encountered. Not in any of the stores. Not in the park, where she had sat in the gazebo with a decadently thick, rich salted caramel mocha frappe and watched the children on the playground. Not when she stopped at *The Neighborlee Tattler* for a copy of the twice-weekly paper to check out the community activities.

The most interesting part of her visit so far was her hotel. The Neighborlee Arms was a grand old building with a quirky history, proudly displayed in a little museum off the lobby on the first floor. She had spent more than two hours there last night after checking in, reading placards on glass display cases or flipping through copies of old newspapers, learning about the early years of settlement. The establishment of the town and the local college, Willis-Brooks. A whole wall and display table had been devoted to when the building had been a bordello, as a cover for the Underground Railroad. There were no claims to ghosts. Jane was especially sensitive to claims of places being haunted.

One man's restless spirit was another's superhero.

All Jane had gained in her leisurely walking tour, besides a little touch of sun color, was a healthy appetite. She had long ago worked off the luscious breakfast she had eaten in Hunky & Dorty's, a little diner near the hotel. Now she needed to refuel. Several people she had asked on the street, including the young woman her age in a wheelchair, coming out of the *Neighborlee Tattler* office, said the Sipping Post was a good place for sandwiches and drinks. She recommended the picnic special: sandwich, cold drink, fruit and a frosted brownie or cookie in a bag she could take to the park.

That sounded like just what the doctor ordered. Jane asked for it when she stepped up to the counter. The woman with a pencil tucked behind each ear, her frizzy white hair caught back in two ponytails high off the back of her head, and a Willis-Brooks College t-shirt in neon pink with neon green lettering, gave her an odd look. Jane glanced at the menu posted on the largest blackboard she had ever seen, filling the entire wall behind the counter, stretching up to the ceiling, covered in a dozen colors of chalk. They must have had to use a ladder—or someone here also had a talent for levitation. Nowhere on the menu was the picnic special listed.

"Umm, a girl I ran into at the newspaper office recommended it," she offered. "Wheelchair, dark hair—"

"Ah, Lanie. Okay, makes sense." The woman nodded and grinned, looked Jane up and down once, and stepped away from the counter. "I'm guessing you're a deluxe-tuna-with-pepper-jack-cheese-on-oat-bread and a brownie kind of girl?"

"That sounds great." Jane waited for that shiver she got when she ran into a Gifted who didn't belong to Hoax, Inc.

"Root beer or peach tea... Or no, chocolate milk?" She reached into the glass-fronted cooler and snatched up a bottle of chocolate milk before Jane could think to answer.

"Definitely chocolate." Still, no shiver. Jane chalked up the woman's ability to guess what she wanted to years of experience.

"Peach, orange, or apple?"

"Apple. As long as it's tart and crisp. No mushy-mealy-sweet apples for me, please."

The counter woman laughed and came up with a Granny Smith, pale green and flawless and as big as her fist. They chatted as she put together the sandwich, about what Jane had seen in Neighborlee so far, and she recommended a few places. She also sketched the city park, south of the town hall complex, on a napkin. Places where Jane could enjoy her lunch in peace and quiet, without the town's "hooligans" disturbing her. Then she laughed and warned her to stay away from a set of triplet boys who were her "grand-hooligans" and the ringleaders of the troublemakers.

"Been to Divine's Emporium yet?" the woman said, as Jane took her paper bag full of food and headed for the door.

"No." That shiver finally ran down Jane's back and wrapped around her lungs, tickling and tightening at the same time. Her mentors hadn't said to stay away from Divine's when she made her survey check, but hadn't said to visit it, either.

"Might like it. Depends on what brought you to Neighborlee." Her smile faded, just enough to be noticeable.

"Memory lane, I guess." Jane shrugged. "I used to live here when I was a little girl. I was in the area and...thought I'd see if the place was like I remembered."

"Is it?"

"Nope." She sighed and grinned. "Better."

"Be careful of Divine's, then. You might like it so much, you'll come back to stay."

Jane strolled down the street to the park and found one of the secluded spots on the napkin map. It was in a little rise near one end of the park, surrounded by big old, gnarled oaks, with branches so interwoven their canopy cast the picnic spot into semi-gloom. The picnic table was old wood, faded and weathered, and spotted with moss. Jane sat on the table and looked down the steep slope on the west, to trees and meadows and a meandering asphalt road. She remembered reading about the park. Much of it had been quarries early in the history of Neighborlee. Some of the quarries had been filled with water, made into fishing and swimming holes. The northern part of the quarries were off-limits, not an official part of the park system.

Jane munched and thought and remembered. Demetrius and Beauregard, nicknamed "the Old Poops" by the children they had rescued from the snatch-and-enslave tactics of the Rivals, had given mixed messages about Neighborlee. A place to be avoided. A place to protect. A place that deserved their loyalty. A place of mystery.

Hoax, Inc., earned a living investigating and debunking reports of the weird, unearthly, and supernatural. Nothing frightened them from uncovering the causes, explaining them, and fixing whatever imbalance in the natural world created the "incident." They dealt with charlatans as the situations dictated. Yet they preferred to avoid Neighborlee. Except for sending in the most sensitive and discrete students twice a year to walk around, to listen, to look for children who might be awakening to Gifts that would draw dangerous attention from the Rivals.

Most of the "family" of Hoax, Inc., including Demetrius and Beau, had come from Neighborlee. Jane was the last child discovered at the orphanage when her Ghost talent manifested. The last student brought to the Sanctum, the headquarters of Hoax, to be trained. The next oldest child was six years older than her.

Jane had chafed, waiting for the day her teachers would give her the duty of testing Neighborlee. She had a talent for sensing when a Gift was being used. Just last summer, she had helped locate a girl in Sydney, Australia, who had started manifesting her Gift at age nine. Demetrius and Beauregard had brought her along to investigate. She had befriended the frightened child and convinced her that being able to manipulate water like clay didn't make her a freak or dangerous.

That had been far more satisfying than the last five years assigned to Fendersburg, the town the Old Poops had put under her care. Jane understood the necessity of generating "odd" occurrences to draw the attention of the Rivals, trick them into making mistakes, to identify and trap them. Her Ghost talent was perfect for the task, allowing her to be in the middle of activities in town while staying entirely anonymous, so the Rivals would never guess she was the bait, even if she talked to them face-to-face. The problem was that Fendersburg's population seemed to be getting more lazy and shed more I.Q. points as time went on. She wanted something more challenging and meaningful. Just how long could she play "catch me if you can" with the Rivals before they gave up and left Fendersburg alone?

Jane paused in mid-crunch and had a hard time swallowing the last bite of her apple. Thinking about going back to that antithesis of Mayberry had just killed her appetite. On the surface, Fendersburg looked a lot like Neighborlee: small town, business district measured in blocks, not miles; weekly newspaper, Mom & Pop businesses. Everybody knew everybody else's business. Underneath... Neighborlee didn't have a suspected inbreeding problem. Here, people cared about good personal hygiene, and everybody graduated from high school and at least tried to go to college. No Gifted child would ever appear in Fendersburg. Most of her duties entailed protecting the town from itself.

That sense of being wasted, of having a useless job, made this visit to Neighborlee feel like a treat. Other than the Sanctum and her little apartment in Fendersburg, this was the only other home she had ever had. Ten years in the Neighborlee Children's Home. She had been happy there. She had friends. What happened to those friends? Did they remember her? She had been a quiet child, with a talent for blending into the background and being unnoticed, even before she discovered her Gift.

Jane threw away the rest of her apple. She was careful to wrap up the brownie, though. Only a fool would throw away three inches by three inches of fudgy chocolaty goodness with frosting as thick as the brownie itself. She might need the comfort of that brownie after she visited Divine's Emporium.

She remembered how to get there, like she had built-in GPS. A big olive and gold Victorian house on a dead-end street overlooking the slope down into the park. Jane dredged up memories of Divine's as she walked the few blocks over there. Outings to town were treats at the orphanage. She remembered competing with the other girls to hold their housemother's hand as they walked from their cottage to the curiosity shop. Or better yet, to hold the hand of Mrs. Silvestri, the orphanage administrator, when she took children into town for shopping excursions or to play in the park or go to a play at the college.

Funny, how easy it was to remember all those little things now, when up until this visit, it felt like her life hadn't really started until Beau and Demetrius took her to the Sanctum. Not that the Old Poops would ever employ memory-wiping.

"Wonder how much trouble I'd get into if I looked for people I knew ... No. Don't be ridiculous." Jane sighed and quashed her grumbling. The last thing she needed was to be caught talking to herself. Even in a town that regularly produced odd incidents, she didn't want to risk catching anyone's attention. Or worse, being remembered. One of the first lessons Beau had taught her was to blend in, to avoid notice. To be a watcher, rather than the watched. The safe, responsible use of her Gift depended on it.

More memories crashed down on Jane as she turned the corner onto the street where Divine's Emporium sat near the dead end. Instead of the usual metal highway guardrail barrier at the high point of the slope, Neighborlee had a pretty wooden gate, and signs pointing to paths people could take to walk down to the park below. Jane studied the building as she walked down the street, remembering bits and pieces. The multiple shelves of penny candy in old apothecary jars. The big brass cash register. The book room. The vintage clothing room, where children could play dress up as much as they wanted. Funny, how it never occurred to Jane until now that adults who came into the shop during their play never seemed upset. Angela, the owner, protected their fun.

"The Wishing Ball," she whispered, and her steps slowed as she remembered the globe just about the size of a bowling ball, dark metallic rainbow swirls, sitting in a stand shaped like a coiled dragon. She had loved simply gazing into the Wishing Ball, on the counter next to the cash register. Jane had always imagined someday the soft swirling of colors in the ball would resolve into images that would answer the questions that haunted her young mind. Who her parents were, how they had lost her, so she had been found, a little more than a year old, sitting by the side of the road just inside Neighborlee's borders. Like the other children, Jane had made her share of wishes on the Wishing Ball. Many had come true, but they were easy wishes: what she wanted for Christmas, to pass an upcoming test, for the bullies to leave her alone.

Was the Wishing Ball still there? What would she wish for, if she could?

"That's easy," Jane muttered as she stepped off the sidewalk onto the flagstone path and through the wrought iron gate that stood open. "To escape Fendersburg."

She grinned at her silliness. She had to grin, or she might cry. Sometimes she absolutely hated the town of lazy, entitlement-attitude mental midgets she had to look after while trying to trick the Rivals into making mistakes so Hoax could identify them.

Then she was at the porch and the front door. She sighed in delight as she pushed the front door open. Bells chimed sweetly, almost like singing, and the sound faded slowly as she stepped down the short entry hallway. The sense of having walked into a familiar place wrapped around her. She smelled fruity scented candles, the dusty perfume of books, and chocolate. Freestanding display shelves invited her to browse a haphazard collection of figurines and decorative boxes, candles, dishes, and numerous other bright, colorful items she ignored as she let memory guide her feet.

Divine's didn't stock all the trendy candy and gimmicks that cluttered the counters at other stores. No novelty candy shaped like aliens. No trading cards and dispensers shaped like garbage cans or cell phones. She saw candy bars and gum, hard candy and licorice whips and funny, funky shapes she hadn't seen since childhood. Jane wandered for a few minutes, looking at all the display boxes and jars. Dolls in lacy dresses, wooden toys, puzzles made of metal and string and wood, pinwheels and bottles of bubbles, sidewalk chalk, squirt guns, balloons, and other fragments of an innocent, happier time.

Jane laughed quietly at some of the strange and unique toys and collectibles, interspersed with necessary things she thought she could never find again. Bottles of perfume no one else carried, hand cream, cooking utensils, spices. Her favorite style of sleeveless shirt in ten different colors--she picked out one in emerald, one in gray and one in cobalt blue. Dozens of things she would regret not buying now, and have to come back to fetch at a later date.

The sign out front promised whatever someone needed would be here. Did that meant *everything* had to be here? Jane grinned, wondering if "everything" could indeed be jammed into this house.

She frowned, when it struck her that the room and the aisles certainly seemed longer than should have fit into the house. At least, not the size of house she had glimpsed from the outside. Maybe it was just an optical illusion. With so much crammed in, it just seemed bigger than it really was.

It wasn't like space could be stretched to accommodate everything shoehorned in here. Could it? Sure, some of the members of Hoax had managed to stretch space and even stretch time when they were under a great deal of pressure, but they couldn't make it last.

Her wandering brought her to the main room. Another sigh, as she saw the marble-topped counter with the brass cash register and shelves full of apothecary jars, just like she remembered them.

Where was the Wishing Ball? Panic shot through her, like the first time she rose three feet off the ground without knowing quite how she did it.

"Welcome to Divine's Emporium." A woman stepped through the doorway behind her.

Jane turned around quickly.

Angela, the proprietor of the shop, hadn't changed in the dozen-plus years since Jane had left Neighborlee. The same long waterfall of hair in dozens of shades of gold, with a hint of strawberry. The same intense, crystalline blue eyes. The same granny-style dress in a blue handkerchief print. Angela had the kind of figure that looked good in the semi-shapeless dress, neither model skinny nor buxom. Just right.

"Uh, hi... I'm — "

"I know you." Angela caught hold of Jane's hand and led her past the counter to a tall, skinny window. The Wishing Ball was right there on the corner, why hadn't Jane seen it?

Angela smiled wider, her expression lighting up as she studied Jane's face. "Yes, definitely. You were that quiet, pale little girl who kept trying to turn yourself invisible." She laughed.

Jane laughed with her. The caress in Angela's voice made her attempts to fade into the wallpaper sound charming. Sensible.

"I still have that volume of *The Jungle Book* you loved to read whenever you visited. Jane Wilson. Or did you change your name when you became a legal adult? Did your adopted parents change your name? Never mind. That's your business." She waved her hand, brushing away the questions before Jane could feel invaded. "What brings you to Neighborlee?"

"Playing hooky." She laughed a little.

It was nearly the truth, even if she was here on official Hoax, Inc., business. The grinding stupidity of Fendersburg, where everyone expected the Ghost to save them from a total lack of common sense, made any brief escape feel like a vacation.

"From what?"

For a moment, that familiar, crooked little knowing smile played across Angela's face. It hinted she knew all the things Jane couldn't say, the things she was feeling and hadn't been able to put into words. She knew her secrets and would wait patiently until Jane was ready to spill them.

"I have a spa, back home. Facials, manicures, pedicures, massages, sauna."

"You do all that? Multi-talented. And probably overworked." Angela gestured with a tip of her head toward a corner of the main room. Jane saw a white wrought iron bistro table and chairs.

Definitely overworked, but nothing I can admit to you.

Angela chuckled as she went behind the counter. "Iced green tea with ginseng and honey?"

"That sounds lovely, thanks." Jane settled down at the little table. "Umm, actually, I don't do all those things. I have people who come in and provide services. I have plenty of room in my store, so... Most of what I do is make appointments and sell all sorts of teas and creams and bath salts. The good kind, the legitimate kind," she hurried to add.

"Of course. I wouldn't expect anything else." Angela came back to the table with two glasses full of ice and two tall bottles of iced green tea in Jane's favorite brand.

Was there room behind the counter for a cooler and glasses and ice? She shrugged away that consideration. Things happened at Divine's Emporium and it was wiser not to ask questions. Answers might destroy the wonder, the sense of "anything is possible."

"We could use a spa like yours. If you ever consider coming back home to Neighborlee, I know just the place. The old

Spindelmutter building. Lots of room, three floors, and the third floor is an apartment. You could add a whirlpool and expand your offerings to include exercise clothes and such."

Jane took the information from Angela and chatted about the possibilities. She had actually been thinking about expanding her merchandise to include clothes and homeopathic treatments. Who was she hurting by playing along? It was a good cover story.

Although, a niggling sense of warning crept through her after just a minute or two. Essentially, she was lying to Angela, and Jane vaguely remembered some unspoken law that no one ever crossed Angela or tried to steal from Divine's Emporium.

"The moment you're ready to make the move, do let me know." Angela rested her hand on Jane's wrist for a few seconds. "I know a good two, three dozen people who would be ecstatic to have a place like yours come into town. In fact, if you started now, you could be open in time to take advantage of the Christmas rush."

"Oh... I... Well..." Jane fought not to yank her hand out from the soothing warmth of Angela's hand. "It's not that easy."

Demetrius and Beauregard would never let her abandon Fendersburg. Even if the Rivals were ignoring the town lately.

"Anything is possible."

Later, as Angela was ringing up the shirts Jane had picked out, and a bag of two pieces from every candy jar, the Wishing Ball caught her attention. Angela laughed and nodded at it.

"Go ahead. Make a wish." A chiming laugh escaped her. Something in her gaze dared Jane, while quashing the automatic, unspoken response: *Wishes are for children.*

Jane waited a moment for the colors to swirl gently in the reflective, black opal surface. They didn't. When she put her hand flat on the top curve, she didn't feel that zip-tingle she had always gotten as a child when she made her wish. The disappointment was thick enough to block any words she might have tried to speak.

Please... I want to get out of Fendersburg. Away from those lazy, greedy, totally oblivious people. I want to find a new place to live, and a spa even better than the one I have now, where people use common sense and don't expect a miracle to come out of a jar. I want... I want there to be magic again. Something beyond me, bigger than me, stronger than me. Something mysterious and awesome.

A single spark leaped off the Wishing Ball as she removed her hand and Jane gasped, staring at her index finger where the spark rested for a moment, a golden-green, swirling ball that seemed to have a core of black, just before it vanished.

She thought Angela frowned at her, but a moment later she wore her usual serene, slightly superior, slightly amused expression. What her friend Katie always called a "Vulcan smirk."

~~~~~

Deep underground, a faint, poisonous green spark zipped along through the cracks and crevices in the bedrock below Neighborlee, following the drip of water and the shivering of crumbling stone. Its movement scratched out a meandering tunnel through bedrock and the fabric of space/time. In a thin place in the rock, a ripple of black light scraped and scratched from the other side of a dimensional doorway that shouldn't have been there. The spark came to a stop. It pulsed brightly once, caught in the vortex stronger than the gravity of a black hole, before the black light swallowed it.

On the other side of the place where Earth and other realms met and clung together, something sniffed at the scent of power and shifted slightly in its years-long sleep.

~~~~~

Jane couldn't sleep. Despite knowing better, she had checked out the Spindelmutter building. The location was perfect. Even with the windows blocked with brown paper, she could tell she would have twice as much space than in her current spa. Now, her brain seethed and churned with possibilities. The ache to put Fendersburg in her rearview mirror added to her restlessness.

When the sounds of traffic through her open window died to nothing and she was sure the entire town slept, Jane gave in to temptation. First stop: check out the interior of the Spindelmutter building and quench her curiosity, even if she couldn't move back to Neighborlee. Jane rolled out of bed and changed into sweatpants and a T-shirt. No need for shoes. She wasn't going to land anywhere, just do an aerial survey of the town now, instead of tomorrow before she left.

A moment of concentration. The Ghost field activated. Phasing out, Jane went invisible. She floated to the outer wall of her hotel room, slid between the molecules, and out into the air. She was on the third floor. In moments she shot straight up, higher than every building in town.

On this clear summer night, she saw all the streets spread out before her. In one direction they fed into the shopping and business center of town, opposite the city hall and police/fire station/courthouse complex. In the other direction, the residential district petered out into farmland. To the west and north of town, beyond the municipal buildings, the quarries were dark blots of stone and moonlight and starlight on water. West and south were the Metroparks, with the fishing and swimming holes and the river meandering among the trees. East and south of her were all the Neighborlee schools and the administration building. Beyond that, the border with Darbyville.

Back home in Fendersburg, just shy of 11pm, the village idiots would be gearing up for a night of stupidity, maybe finding a blank wall to fill with misspelled graffiti. Then if they hadn't already guzzled enough beer to drown in, they would race down the back roads and try some vandalism.

Jane sighed in satisfaction as she looked around, slowly rotating in her bubble of invisibility, and enjoyed the peace and quiet. The only movement came from four police cars patrolling different areas of town. One toured the downtown/shopping district, the other in the industrial park east and north of town, another meandered around the school buildings, and the fourth wove through the main residential district. She caught a few dots of light on top of cars driving around the sprawling campus of Willis-Brooks College, and assumed that was the campus police, probably preparing for fall semester.

A truck drove down the slope behind the municipal complex, taking an access road into the Metroparks. That didn't look like a police car or a ranger's car. Her finely tuned sense of "something is about to happen" urged her to investigate, even though whatever happened in Neighborlee really wasn't any of her business.

Chapter Two

The truck stopped just within the edge of the park, among clumps of bushes. That was a bad sign, no matter where it took place. Jane dropped a little closer, enough to see three people in the truck when a door opened and the inside light came on. The driver got out, and two people slid out of the passenger door. The three linked arms. Her fingertips tingled faintly, and a soft rainbow-tinted shimmering hovered in the air around the trio.

"Oh heck heck heck," Jane muttered, and threw herself backward as the trio rose straight up in the air. She knew they couldn't see her, but logic said if she could sense the vibrations of Gifted energy in use, someone else might be sensitive enough to sense *her* using her Gift. Shivering, she flew straight back to town, glancing over her shoulder, ready to change course if those three followed her. Being invisible might be no help at all.

Oddly, she felt vaguely disappointed when she got back to the airspace above the Neighborlee Arms and there was no one within sight or sensing. She sank down through the roof, down through an empty room, into her hotel room. Distracted, she almost didn't phase back into solidity before changing back into her pajamas.

"Get a grip," she scolded herself, and laughed a little when she realized she had forgotten to go check out the Spindelmutter building.

She stayed up until nearly 3am, curled up on the chaise lounge in front of the balcony door, searching to feel the presence of the flying trio. Whoever they were, wherever they were, she didn't feel any Gifted energy being used. When she finally climbed into bed, Jane knew what she had to do. This wasn't something to report over the phone.

Which side of the decades-old battle were those three strangers on? Agents of the Rivals. Allies of the Gifted old man whose family ran Sheridan Communications? Residents of Neighborlee who had escaped the notice of Hoax and the Rivals?

Her dreams, when she finally slept, were fragmented. When she woke, she had a headache, as if she had stayed awake all night, listening for something. She jumped into her car before breakfast, and headed back to Fendersburg, by way of the Sanctum.

~~~~~

Amelia Quinn and Theo Brickman were the only ones home, when Jane drove up the long, gravel drive through the woods to the old mansion of the Sanctum. Demetrius and Beau were meeting with some friends at a think tank that monitored world events. Amelia sent Theo to contact the Sanctum's leaders, then herded Jane into the kitchen for a late breakfast.

"Something has you rattled, lovey, and that's rare enough to be worrisome," the dainty, elderly woman said, just before plunking down a huge cast iron skillet on the stove, big enough to cook a dozen eggs at once. "You had the Neighborlee evaluation. What happened?"

Jane told her in the time it took to crack and scramble the eggs. Amelia nodded and pursed her lips, and her eyes went vague with thought for a few moments. Then she sent Jane to get ingredients for brunch for the three of them. Theo joined them in time to help set the table, and Jane had to repeat her story. She had new doubts. Had she fled too soon? Should she have investigated, and risked being caught?

"You did the right thing," Theo said. "Get out of there, avoid notice. Let the professional worriers chew on the questions and send out feelers." He winked. "My personal theory is that some Gifted got overlooked. They've dug in and know how to stay safe. Neighborlee has its own means of defense. You don't want to run afoul of those who belong there, do you?"

"Of course she doesn't. She's a good, smart one." Amelia reached across the table to pat Jane's hand.

Jane wrote up her report before she left. Amelia loaded her down with treats members of Hoax brought back from their world travels. Jane was glad she had driven there instead of flying in. She had never tested the limits of how much weight she could carry while flying, but a dozen boxes and bags and tins could be awkward. She could just imagine losing her grip while flying over heavy traffic and dropping some decadent treats. As the youngest member of the family, she felt like she had several dozen aunts and uncles, all intent on spoiling her.

~~~~~

Nobody in Fendersburg had gained any common sense while Jane was away. The usual routine had gone on without the Ghost to remedy problems a little common sense could have prevented. Joe Conrad had run out of gas while picking up milk from the cooperative's four small dairy farms. He sat for half an hour, yelling for the Ghost to help him, before he used his cell phone to call his brother to come with the gas can. Georgie Tupper decided he could fly with just a blanket tied to his shoulders for a cape. When he climbed up the tallest tree in the center of town, the blanket got tangled on a branch. He hung there, kicking and screaming, while his mother sat on a park bench a few dozen feet away, working on her nails. Someone finally got tired of hearing her complain about the Ghost taking so long to show up, and they called the fire department. When the fire department presented Mrs. Tupper with a bill for rescuing her son, she told them to charge the Ghost, since he was "shirking his responsibility."

Various assorted other foolishness happened. People ignored stop signs and ate food from swollen cans. When the Ghost didn't show up to stop them, they dented their cars or rushed to the hospital to have their stomachs pumped. Jane got to her spa in time to open the doors for business at 10am, and by 2pm she had heard about every incident in the two days since she had gone to visit Neighborlee.

The newspaper the next morning listed all the minor disasters on the front page and the complaints from the people who expected the Ghost to do their thinking for them. Same old stupidity. Jane supposed the incredulous fascination of people who rubbernecked at traffic accidents kept her reading. When she unfolded the newspaper, to continue reading down the double-wide column, the headline on the bottom half of the front page stopped her cold. She stared, blinked, shook her head, and balled up the newspaper.

Legal action against the Ghost? The nerve of those lazy, self-righteous —

"Hey, did you hear?" Sylvia Daystrom squealed as she bombed through the propped open door into the spa.

Jane stopped in mid-crumple, her hands shaking.

"Yeah, I guess you did." Shaking her head, Sylvia made her way across the large main room to the nook where she had her manicure and pedicure station set up, open for business four days a week. "Can you believe the nerve of those morons?"

"Nothing about this town surprises me anymore." Jane managed a smile. Sylvia was one of the more commonsense people in Fendersburg. Knowing she was disgusted by the story on the bottom half of the page helped release some of the pressure that threatened to take off the top of her head.

The Old Poops need to see this.

The town was abuzz with the story. Jane's spa sat in the middle of the tiny business district. She kept her door open all day in the summer and the biggest gossips in town always sat on the benches in front of her store, so she heard everything. All day. Speculations and reminiscences and laughter and criticism. Every time someone agreed with her assessment of the irresponsible, immature twits in Fendersburg, someone else came along to dump everything back into the Ghost's lap. Jane watched the clock as the hour hand inched around, until she could finally close her shop.

She mentioned to half a dozen people, including one of the gossips out front, that she was tired, had a headache, and was going to take a sleeping pill and take her phone off the hook. That would ensure everyone in town knew by nightfall that no matter how many times they called or knocked, no one was going to get through to her. People who ignored posted store hours would just have to wait to get their detox cream or a new lipstick tomorrow.

Jane went to her apartment and made a sandwich. She needed the energy even if she wasn't hungry. While eating, she tucked the newspaper into her backpack, then phased into Ghost mode and went up through the roof. She took her last bite of sandwich while hovering in the air, looking down at Fendersburg and wishing it could be as quiet and friendly as Neighborlee. At eighty feet higher than the tallest building in town, she headed west and north for the Sanctum.

Thank goodness for secret identities. None of those idiots can follow through on their threat to sue the Ghost, because they can't find me. Jane snorted and grinned into the setting sun. *Not to mention they think I'm a guy.*

"I have never been so happy to be the Ghost in my entire life," she grumbled as she tossed the newspaper down in front of Beau and Demetrius less than an hour later.

Beau smoothed it out on the desk the size of a small swimming pool while Demetrius settled down in his easy chair in front of the massive fireplace big enough to roast an entire cow. One drawback to their Gifted longevity was feeling chilled even in the muggy warmth of summer. Jane used just enough Ghost field to let her get close to the roaring fire without dripping in sweat.

The headline read: "Fendersburg Uses Samaritan Law to Sue Ghost." Jane snorted as she glanced over the big, black letters in slightly runny ink. The complaints lodged against the Ghost, her alternate persona, were printed in fourteen-point font instead of the standard ten, and took up the bottom half of the front page and most of the second page. Mrs. Crookins must have been furious when her society column got pushed to page three.

"I'm sorry, my dear. Obviously these..." Beau scowled, searching for a better word.

"Throwbacks? Inbred morons? Hicks?" Jane suggested.

The proper old gentleman glared at her, but a few seconds later the look dissolved into merriment. He sighed and shook his head. "Obviously, these benighted folks have chosen to ignore your regular warnings, posted in this very newspaper, stating you are not responsible for the everyday incidents and accidents in their lives. You are one person and therefore cannot be everywhere at once. No lawyer in the land will agree to take the lawsuit."

"I wouldn't count on that," Demetrius grumbled around the stem of his pipe. It was empty, and had never held tobacco for as long as Jane had known her teachers. "For every ten good lawyers with common sense, there's one who makes ambulance chasers look reasonable. Someone will take up the case, just to make a name for himself."

"You have no legal responsibility. They can't force it on you," Beau insisted, patting Jane's shoulder. "As the Ghost, you are there to handle large accidents and emergencies. Floods and tornadoes, water main breaks, fires, that sort of things. Not to retrieve improperly disciplined boys from trees twenty times in a day and protect idiots from their own stupidity." He folded the newspaper in half and slapped it on the desk in front of him for emphasis, tumbling several scones off the pile with the force of the blow.

Beauregard might have been white-haired and paunchy and wrinkled, but he still had a lot of *oomph* left in him.

"However..."

Jane sagged, knowing she was in trouble when Beau used "however." She had overlooked something, and he had seen it. The fine print, so to speak, in her unwritten superhero contract with the town of Fendersburg.

"Well, part of this problem, you brought on yourself," he said, softening his voice.

"Kick the girl while she's down, why don't you?" Demetrius grumbled. *"We* did it to her, sending her there to bait the Rivals. The same stupidity that lets these half-wits shift all responsibility to her is what we depended on to keep our enemies stymied."

Jane sighed. She knew he was right. She also knew she was stuck in Fendersburg until the Rivals got so frustrated they carelessly left clues for Hoax to track them to their headquarters. If that ever happened, they could at long last settle the problem and the war the Rivals had declared with their actions, if not words.

"If she wouldn't wear herself to a frazzle pulling their nuts out of the fire, day in and day out, if she'd just let them fall down and bloody their noses a few times, they might learn to stand on their own two feet and not sit around on their fat backsides, expecting her to come to their rescue." Beau gestured with his scone. "You have to admit I'm right, Janie-gal."

"Yeah, you're right." She sank into a chair. "But honestly, it's easier to take care of the mess right away, instead of listening to them scream and whine and make it even worse."

"You're stuck, Cookie," Demetrius growled, twisting around in his overstuffed chair to turn it without actually getting out of it. "I'm sorry, but that's how it is."

"Is she?" Beau said. "Every lead generated from her acting as bait has evaporated. No suspected Rivals have come back, and no newcomers have been spotted in town in nearly four months. I'm inclined to think they've given up."

"Or?" Jane said, hearing the unspoken qualifiers.

He sighed and seemed to deflate a little. "Or they've moved on to more fruitful hunting grounds."

"Neighborlee?" she whispered.

"Who can be sure? None of the other potential arrival spots for Gifted have panned out. You were the last one from Neighborlee."

"What do we do?" Jane thought of the lovely town that felt like home, the warm, friendly people, and the Rivals finally making a move. Something worse than leaving those arrogant, power-grubbing Grandstones like a rusty spike in the town, to mark their spot and give them a foothold when they finally decided to act.

"Other than hope for a nice, tidy explosion to wipe the whole moronic town of Fendersburg off the map and set you free?" Beauregard winked. Demetrius snorted.

A bottle of whiskey levitated over from behind a stack of books that didn't hide it very well. Jane waited, holding her breath while the bottle tipped and poured three fingers' worth into the glass-bottomed tankard Demetrius always used, no matter what he drank, hot or cold, common beverages or scientific experiments. She was grateful his telekinetic talents were at full power right now. Depending on the phases of the moon and whatever problems he had, his energy levels could be high enough to be dangerous to everyone around him, or so low he couldn't even get out of his own chair without help. Another price of getting old, along with losing the ability to heal from anything short of amputation.

"Now," Demetrius said with a sigh. "Tell us about those flying people you saw in Neighborlee."

He had taught all his students how to tell a story. A spark of interest and new energy came back to the eyes of both elderly men when she described flying over Neighborlee and seeing the trio park and get out of the truck, link arms, and rise up in the air. And the tingle of energy, the visible-but-not-visible shimmer, that were clear signs of a Gift in use.

"Adults, you think? So they developed or were already using their Gifts around the time you did." Beau thumped his fist on the table. "We missed them. How could we have missed them?"

"We're set in our ways." Demetrius smiled as he interlaced his fingers over his belly and slouched in his chair. "Haven't we been using literature to teach our students how real superheroes should act, how to hide their talents, how to live double lives? Who's to say that these three didn't discover similar stories before they found out what they could do, and were clever enough to apply those principles when their Gifts emerged?"

"You don't think that book thief you tussled with, fifty-some years ago..." Beau shook his head. Jane caught the tail end of a glare Demetrius shot him.

"What book thief?" She followed gut instinct. "You ran into

someone in Neighborlee who might have had a Gift, and you got in trouble, so you left him there?"

"Too old," he muttered, frowning at a spot on the table. A sure sign he was lost in memories or thinking up some new theory.

"Too old?" She turned to Demetrius.

"Too hard nowadays to swoop in with falsified paperwork and whisk young ones like you away anymore," Demetrius said. His relaxed posture looked rock hard now.

"We have to do something to protect Neighborlee. Why do the Rivals always go back there? Why do you think they're going to focus there and not somewhere else?"

"Neighborlee, my dear child, is unique in one specific aspect: an unusually high ratio of lost, unclaimed children found within the town's boundaries. And, if you think about it, an inexplicable tendency for all of them to end up in the orphanage there, instead of being snatched up by other child welfare agencies throughout the county or even the state. Yet, out of every ten such children, nine display not a smidgen of anything unusual."

"Who says?" She grinned when both old men cocked an eyebrow at her in almost perfect synchronization. "If those three I found stayed hidden from you, and from the Rivals, what if there are others, with much smaller, less noticeable Gifts? What if Neighborlee stays safe because ... I don't know ... they work together, to protect each other? Only a fraction of us have visible Gifts. The rest could still have the *genetics* for something amazing. How many grow up and stay in Neighborlee, and marry others like them, and maybe produce Gifted kids?"

"We have noticed some who might be Gifted," Beau admitted slowly, "but they weren't orphans. We had to leave them alone." He smacked the middle of his forehead with his open palm and slouched. "If their parents or even grandparents are just slightly Gifted, then they have enough experience, enough understanding, warning, intelligence, to teach them to hide what they can do."

"What about this book thief?"

"What about him?" Demetrius said with a grunt.

"How did he catch on to what you were doing?"

"He was more aware than the others," he said, the words coming slowly as if he didn't want to let them out. "And we noticed that energy levels fluctuated around him. Lights would brighten, small power surges, nothing that would damage any equipment, whenever he walked into a building. We watched him, tried to find out more information about him. And yes, we learned he was another lost child. He had already graduated from the orphanage and had set himself up in business. Hmm, can't remember what exactly."

"Buying and selling," Beauregard said. "Rattletrap truck, went around to estate sales, bought junk and fixed it, or refinished furniture. Had an amazing talent for finding treasures hidden under layers and years of filth and abuse. He had a fondness for books. Made him stand out from the other collectors."

"Not a fondness. Passion. Obsession. He rarely resold any books." A half-grunt, half-chuckle escaped Demetrius. "He loved libraries, but he hated giving the books back. As I recall, there was a feisty young librarian who took him down like a fullback."

"The point is," Beau said, and rolled his eyes in barely disguised amusement, "he noticed us watching him and he got in our faces, as you young folk put it. Any time we went back to Neighborlee, we had to make sure he didn't notice us before we could check on the latest crop at the orphanage."

"So you've never checked on the next generation," Jane said.

"Hmm, no, unfortunately." Demetrius reached for his tankard. "It's not like we can pop in and snatch the children from their families for training, like we could with the orphans."

"How about some honesty?" she asked, when she sensed that thoughtful silence settling back over the room.

"Oh, yes, of course. Drive into town and introduce ourselves and ask if any of them have developed mutant powers like in the comic books. That won't get us run out of town," Beau grumbled. "Especially since we have been confronted several times by people who seem to at least suspect what we were up to."

"Why couldn't you go in with your Hoax identification?" Jane said. "You have quite a reputation for debunking the fakes and con men. Wouldn't that give you some credit, some standing so people have to believe you when you present your theory?"

"Problem, Cookie." Demetrius locked gazes with Beau as he spoke. "Hoax has too public a face. We did it to ourselves, taking down the Rivals to defend the innocent. Whenever we roll into town, people are watching. We don't want to draw attention to

Neighborlee or the Gifted we might find. We need to be represented by someone they consider their own, who will be believed when the truth is revealed." He sighed. His gaze stayed focused on Jane, and his eyes slowly narrowed. "Or at least given a fair hearing. Beau, old boy, I have an idea. Definitely something the Council needs to discuss."

"Could take months, getting everybody here from all over the world. Depends on how busy they are," Beau offered.

"Speed is never wise in these circumstances." He nodded. "Thank you, Janie. This has been a most ... enlightening evening." He chuckled and saluted her with the tankard before tipping it back and emptying the last mouthful.

~~~~~

"And here's the Ghost, defender of the weak and defenseless and ... the really stupid," Jane muttered as she made her nightly rounds a week later. She spread her arms, stopping her leisurely glide over Fendersburg. Her mood was down because no word had come yet on the results of the Council meeting. Most likely they hadn't met yet. She had hoped part of that meeting would result in a change in her assignment.

"What did you expect?" she muttered as she looked up at the moon and turned over for a few seconds to fly on her back. "To be given instant permission to hop the next train out of town?" Sighing, she turned over to study the layout of streets she knew so well, she swore the grid was imprinted on the inside of her eyelids.

A typical late August evening in Fendersburg meant not a cloud in the sky, and everybody under the age of thirty out on their bikes, motorcycles, scooters and junker cars, cruising until the moon started to set. Didn't anybody believe in sleep? Just once, Jane wished she dared settle in for the night before midnight. The longer she lived in this nowhere town, the lower the IQ points dropped, and the higher the self-destructive tendencies. And that meant more work for her to do.

Beau and Demetrius were right. It was her own fault. The more she protected the people of Fendersburg, the less responsibility they felt for their own welfare, and the more risks the idiots took. Why not be daredevils, when they knew the Ghost would swoop down just in time to save their worthless hides? She wondered: did Superman ever get disgusted with Lois Lane for taking all those stupid risks, knowing he would save her? Unfortunately, Lois Lane had some good points to make up for sticking her nose where it didn't belong. Jane couldn't think of more than ten people in this town she liked helping. The rest weren't worth the powder it would take to blow them to Kingdom Come.

For instance, the McCreedy boys driving around below her. Poster children for mandatory sterilization. Someone should have dumped chlorine into that particular gene pool long ago.

The six McCreedys crammed into Willy's rust-bucket truck, four hanging out the windows and two standing up so their heads poked through the sunroof he had cut out six years ago. That sunroof proved the unfairness of life in general because no McCreedy ever came down with tetanus. Jane swooped down to watch the boys, sure they were up to no good.

Tonight's target appeared to be the reservoir. Even from twenty yards above the trees, Jane smelled the stink of scummy water through the protective field enclosing her. The dry summer, low water level and recent police budget cuts were all invitations to trouble. The reservoir was a neglected sitting duck.

"Looks like another busy night," Jane muttered as she swooped down through the stifling night air. "Goody gumdrops."

Bald tires, a road badly in need of patching, and overgrown bushes and trees hanging over the edges of the crumbling blacktop meant the McCreedy boys had to drive slowly up the steep hill and follow the hairpin turns instead of bouncing up and over. Jane appreciated their caution. She was in a bad enough mood without carrying the guilt and dismay of saving a McCreedy's life. She had just painted her nails and didn't want to risk chipping them, if she had to lunge to catch a rusty bumper and keep the truck from going over the edge. Her telekinetic ability had a weight limit. Cookie jars, yes. Trucks full of morons, no.

With her luck, she would get tetanus or hepatitis or any of a dozen diseases hiding in the thick coating of filth that kept the truck from falling apart. Jane wasn't bulletproof or made of steel. She could fly, she could go invisible. She could walk through solid objects and heal broken bones within a couple hours. That didn't mean she was impervious to pain or disease. She needed a decent night's sleep even more desperately than most people. Or at least, most people in the backward town of Fendersburg.

"Told ya it was broke," a whiny McCreedy voice crowed, just before the truck crashed into the lopsided gate of the reservoir.

"Told you to get it fixed," Jane muttered as the truck skidded to a stop in the gravel yard. How many times had the Ghost listed the necessary repairs, the accidents waiting to happen on all public property, and given the list to the town council? She had lost count. She had even sent the list three times to the *Fendersburg Trumpet*. The newspaper printed the lists and demanded action. Nothing had happened.

As evidenced by the broken lock on the fence and the lack of a single spark when the truck hit it open. That fence was supposed to be electrified, to stop the mutants from breaking in. Granted, calling the McCreedys mutants insulted mutants. Especially since Jane was pretty sure she was one herself.

"Let's go have some fun!" Willy chortled and slid out of the driver's seat. He reached into the back of the truck and pulled out tools for his brothers.

Most of the tools had price tags still attached. Jane sighed at that evidence that Joe-Bob still hadn't repaired his hardware store's burglar alarm from the last time someone broke in. She supposed she'd hear an angry tirade in the morning, about how the Ghost hadn't stopped the burglars. Honestly, how could anybody resist when the door wouldn't lock and Joe-Bob left the lights on, so anybody walking by could see what was waiting to be stolen?

How many times had she retrieved Joe-Bob's property for him? How many times had she heard him bragging about reporting the thefts to the insurance company and getting money for his claims, even though the merchandise was returned? Jane decided now was a good time to make an honest man of Joe-Bob.

Another letter was due at the *Trumpet*, scolding the people of Fendersburg to use some common sense. Such as making sure doors were locked, irons and coffee pots were turned off, and they kept their gas tanks filled. People grumbled, but they did act a little more responsibly. For a short time. How many letters could she send before people got used to being scolded and ignored her, continuing their lazy, oblivious practices?

Chapter Three

Jane floated up over the McCreedy boys' heads and snatched three shovels, two picks and a bag of blasting caps from outstretched hands. The items turned invisible the moment she pulled them inside her Ghost field. Jane snorted, muffling laughter as the McCreedys just stood there, hands grasping at empty air, their mouths dropping open. She didn't pause to hover in mid-air and enjoy the moment, but darted away to the crumbling face of the reservoir. A little extra *oomph* to her Ghost field, and she parted the cement molecules enough to shove the tools into the center of the reservoir's retention wall. There they would stay until she retrieved them, or the sub-standard construction finally eroded. Without the pressure of the scummy lake behind it, Jane estimated the wall would last another four or five years. More's the pity.

Returning, she found the McCreedy boys stumbling around, looking for their tools. Did they actually think they had dropped their stolen booty and it was there, hidden, despite the light of the nearly full moon clearly illuminating the gravel yard? What kind of idiots was she dealing with tonight?

"That's a rhetorical question if I ever heard one," she said, and didn't bother to keep her voice down.

"Who's there?" Slick, the oldest McCreedy bellowed.

"Who do you think?" she shouted back.

Coming through the Ghost field, her voice dropped nearly two octaves. Until she altered the field so it didn't alter her voice, Fendersburg would continue to believe the Ghost was a man.

"Hey, Ghost, long time no see," Jeff said with a vacuous grin.

"Idiot," Clint snarled. He elbowed his brother, misjudged the distance, and nearly fell off his feet. "Nobody can see the Ghost."

Jane didn't wait for the usual fight to break out among the McCreedys. She swooped down among them and picked up the rest of their demolition tools. Spray-paint cans, two hoes, charcoal lighter fluid and three boxes of matches. Those joined the other tools in the center of the retaining wall.

When she came back to the truck, the boys had scattered,

running along the edges of the reservoir. Ten IQ points higher, and they might have had the sense to jump back in their truck and get out of there. But no, McCreedys had to do damage. Maybe they considered it their civic duty. If they could spell "civic duty." Jane flew over the water, trying to ignore the smell of pea soup algae gone out of control, and listened to the boys shouting directions to each other.

Some people seemed to think if they couldn't see the Ghost, then the Ghost couldn't hear them.

She stopped Slick from climbing down the rusty ladder to the control house. She caught Hill and Roddy as they ran along the top of the retaining wall, trying to find the sluice gates. She picked up Willy and Jeff when they found some chains and tried to use them to climb down into the main channel of the outflow. Clint fell into the slimy, knee-deep water of the reservoir. Jane left him there and flew away to call the police.

"One of these days, I'm going to send a bill to these morons," she told the starry night. "The only problem is, they'd probably try to take me to court for overcharging."

She sighed when she reached the highway payphone she always used to call the police, and made her voice falsetto. As far as she knew, no one yet had tried to set up a tracing program or record the voice of the "female assistant to the Ghost," according to the *Trumpet*, who always notified the police of his latest activities.

Jane flew away and reflected that idiots needed twice as much watching as anyone else, to protect the rest of the world from them.

An hour later, she wondered if she was the idiot here. She had flown back to the reservoir to make sure the police actually showed up to take away the McCreedy boys. She had left them trapped by their own stupidity, tangled in chains, wedged inside the control room, slipping around in slimy water. They lost the keys to their truck. It never occurred to them to run when the police finally sauntered in through the broken gate, without lights flashing or sirens blaring.

"Hey, Ghost!" one of the officers shouted. "When are you gonna fix this gate? How many more kids have to get in trouble before you do something about it?"

Jane groaned and shook her head and flew away. The first time someone had demanded that the Ghost take care of something that was their responsibility, she got into a shouting match with the idiot. After that, she regularly sent letters to the editor, pointing out the town and property owners' responsibilities. Half the town had laughed. The other half regularly yelled at the Ghost for allowing burglar alarms to stay broken or tires to go flat or their cars to run out of gasoline. Jane gave herself a mental slap on the wrist for being foolish enough to revisit the scene of her latest rescue.

Did she really think, after all this time, she would hear a single word of gratitude?

She repeated the question, aloud, when she got back to her apartment and Katie, nearest her age at the Sanctum and her closest friend, called to make arrangements for a visit on her way through town.

"I bet those kids brag about the Ghost catching them," Katie said, when Jane related the events of the evening.

"Yeah, they're just dumb enough to do that." Jane sighed and stretched out on her back on the futon in her tiny living room. "The people here are lazy or stupid. Usually both. How come the superheroes in the comic books never go through this?"

"They do," Katie said with a snort of muffled laughter. "It just never gets written into the comics because it's boring."

"Boring is a nice way of describing what I'm going through."

"Hey, at least you get a little variety, even if it's mostly frustration. I spend my whole life zipping from one town to another, playing Pony Express without a pony. It amazes me how much paperwork we generate, but we still don't make any headway dealing with the Rivals."

"I'll trade places with you." Jane closed her eyes and contemplated, just for a few seconds, the glorious thought of walking away from this assignment. Beau had nearly admitted it was a waste of time. "I almost asked the Old Poops to let me retire."

"When? What happened?"

An hour later, after discussing the visit to Neighborlee and the meeting with their teachers, Katie promised she would ask discreet questions and find out if anybody else had heard about a Council meeting. The idea of descendants of other lost children marrying and raising up a new generation of Gifted, outside the guidance of the Old Poops, fascinated her.

~~~~~

"Did you see what that Ghost did last night?" Even without the nasal twang, the accompanying *hack-splat* identified the speaker as Rufus Holcomb, deep into today's first pouch of chewing tobacco.

Despite herself, Jane's ears pricked up. She shook her head and deliberately turned her back on the big bay window of Lazy Days Spa and the wide-open door that let fresh air and conversations through. No, she did not want to hear any gossip about the Ghost. It was bad enough *being* the Ghost, without hearing all the misconceptions people spread about her alter ego.

"That boy's gonna get himself in trouble, one of these days," Junior Barnes' gravelly voice drawled. "Interfering where he ain't wanted. Ain't normal for people to get yanked out of trouble they brought down on their own heads."

Jane sighed. She hated it when she agreed on anything with the geezers slouched in front of her shop. She turned back to her work, resisting once again the temptation to sabotage the support posts for the awning out front. The lack of shade might make the August heat inside the shop unpleasant, but that was what air conditioners were for, right? She might have heat, but she wouldn't have green-black tobacco stains and the stink of tobacco juice all over the sidewalk. The trade was definitely a step up, in her favor. With her luck, Junior and Rufus wouldn't let lack of shade make them move.

"What'd he do this time?" Junior continued.

"The McCreedy kids went down to the reservoir and broke through the fence—"

"Ain't it electric?"

"Was. McCreedy might be raisin' a bunch of juvenile delinquents, but he's raisin' smart ones. They un-electrified it, cut themselves a nice door through the fence, and went swimming. Right near the sluice gates, which were wide open, thanks to the water level goin' down."

Newspapers rattled. Jane rolled her eyes and tried to focus on her inventory of aromatherapy candles. Only Rufus could read a two-inch newspaper account and turn it into big news, with details the reporters never gave. The fact the details were totally wrong proved yet again that Rufus' claim to know everything in town was a big enough lie, his nose should have grown all the way out to the Interstate.

"Nearly got sucked into the turbines or whatever you call it for the power plant. The kids claim the Ghost stopped the water and made it go backwards, then flew them up onto the cement wall and left them hanging there until the police came." Rufus snorted. "Smart boy, the Ghost. Got some girl to call the police with an anonymous tip about the ruckus at the reservoir."

"Lucky girl, having the Ghost for a boyfriend," Junior said.

Lucky girl, nothing, Jane fumed silently. She took a deep sniff of the lavender serenity candle. It didn't help.

Nothing helped. She had the biggest shop on Center Street, with a vaulted ceiling and lots of plants hanging from hooks, lots of open floor space and windows down the north wall because it was the end unit. Still, that didn't fight the growing feeling of living in a box, a cage, with half the town crowding in around her. She had to get out.

"Yeah, lucky girl, whoever she is. Right handy, having a boyfriend who can fly and walk through walls and whatever other hinky things the Ghost can do."

"Hinky?" Junior snorted. "How about kinky?"

The two old men wheezed and snorted and guffawed until Jane wanted to take a fire hose to them. She prayed they never needed CPR. She wouldn't be able to get past her revulsion to touch either one of them, let alone perform mouth-to-mouth.

"What I wouldn't give to have the kind of girl the Ghost could get, with all his superpowers," Rufus grumbled.

The Ghost didn't have a girlfriend. If the Ghost were a man, he wouldn't be desperate enough to date one of the town twits. Last night had proven once again the local genetic deterioration.

"Probably wasn't too smart, hiding the evidence," Jane muttered. "Even to get back at Joe-Bob. It still isn't a crime, is it, to be so stupid?"

"What was that, dearie?" Mrs. Tarvish called from the back of the spa.

"Just thinking out loud." She cast a fond glance at her pixie-like favorite customer.

At ninety-seven, Mrs. Tarvish insisted on trying all the latest fads and the most garish colors for her makeup, nails and hair. Right now, she reclined in Jane's spa chair, her feet soaking in a warm whirlpool bath, her hands encased in scented paraffin and a bottle of magenta nail polish waiting to be applied. A honey-oatmeal-avocado self-heating facial mask covered her face. Her freshly dyed hair — metallic gold — was wrapped in teeny tiny curls.

Otis Conroy sauntered through the door, thumbs hooked in the pockets of his jeans and biceps threatening to tear the sleeves of his too-tight T-shirt. "Big night last night, huh, doll?"

Jane knew most girls in Fendersburg thought the sun rose and set on Otis Conroy, football, baseball and hockey star. He was handsome enough, in a Christopher Reeve kind of way. He understood basic hygiene, didn't chew tobacco, and had come home from college with a business degree that hadn't taken eight years to earn. He inherited his father's car dealership and turned it into a multi-million-dollar business, with car lots in three counties. Any girl in Fendersburg would consider him a catch. Except Jane.

Which, she supposed, was the sole reason Otis kept harassing her, instead of settling down with one of his adoring fans. That said something for his taste, and preferring girls with more than a single-digit IQ. Maybe he had enough brains to want to improve the gene pool, but Jane had no intention of being a donor.

"What happened last night, Otis?" Mrs. Tarvish said.

"Big doings down at the reservoir." He waggled his eyebrows at Jane and settled down on the little stool she used for giving manicures. It creaked but didn't give out under him. "I never saw kids so scared in my whole life. They shouldn't have tried to go swimming. Good thing someone — " He winked at Jane and puffed out his chest another four inches. " — saw they were in trouble and flew down to help."

"The Ghost doesn't fly," Jane said, just because it was a knee-jerk reaction to contradict Otis.

"How do you know, dearie?" Mrs. Tarvish said with a girlish giggle. "That's why they call him the Ghost. Because nobody ever sees him. Just the things he does. If I were thirty years younger..." She sighed and her tiny bow-shaped mouth widened in a grin like a cat about to pounce on a canary.

Otis shuddered, and stared, horrified, at the little old lady.

"Maybe they should call him the Wind," Jane said.

"What's it gonna take to let a guy blow into your life and sweep you off your feet, huh?" Otis' usual leer was only half the usual wattage. He turned on the stool, following Jane as she moved over to the display of nail polish, to continue her monthly inventory.

"I'll keep my feet firmly planted on the ground, thank you." She could almost feel his hot breath on her back. She could definitely feel his gaze boring holes in her roomy white cargo pants. She wore a white leotard under her neon green gauze shirt, but Otis always made her feel like she went commando, with her buttons loose in a high wind.

Jane stepped away from the display rack. The inventory could wait until Otis left the spa, or got up from the stool only three feet from her rear end. He had no superpowers, despite his broad — make that wide load — hints that he could be the Ghost's alter ego. Yet sometimes she could feel a supernatural touch on her bottom when Otis was around. She had to constantly fight the temptation to make some rapid, much-needed improvements in his anatomy.

As she passed him, she saw his smirk widen. He knew his presence made her uncomfortable, but the jerk took it as a compliment. Jane gritted her teeth, and then decided, *Why not?* She paused just long enough to press her foot against the leg of the stool and give a mental nudge to the legs and crossbars. The wood lost its density just long enough for the screws to fall out with soft chimes on the white floor tiles. Otis swore as the stool collapsed under him.

"Now look what you did," Jane said. "That's the fourth piece of furniture you've broken in the last month. Honestly, Otis, just stay away. You're bad for business."

"I didn't break —" He sputtered to a stop and hauled himself to his feet. Otis backed away from the pile of wood and rubbed at his bottom as he headed for the door. "I didn't break it."

"Then how do you explain it falling apart? No, wait." Jane put down her clipboard with her inventory list and tapped her chin, making a show of thinking deeply. "The Ghost could do something like that, couldn't he? Just manipulate matter, reach through things, unscrew screws, evaporate glue. Why, Otis, are you trying to prove you're the Ghost?" She batted her eyelashes at him.

Muttering, Otis stomped out of the spa. Mrs. Tarvish giggled and opened one eye. Her purple contacts contrasted strangely with the green facial mask.

"If that hulking idiot is the Ghost, then I'm Beyonce!" The little old lady chortled.

"You dance better than she does, anyway." Jane fought the urge to go lie down in the back room. One of the few nice things about Fendersburg was that the people were so incredibly dense. She could pull tricks like she had just done on Otis, in broad daylight, and nobody ever caught on that she was the Ghost.

The lack of smarter people catching on just proved the Rivals had stopped coming around. She was wasted here.

~~~~~

Today was Timmy Higgs' turn to get himself stuck in a tree, when Jane retreated to the park to eat her lunch. Timmy Higgs and Georgie Tupper got themselves stuck in the same gnarled century oak at least three times a week, during the summer. If the boys didn't loathe each other so much, Jane would have accused them of cooperating and taking turns getting in trouble. Her ribs ached at the memory of the last time the ungrateful little snot kicked her when she got him down out of the tree. Sometimes her rapid healing ability just wasn't fast enough.

She reminded herself of the aches and bruises and temporary nosebleeds and cuts and burns she earned in rescues, and tried to ignore Timmy's shrieks. Very hard to do, when her memory replayed Beau expounding on the duty that came along with the unusual talents in the blood and bone of the Gifted. Why couldn't she ignore him? Weren't his mother and aunt responsible for him? They were doing a wonderful job ignoring him. They were only a dozen or so feet away from him, while Jane was at the far end of the tree-lined park at the center of town.

After ten minutes of trying to eat her apple and concentrate on the latest Young Wizards book, she couldn't ignore the boy's piercing shrieks. They made her nerve endings shrivel, like hairs touched to a flame. She looked over her shoulder, down Center Street. Maybe Maribeth, who filled in for her at lunchtime, would dash out of the spa and urgently flag her down for an emergency of some kind. Jane's conscience kicked her. What would be a greater emergency? The town snot breaking an arm or leg, or a woman needing a manicure or massage in the next five minutes, before her world imploded?

Jane slid her book into her shoulder bag and flung her apple fifty feet to the trash barrel. The molecules of the barrel phased out just long enough for the apple to pass through and clang against the opposite side. She took a step and the automatic blurring of her entire physical form kicked in. So what if she didn't look around to make sure no one saw her? Maybe an obliviousness virus had infected the whole town? That could explain why the Rivals didn't react to her Ghost activities anymore. Unless someone needed her advice or to buy something from the spa, she was invisible even without the Ghost field. Jane never needed a costume.

Blessing or rip-off?

Three steps vaulted her across the length of the park, to the tree where Timmy's mother had finally sauntered over to look up at her dangling son. Jane leaped. Her blurred form had no mass or density to resist gravity. She shot up through the branches and leaves, to the topmost, swaying branch where the boy screamed and kicked and contorted his face into a snot-smeared, red mask. No way was Jane going to sacrifice her new gauze shirt to wipe that filthy, slimy face clean. Some things went beyond the call of duty and Timmy Higgs made up about eighty percent of the list.

"Let go, Timmy," she said through clenched teeth.

As usual, the moment she touched him, Timmy kicked harder and held on tighter.

"My plane!" he shrieked, and wriggled like a greased pig until she nearly lost her grip on him.

Jane sighed. Of course, it was his plane. As many times as he broke his favorite toy, someone fixed it for him or bought him a new one. He then launched it up into the air, straight into the branches of this very tree. This always required Timmy to risk life and limb to retrieve it. Jane wondered if his parents had ever considered introducing him to rock collecting.

She thought of all the broken windows resulting from that hobby, or visits to the reservoir or the nearby ravines, in search of specimens. No, twice-weekly flights were much easier to handle.

She spotted the missing, mangled plane, shot up through the branches to snag it, and floated down with Timmy still kicking in her arms. He did the most damage when he was wrapped in her blurring field and his density matched hers.

Irony? Timmy was in a neck-and-neck contest with Georgie to be the densest child in Fendersburg.

"What took you so long?" Mrs. Higgs snapped, the moment Jane let go of Timmy and the boy bounced to the ground. "Do you know how long my boy has been hanging there, waiting for you to do your job and get him down out of that tree?"

For a change, she aimed her diatribe *at* Jane, instead of two or three feet to the left. Jane stood still, fists clenched, wanting very much to become visible just long enough to slap the woman's face. But Anabelle Higgs bought pounds of makeup and exercise clothes, cleansing spray and body butter from Lazy Days Spa every month. Jane knew better than to irritate the customer who always put her into the black.

"Men!" the woman snapped, and reached down to grab hold of her son's hand before he headed up the tree again. "If superheroes were women, they'd pay better attention to children."

"Why don't you pay attention to your own child for a change?" Jane muttered, and floated away.

After her little exercise, the half apple she had eaten didn't satisfy at all. She landed, looked around carefully, and phased back into view. Then she headed down the street to Gertie's for a chicken barbecue sandwich and peanut butter chocolate malt.

One of the few side benefits of the energy consumption of her Gift was the freedom to eat just about anything she wanted, and never gain a pound.

That afternoon, Jane tuned into the local radio station, with barely enough wattage to be heard at the borders of the county. Just her luck, she had tuned in for another chapter of the endless debate on whether the Ghost really existed or not. Many people blamed the Ghost "delusion" on pollutants in the water, radiation, heat stroke, and inebriation of the witnesses. She snapped the radio off with an angry flick of thought and didn't glance guiltily around the spa to see if anyone witnessed. Her current customer in the massage chair didn't notice, nor did the woman with her head under the dryer hood or the two in the tanning booths. Jane wondered if she had played the Ghost so often, nobody noticed her even when she was herself. Maybe she was becoming invisible even when she didn't want to be?

That wouldn't be good for her business.

Sad. Her day job meant more to her than saving lives, and doing her part to take down the Rivals before they brainwashed enough Gifted to take over the world.

~~~~~

"Well, what do you expect from a man?"

Jane cringed with one hand on the light switch and the other reaching for the bamboo shades to lower across the big bay window. Closing time hadn't come fast enough. She had done enough business today to make up for the last two slow weeks, but she couldn't close the door with customers coming in at the last minute. Stepping back, she waited for the owner of the familiar, stinging voice to step into the recessed doorway of the spa.

Mrs. Slodoski stomped past, complaining to Mrs. Simperton, her best friend by virtue of never daring to interrupt or contradict her. Jane breathed a sigh of relief, then choked when the next words slammed back at her.

"You'd think the Ghost would appreciate how important that bake sale was to the Parks and Recreation fund. How can we build a decent swimming pool if we don't raise enough money for it?"

Jane avoided City Council meetings because Mrs. Slodoski had turned the last three into shouting matches. She insisted that no money had to be taken out of other areas of Fendersburg's budget to pay for the pool, as long as people were willing to donate. Each time, she paused dramatically and gave a meaningful glare at Homer Bedlow, Fendersburg's resident millionaire.

Homer was a millionaire because he never gave any money away. He rarely spent it on himself, as proven by his skeletal frame, threadbare clothes, homemade haircuts, and the fact he walked everywhere instead of driving a car or bike.

Mrs. Slodoski kept organizing fundraisers, in spite of the underwhelming apathy of the general community. She ignored the fact that Fendersburg High School had an Olympic-size swimming pool, open from 8am until 9pm every day during the summer. Jane would bet her favorite new nail polish that Mrs. Slodoski had rammed the bake sale through by force of intimidation. People avoided her bake sales so she couldn't make them buy overpriced plates of bland cookies and cupcakes that someone always sabotaged in an attempt to make them dietetic.

"We were told not to set up there," Mrs. Simperton said, when her imperious leader paused for a loud, sighing breath. "Everybody told us it was a bad traffic area, children and dogs and bikes and whatnot racing through all day long."

"The Ghost could have stopped those nasty little brats from knocking over our table and kept the dogs from eating my lovely sardine pork balls and bran muffins, but did he? No, he couldn't be bothered to help out. What kind of civic pride does he have?"

"Civic pride doesn't mean a thing when common sense says not to come within twenty yards of you when you're in a snit," Jane muttered, and flipped the light switch. She let the shade drop with a bang and retreated out the back of the shop without opening the locked door.

So, it had finally happened. The Ghost was being blamed for things he *didn't* do, as well as the things he did that didn't suit the persnickety folks of Fendersburg. Jane wondered how long it would be before people blamed her for the heat, the fall rain coming too early or too late, and the noise of traffic on the Interstate.

"Half of them think I don't exist, and the rest of them think I'm a man," she grumbled when she got home to her fourth floor apartment on River Road. Jane tried to laugh, but that sour frown had claimed territory on her face. "You're an idiot, you know that? Sticking around where people would as soon kick you in the teeth as say a kind word. And when you are visible, the only people who pay any attention are either slimebags like Otis, or people who want miracles."

She sighed and sank down on the floor with her back against the door from the hallway.

"You're out of the miracle business, girl. Time to find some place where you can be normal."

And though she didn't say it, the thought echoed through her head: *And where you can meet some normal men and go on normal dates and maybe fall in love the normal way.*

Was that too much to ask?

"Is there such a thing as a town where people are normal? If there is, would I ever be allowed to settle there?" She sighed, and her sense of humor finally woke up. "Define 'normal' please?"

What would happen if she just picked up and left Fendersburg? It was a given the Rivals wouldn't notice because they certainly weren't paying attention to the Ghost's presence and activities now. Why stick around any longer? Why not leave?

Her heart skipped a few beats. Could she do that?

She got up and fixed dinner without really paying attention to what she pulled out of the refrigerator while she examined idea from all angles. Beau and Demetrius had certainly seemed sympathetic. They had been disgusted with the town long before the proposed initiative to sue the Ghost. Would they let her quit?

What then? Would they just assign her somewhere else? Or would they let her pick where she wanted to live?

"Convincing them is going to be the easy part," Jane told her peanut butter, salami, pepperjack cheese, spicy mustard on oatnut bread sandwich. With a full bag of barbecue chips to wash it down. "Escaping this place without it going up in a nuclear reaction before I step over the city limits will be the hard part."

Even though Fendersburg thought the Ghost was a man, Jane knew better than to think she could just leave town at the same time the Ghost stopped operating. She also couldn't just stop responding to every cry for help or crash or ripple of panic. For her own peace of mind — forget that threatened lawsuit — she had to warn Fendersburg no one was going to come racing to save their necks.

Then, after a month or two of no Ghost in Fendersburg, she could leave town.

It wasn't like anyone was going to suddenly wake up in a flood of remorse, realize they had taken the Ghost for granted, and mend their ways. No, Jane had no illusions on that score. She fully expected to hear complaints, maybe some people laughing, convinced the Ghost was playing a joke on them. Then as the days went by and people suffered the consequences of their bad choices, the groundswell of sniping and placing blame would be overwhelming.

Petty criminals would be more overt in their activities, and people would stand around and scream for the Ghost to do something instead of helping themselves. Finally, the police would become more active. Some people would get so fed up with the Ghost ignoring their demands, they would resume responsibility for their own lives.

"Tough love," Jane mused through a sticky mouthful. She grinned. "The problem is, there was never any love on either side. Selfish brats."

The thought of getting away, the relief she anticipated, soothed the deeply ingrained sense of guilt that seemed to be mostly asleep. Frustration was a powerful narcotic.

Even if the Council disagreed with her decision, they couldn't really stop her. Could they? At least they couldn't haul her up on charges of endangering the ordinary Humans who depended on her if she *warned* Fendersburg the Ghost was leaving town.

Step one — go through proper channels.

Chapter Four

"Hello there."

Beauregard remained hanging by his knees from the bar sticking out from the far side of the massive fireplace. The heat and gravity eased the stiffness in his back. He watched Jane settle into an easy chair where they could have a comfortable conversation without either of them twisting their necks too far. Demetrius was absent.

"If you're coming about that meeting of the Council, you're premature."

"You are meeting, though?" she asked. Hopefully not too quickly.

"Oh, absolutely. Demetrius and I had a long talk after you left. We're pretty much agreed that maybe it's time we assign someone to watch Neighborlee, track down every lost child who stayed in town and married each other, and see what has developed among their children. If they had any children. If they didn't lose their minds when odd things happened. Neighborlee has a tendency to act like itching powder if you don't quite fit in. It's like the town is aware, and it rejects you or welcomes you with open arms. Whenever we spent any length of time there..."

"It's like the people who live there, who fit in, they don't notice the weirdness?" Jane offered. Since her visit to Neighborlee several weeks ago, she had done a lot of thinking, a lot of remembering, and contacted a handful of friends who were willing to share their memories from life before the Sanctum.

"Exactly." He tipped his head to one side, which looked odd, hanging upside down. "What do you think of the town?"

"I like it."

"Hmm. Good. I'm of the theory that places where people like us show up are different enough, so embedded with whatever it is that empowers us, they develop awareness. They choose who they want around. And they let us know if they like us or not. Take this old pile of bricks." He reached out and patted the facing of the massive fireplace. "It was falling down when Demetrius and I

39

found it more than a century ago. Practically dragged us through the shattered doorway, begging us to make it a home. Did you ever hear the stories about this place being haunted?"

"No." Jane shivered, earning a chuckle from him.

"We heard lots of stories. Made it easy to buy the place. The locals almost begged us to take it. But not a peep, not a rumble, not a flicker of an apparition from the moment we crossed the threshold. Over the years, we've been waiting for one of you to learn to move back and forth through time. The most logical explanation was that the ghosts were students from the future, learning time travel." He shrugged — also interesting while hanging upside down. "Hasn't happened yet."

"But it might."

"Anything is possible in this place. So much of our personal energy has soaked into the granite, the soil, the very air... Anyway, what brings you here? Besides curiosity."

"I want to quit, Beau. Fendersburg. Just hand in my resignation letter and walk away. After a suitable wait, so no one will ever link my leaving town with the Ghost going out of business," she hurried to add, as he opened his mouth to protest.

"Thought about it a lot, haven't you?" He winked, and then he reached up to grasp the bar with both hands. With a grunt, he unhooked his legs and dropped to the floor, landing lightly despite his bulk. "What do you want to do? Where will you go? Can't see you coming back to this pile of bricks as a teacher."

"Who is there to teach?"

"Exactly. I pray every day there are others like us out there, scooping up children and training them so they don't make a big splash when their Gifts activate. Protecting them from rotters like the Rivals. With the world getting smaller every day, all this online folderol, it'd be impossible to hide when some wannabe superheroes take their adventures out of the comic books."

"Beau... What if whatever sent us here, to do something or hide from something ... What if that reason isn't there anymore?"

"What if wherever we came from isn't there anymore, so the door has closed?" He winked and settled in his easy chair.

"All I know is that I need to get away. I need to quit being the Ghost, because we wove together the whole stupid persona to play tricks and trap the Rivals. That hasn't worked. If they've only pulled back, they could be watching and waiting, and they might follow me wherever I go, so I have to *stop* being the Ghost. But at the same time … God gave me these talents, so I'm supposed to use them for something, right? So what am I supposed to do?" She spread her arms, palms up, half-hoping the answer would fall out of the air and land in her hands, maybe with a ten-step plan and pictures to make things clear. Was that asking too much?

"Uh huh. And that brings us back to Neighborlee."

"How does that bring us—" She shivered, as her mind latched onto the time spent in Divine's Emporium. Angela's suggestion. The sensation she knew far more than she was letting on.

"You've read Charlie and Rainbow Zephyr's books, haven't you?"

"Required reading … oh. Right. They're from Neighborlee." Another shiver, but this one felt like waking on Christmas morning or her birthday, knowing something incredible was about to happen. There were some benefits to being the adopted niece or granddaughter to a mansion full of Gifted.

Jane called their images to mind. A tall man with a receding hairline and a long, snow white ponytail, wearing a tie-dyed T-shirt. His wife came up to his shoulder, Asian, with long, straight hair dyed a different color of the rainbow in each picture Jane had seen on the backs of their books.

"Have you ever considered working with them, asking them to join Hoax?"

"We have, but several times when we prepared to approach them, we always encountered strange incidents. Too many coincidences. Either they were being watched by suspected Rivals or …" He shrugged.

"They could be Rivals, and all their books are just a cover for investigating? Just like Hoax is a cover for us searching the world for Gifted?" Jane ached a little for her teacher, who had been carrying this burden so long.

"Besides, they have military connections. One is a lost child who was nearly snatched up by the Rivals, when we rescued Charlie. We had been investigating him for some time, especially since he seemed to be aware of Charlie's Gift about to bloom. We gave him the choice of coming with us. He chose to go into the military. Sometimes I wish …" He sighed.

41

"If we don't give people a choice, what makes us any different from the Rivals, even if we're doing it for the right reasons?" she whispered.

"What we *believe* are the right reasons. Never forget, Cookie, despite our Gifts, we are Human and that means we are fallible."

"So you can't take the risk of approaching the Zephyrs to get that inside connection?"

"Hmm, somewhat." That shadow of sadness flicked out of his eyes and a sparkle of promise and a touch of mischief returned.

Jane relaxed a little, glad for his rising spirits. Then a new thought seemed to slap her between the eyes and she gasped.

"Beau ... Are you assigning *me* to investigate the Zephyrs? Test them? Make friends with them?"

"Reweave your old connection with them. They were regulars at the children's home, after all. Their daughter is close to your age. You were probably in school with her."

"She was four years ahead of me, I think. The track star. Lanie?"

"She's probably your best connection point. Once you're settled, get involved with the town. The children's home has a mentoring program. Former residents come back and work with the children. Get involved there. That will put you right in the center of things if any Gifted start blossoming." He shrugged. "Hope springs eternal and all that rot."

Jane snorted and they shared a conspiratorial grin. "Definitely have to quit Fendersburg. Can't just commute back and forth."

"I'm going to go out on a limb and give you permission. If Demetrius and the rest of the Council disagree, they'll have to deal with me." He chuckled when she nearly leaped on him and hugged him hard and tight for many long moments.

~~~~~

Jane was only slightly disappointed when she started her research in preparation for relocating and discovered that Charlie and Rainbow Zephyr were heading out of town on a research trip that would take them at least six months. The news wasn't a setback. She was going to take her time uprooting from Fendersburg. As Beauregard had said, she should connect with people who might remember her from Neighborlee Children's Home, especially Lanie Zephyr, and work her way up to meeting and getting to know the older Zephyrs.

The results of investigating Lanie slapped her in the face with the realization that she hadn't kept up with events in her hometown. How had she missed the tragedy from four years ago, when Lanie, a teacher, had rescued one of her students from his own stupidity and broke her back? Jane remembered the tradition of Senior Prank Night. She remembered Lanie being a star athlete, and ached for her, sentenced to life in a wheelchair. She wasn't surprised when she bought a subscription to the *Neighborlee Tattler*, to follow the town news, and found Lanie was a sports reporter for the paper.

"You made a new life for yourself. Is there room in it for me, and can we be friends? Will you be glad we're friends?" Jane mused, and moved on to her next topic of research.

Jane liked the feeling of anticipation as she made lists and prioritized the chores and steps necessary to change her life.

~~~~~

Katie came to see her several days later, arriving with a leap from the street, a muffled boom and a wall of air that ruffled the curtains of Jane's open balcony door. She paused. The brilliant Sunday afternoon light spilling over her shoulders wavered a little as the dying force field enveloping her aggravated the photons.

"Writing the story of your life?" the spike-haired platinum blonde asked. She gestured at the drifts of crumpled paper all around Jane's chair in her tiny living room.

"Resignation letter."

"How can you resign? You're self-employed." She snorted and settled down on the floor and reached for the closest crumple.

"Things quiet in Metropolis?" Jane snatched the paper away and twisted her wrist, forming a brief whirlwind that clumped all the papers together into a lump slightly denser than coal.

"Deadly." Katie grinned and held out her arms, shaking them so her multiple silver rings flashed and her charm bracelets jangled. She currently lived in Fredonia, Kansas, just because it was equidistant to all the places she needed to travel to in her duties of carrying messages. She joked about having to put up with the Marx Brothers, when she didn't call the town Metropolis and joke about looking for Superman.

Jane knew there was no Superman, except in lonely dreams

late at night, and comic books. Her life was no comic book. She had long ago faced the fact that all the Gifted men she had ever met were too old for romance or looked on her as a daughter or little sister. The only interesting ones were taken, somehow striking the jackpot by finding an ordinary Human woman who didn't freak out when she learned the truth. None had produced children yet. Jane knew she was crippling herself with her high standards, but she wanted romance, she wanted marriage, she wanted children. She wanted it all. Based on the track records of everyone in Hoax, she needed to get out of the hero business if she was ever going to find a man worth running all the bases for. One worth making that home run for—and staying home.

Every orphan dreamed of home, and superpowered orphans wanted one more than most.

She wasn't ever going to find that home, or that man, in Fendersburg.

"If only there really were a Metropolis." Katie sighed, and that mischievous light flashed in her eyes. "Do you know how easy life would be for us if such a place existed?"

"One: there is a Metropolis, in Illinois. And two: I have no idea."

"In all the comic books, the villains are all polite enough to live in one city. They don't bother the rest of the country."

Jane snorted. That theory was ridiculous. Still, she felt better already. Leave it to Katie, her big sister, who had helped her in those awkward, wonderful, slightly frightening months when she first joined Hoax. Maybe her timing was great, as usual? Maybe she could help write this frustrating letter?

The task had felt so easy, so simple, when Jane got up that morning. Then when she finally sat down to put pen to paper, a sense of shame started to creep over her. The first ten letters sounded spoiled and temper tantrum-inclined. Not the lasting impression she wanted to leave, even if it was moronic Fendersburg getting a Dear John letter.

"So, what are you doing? Really," Katie prompted.

"Like I said, I'm resigning. I'm going to deliver a letter first thing tomorrow morning to the *Trumpet*, announcing that the Ghost is retiring and everybody will just have to look both ways before crossing the street and get their own brats out of trees and the police will have to get out of their patrol cars for more than coffee breaks."

"Wow," Katie whispered. She went perfectly still, not a charm jangling, not a platinum strand waving. That showed the depths of her shock. She was constantly on the move. "You think they'll let you get away with it?"

"Do you really think I care what the lazy twits of Fendersburg think or want?" Jane jammed her pen straight through her much-depleted notebook.

"Not them. The Old Poops," she whispered.

Jane snorted. She tried not to, but a grin cracked her face. She met Katie's dancing gaze and the two of them slouched, giggling, the rebellious laughter of children who had mocked their pompous elders. Underneath that laughter, she sensed a vein of nervousness in her friend. Jane knew it wasn't nice, but she wanted to milk the moment for everything she could get, griping-wise, before she revealed the truth.

"Tough. I have every right to a life of my own. Getting kicked by snot-nosed brats and yelled at by irresponsible mothers and hit on by libidinous morons isn't part of that life. After all I've done for them, don't I deserve some respect, some free time, some normality? Nobody even bothers to say thanks. Is it so hard?"

"What we need to do is get the people who write the comic books to insert some lessons on superhero etiquette in their stories."

"The dweebs in Fendersburg don't have high enough IQs to read comic books." She sighed, feeling tired. The joke had definitely fallen flat. "Anyway, Beau knows."

"Uh huh. You're not the rebel I thought you were."

"Well, he gave me permission without going to the Council. They could still say no. I haven't heard anything, so either they agreed or they haven't met yet." Jane thumped the table. "Doesn't matter. I'm quitting the hero biz. As soon as I get this letter written, anyway."

"What's the game plan?"

"Write the letter, deliver it to tomorrow's editorial meeting, in a way guaranteed to make plenty of witnesses. Then sit back and watch life go on without me." Jane closed her eyes and smiled, imagining the utter bliss of the freedom to pretend she was ordinary and oblivious.

"You're going to stay here in town and just watch everybody make a mess of their lives without you?" Katie's mouth dropped open and she sat perfectly still for twenty-four seconds.

"No. I'm going to move away after about a month. I know everybody thinks the Ghost is a man, but I still have to cover my tracks. With my luck, if I announced I was leaving town and vanished the next day, the light would finally dawn and somebody would link the Ghost's disappearance—ha!—with my leaving town."

"Such as the Rivals."

"My staying here and making a ruckus, rescuing every candidate for the Darwin Award hasn't done any good. Not a single rat has even tried for the bait in the trap." She opened her eyes and shrugged. "With my luck, someone would think I'm the Ghost's girlfriend, the real reason he's leaving town, and then I'd never have any peace."

"Where are you going?"

"Back to Neighborlee."

"But that's--" Katie nodded slowly. "Another assignment? Going quiet and waiting for the Rivals to make a move?"

"I hope not. No, this is more like putting down roots and becoming one of them and doing some research into the others like us, lost but no Gifts. Find out what happened to them."

"Sounds … fun."

"Could be." Jane stood up and snapped her fingers, and then held out her hands in baseball catcher pose. The cookie jar obligingly zipped across the room and into her hands. She sat down and took the surfer figure off the wave, which let out a roar like the ocean. Then she related to Katie everything that had happened in the last few weeks since her visit to Neighborlee, and what she and Beauregard had discussed on her last visit.

~~~~~

"Beau, it's finally happened." Demetrius stomped into the library and slapped the *Fendersburg Trumpet* down on the three-foot-high stack of suburban newspapers in front of the other man. Wisps of smoke curled up from the blackened edges of the pages that had burned away until the page he wanted was uppermost.

"Hmm, can't imagine what would happen in Fendersburg that would upset you like that," Beau murmured around the lip of his bottle of Perrier. He put the bottle down, fumbling it at the last minute, so he had to mentally nudge it away from the edge of the table. "Janie does an admirable job dealing with those poster children for involuntary sterilization."

"It's always the quiet ones who shock you."

He cocked his shaggy gray head to one side and studied his old friend for a few moments. Their many pupils through the years had never learned to stand up under his searching regard, always growing restless in less than a minute. Gazing at a suspected troublemaker or rebel had often wrung a confession, without the painful application of telepathy to read the short-term memory and emotions. Demetrius, though, was immune. He simply stood and fumed, little wreaths of smoke emerging from his ears in rhythm with his sighing breaths.

"Now, let's see what trouble has found the little gal," he muttered and reached for the paper.

"You sentimental old fool." Demetrius snatched the paper out from under his hands and stepped back, holding the paper up to the light slanting through the skylight. "'To the people of Fendersburg, a warning,'" he read slowly. "'From now on, you're responsible for the messes you get into. Just like when you moved away from home, your mother didn't keep doing your laundry and picking up your socks. You learned to clean up after yourself. Over the last few years, you've become lazy. Maybe part of that is my fault. Well, folks, that ends today.'"

"Hmm. She sounds a little peeved. It takes a lot to irritate her." Beau grinned when Demetrius glared at him and rattled the paper. "Sorry, old boy. Do go on."

"'Stop wasting time debating whether or not the Ghost exists. You won't see evidence of my work from this day forward. No more flying you to a job interview when your car died because you couldn't be bothered to put gas in the tank. No more pulling children out of trees because their parents can't be bothered to keep them on a leash. No more pulling your fat out of the frying pan because you couldn't be bothered to pay attention to the weather or lock your door when you left the house or turn off the iron or the stove or a thousand other problems that normal, responsible adults handle every day without thinking about it twice.

"'You've gotten lazy, Fendersburg. You think since the Ghost is here, why should you act like adults? Why should you look both ways before you cross the street? The Ghost will stop the cars. Don't deny it. When smarter people ask why you took stupid risks, "Oh, well," you say with a shrug, "if something goes wrong, the Ghost will rescue me.""

Demetrius paused to shake his head. Beauregard reached out as if to take the paper from him. He glared, rustled the paper, took another step backwards and continued.

"'Well, folks, those days are over. The Ghost is gone. Good-bye. I quit. I'm leaving town as of today. You're on your own. Grow up. The baby-sitter has left the building.'"

Beau burst out laughing, the sound somewhere between a donkey's bray and rough, deep barking. He shuddered so hard he nearly tumbled out of his throne-like easy chair. "Good for her!" He slapped his knee. "She picked up those lazy bums by their collars and shook them hard. She warned them, didn't she? Put them on the alert that they're responsible for their own lives. Good girl."

"Yes, but the way she said it—" Demetrius folded the paper into a small bundle and slammed it down onto the table. He dropped down into his chair. All the starch went out of him. "No dignity. Even if those ungrateful wretches in Fendersburg have no dignity, as our student, entrusted with her superhuman powers, Jane should show some dignity."

"They deserved it. You said it yourself, Dem. The people don't have the common sense of a rock. Like Janie said, they're lazy. Give them a few weeks of burning their fingers and stubbing their toes and they'll realize how good they had it."

"I wouldn't bet on it," Demetrius said, punctuated with a sniff of disdain. "If they stay true to form, instead of apologizing and hoping the message gets to the Ghost, those entitlement-attitude morons will follow through and sue for dereliction of duty. Serve them right if they publicly humiliate themselves. Wouldn't be surprised if a dozen shyster lawyers get involved, trying to make a name for themselves by handling the case."

"Might be entertaining to watch. How sure are they the Ghost wrote the letter?"

"There was a preface saying it was delivered by an arm coming through the wall during an editorial meeting, and dropping the envelope on the senior editor's desk." He chuckled. "The girl has style."

~~~~~

"That ingrate!" Mrs. Higgs shrieked, almost on the threshold of Lazy Days Spa.

Rufus and Junior burst out in cackles and hiccups of laughter. Jane winced at the blare of sound, but consoled herself that if the two old coots were laughing, they weren't spitting. She glanced at her calendar. Twenty-nine days and counting until she put the closing sign in the window. She wondered if she could arrange for them to take a long vacation, until someone agreed to sign the lease. She didn't like leaving her landlord in the lurch. Arabella Jones was a nice old lady, even when she dressed in leather and studs on the weekends and went to Harley rallies.

"What's wrong?" Jane hurried forward to catch Mrs. Higgs as she staggered into the shop.

"Did you read the paper?"

"A little." The letter to the editor section was the only one Jane had looked at. She wanted to make sure the *Trumpet* had printed her letter in its entirety and had been braced to make a return trip to the editorial offices to reinforce her wishes. To her surprise and delight, the editor hadn't changed a thing, and even related how the letter was delivered. Maybe someone was taking the Ghost seriously for a change.

Too little, too late.

"What is wrong with that man?" she wailed, and sank down on the bench strategically facing the display case with the latest shades of makeup, and the newest wonder-working clarifiers and vanishing creams.

"What man?" Jane bit her lip to keep from grinning.

"The Ghost, of course. Who does he think he is, leaving this town? After all he owes us!"

"What does the Ghost owe us? Has anyone paid him for stopping fires and catching bank robbers and pulling children and cats out of trees?"

"No, but he —"

"What has anyone ever done for him?"

"Why, we..." Mrs. Higgs' angry flush faded into a thoughtful frown. "But we were talking about...no, we didn't do that, either. Surely somebody gave him...and then the mayor...no, I don't remember that being done, either."

"Has anyone ever said thank you?" Jane kept her voice soft to fight down the angry trembling that still hit her at times.

It had taken nearly all day Sunday to write her letter, and she had gone through a long, frustrating list of all the things she had done for Fendersburg without a word of appreciation. The bruises and cuts and burns, the kicks and slaps from nasty brats who didn't want to be rescued. The scratches from cats, the stink of drunks who had puked on her shoes, the smell of smoke and spilled oil and a thousand other unpleasant memories and sensations. In the end, she had ripped up the list instead of including it with the letter. She felt like a whiny brat the more she looked at it.

"Why should we thank him?" Mrs. Higgs' voice wavered. She didn't sound half as indignant as Jane knew she could. "He's only doing his job."

"Who hired him?" She brought up the fake smile she had learned to use on customers she thought were vain and ridiculous, when she had to be nice for the sake of her business.

"That's true. Nobody asked him to come here. Let him leave. Good riddance." She started to get up, but her attention snagged on the display of sable cosmetic brushes and the pearl-toned eye shadow in six new shades. Avarice made her eyes gleam and she reached for the nearest box. Jane sighed and heard the cash register ring. One disaster averted. Maybe.

Otis sauntered into the spa half an hour later, as Mrs. Higgs scurried out with $80 of war paint clutched to her chest.

Jane smiled. In a month, she would never have to look at him again. Unfortunately, Otis took it as welcome rather than relief. His obnoxious grin widened and his swagger threatened to broadside a semi-truck.

"Hey, there, babe." He rested sweaty arms on the glass display case and breathed beer fumes in her face. "What's the good news?"

"Did you hear what the Ghost did?" She fluttered her lashes, knowing instantly how to pay back some of the years of ogling and leering. If she was lucky, Otis would do it to himself.

"Hear?" He smirked and stood up straight, pulling his shoulders back and thrusting his chest out. Fortunately, he was still in good enough shape not to need to step back to keep his belly from rubbing against the display case. "Honey, I was there."

"Really? What are your plans?"

"Plans?" His smile shortened a notch. "For what?"

"Leaving town. Rufus," she called, pitching her voice and adding a little Ghost *oomph* to change the acoustics in the shop so everyone out on the sidewalk could hear. "Isn't the Ghost leaving town? Otis has been hinting for years that he's the Ghost, so, he's leaving town. Right?" She batted her eyelashes at him again.

"So, what's the scoop, Otis?" Rufus leaned against the doorframe but didn't come inside. "Why're you leaving town?"

"I'm not leaving town!" Otis staggered back two steps, his head turning, looking back and forth between Jane and Rufus so fast, she thought it might just snap off his neck.

That'd be an improvement.

"So... You're just gonna hang around and watch everybody suffer," Junior drawled, leaning in to look through the door. "Just sit back and laugh at us poor helpless folk, because you're too high and mighty to help. Kinda makes a fella wonder how you and your daddy made your big bucks in the first place. Y'know?" He leaned against the opposite side of the door from Rufus, then turned his head aside to spit with a loud splat.

"I wouldn't—I didn't—"

"It's right here in the paper. Ghost is retiring." Rufus waved the folded paper at Otis.

"Whoever said that is lying!" He snatched it and unfolded it with shaking hands. His face went from embarrassed red to panicked white to angry red to terrified white in the time it took to read the letter. Jane noticed his gaze tracked back to the opening, italicized paragraph three times.

"Somebody is lying," she said. It took all her self-control not to gloat, not to let years of frustration and disgust creep into her voice and face. "If you didn't deliver that letter to the editor, who did?"

"I didn't—I never said—" Otis dropped the paper and staggered toward the door. Rufus and Junior blocked it.

"Are you the Ghost, Otis?" She smiled as sweetly as she could manage. "Please, honey, tell me it's true." She reached out and stroked her fingertips down his bared, sweating arm. His skin felt greasy, and the muscles twitched as if he'd just been zapped with about a thousand volts. "I just adore the Ghost," she added on a whisper, and sidled up next to him. Another step would have them sharing the same space.

As the Ghost, she could do that, but Otis would totally lose his mind and she would have destroyed all the years of hiding her identity. Jane depended on Otis' basic sense of self-preservation and terror winning out over ego and lust.

"I ain't the Ghost!" He staggered backward, clutched at the doorway and misjudged. Rufus and Junior leaped out of his way with more agility than Jane ever would have credited to the two oldsters. Otis twisted around on one foot and nearly ran into the bench just in front of her bay window. "I'm not the Ghost. I ain't leaving town. You can't make me!"

People on the street stopped to stare. Since it was the lunch hour, Otis had the biggest audience he had played before since being a sports hero in high school and college. He never noticed. Face pale and sweating, he ran down the street.

Somewhere out there was a man who was exactly what he said he was, no hinting, no mental games, no bragging, no resting on someone else's reputation. No lies. No pretenses. Somewhere out there was an ordinary guy Jane could be comfortable with, who would let her be herself. Maybe he was the kind of guy who, if he found out about her Gifts, about her former secret identity, he would shrug, think about it a minute, then tell her she was beautiful and ask her what she wanted to do Saturday night.

Chapter Five

Timmy Higgs got stuck in the tree, chasing his balsa wood plane two days after the letter appeared in the paper. He hung there for nearly half an hour before his mother called for the fire department. Ginny Piper, Fendersburg's fire chief, laughed about it when she came into the spa that afternoon for her weekly therapeutic massage.

"Kind of nice, you know? Using our equipment and training." She sighed as Jane rubbed deep into her shoulder muscles. "That kid was actually scared, just hanging there, kicking and starting to blubber. And you know what he told me when we got him down to the ground? He said the Ghost was his friend, and he wanted to know what we did to scare him away. The Ghost has too much sense to be friends with that brat. He kicked me in the ankle when I told him not to climb that tree again." She snorted. "His mother swatted his bottom before she dragged him away. I bet that's the first time that ever happened. For both of them."

"Probably," Jane agreed. Inside the privacy of her head, she wavered between shrieking and laughter. Timmy thought he was her friend? Not for all the tea in Asia!

The usual bi-monthly diatribe about vigilantes and people living in fantasy worlds ran in the *Fendersburg Trumpet* a week after the Ghost's resignation letter. Instead of the usual demand for intensive psychiatric evaluation for the Ghost, the letter writer, Marijane Hunter, congratulated the Ghost on finally gaining some perspective and a grasp on reality.

Three days later, her house was burglarized. She wrote a scathing letter to the editor, blaming the entire town for the Ghost's retirement.

Other than Marijane being robbed, Jane didn't notice any change in the crime rate in Fendersburg. She suspected someone had struck Marijane because of her letters to the editor. For all she knew, people blamed her vitriolic letters for the Ghost leaving.

The accident rate went down, now that people no longer took their safety for granted. Jane would have laughed, except she felt an odd little twinge of guilt. Had she encouraged people to be careless about their own welfare? Maybe her leaving was good for Fendersburg. Maybe it was good for the world that there really weren't any comic book style superheroes.

It didn't matter. She reminded herself of that firmly every time she heard someone discussing the Ghost's reasons for quitting. She reminded herself of that every time she crossed a day off her hidden countdown calendar.

~~~~~

At the three-week mark, Jane took off Saturday night after closing up the spa and headed for Neighborlee. She walked around all day on Sunday, glorying in the quiet, the fall sunshine, the people who smiled at a total stranger and offered advice on where to get the best burger, the best bed & breakfast, and recommended she attend the college's newest theatrical production. She made an appointment with the realtor to look at the Spindelmutter building, and laughed at herself, remembering last time she thought about doing it the Ghost's way. It was perfect. Huge picture windows and a recessed doorway, old brick, in the middle of the business district, in a long row of quaint, fifties-style buildings.

The realtor, Debbi Kunardi, answered all Jane's questions. She couldn't take over the building right away. The county building inspector had found major foundation damage that needed to be repaired. The owner was in the middle of gathering estimates and determining what he wanted to do, how extensive he wanted to make the repairs. When Debbi told him that Angela at Divine's Emporium had recommended the location to Jane, the owner promised the repairs wouldn't impact the lease price at all. He would even sign a paper locking in his price before he found out the cost of repairs, guaranteeing Jane would have first refusal after the renovations had been made. He also promised a power wash to freshen up the outside of the building.

"Definitely weird," Katie agreed, when Jane reported on the results of her first foray into resettling to Neighborlee. "But nice."

"It's kind of like what Beau told me. The town is alive and reaches out to welcome you, if you've found your place there."

~~~~~

As the weeks crawled by and fall turned into winter, the reactions in Fendersburg wavered slowly back and forth. Glad the

Ghost was gone, because it meant he wasn't interfering with their lives. Glad the Ghost was letting them grow up and think for themselves. Suddenly, the Ghost showing up to fix or prevent every minor catastrophe was seen as interference with the rights and freedoms of the people of Fendersburg. Then someone would make a mistake, cause an accident, take a stupid risk, essentially thumb their nose at the warnings of people with more common sense, and suddenly everyone was furious again. The Ghost had no right to abandon his responsibilities. The race resumed to blame someone for driving the Ghost away.

There was always someone who spoke with an almost homesick fondness for the days when the Ghost showed up within a few seconds of a call for help or the sound of squealing brakes. Girls who had never been within a hundred yards of the Ghost talked about the sound of his voice, the touch of his hand, feeling his arm around them as he carried them away from danger. Jane wondered how many times she could hear such outright lies in her shop before she became physically ill. As time went on, the worst of the airhead liars got into fights with each other over who the Ghost would have dated and eventually married.

She found some amusement in the torments Otis went through, when people remembered the broad hints he had dropped that he was the Ghost. Girls wanted him to prove his secret identity. People wanted him to pay for damage that he, as the Ghost, hadn't prevented.

Her teachers found some amusement at the vagaries and stupidity of the people of Fendersburg. Jane was touched that they were concerned about her feelings and her progress in getting out of town. The Council finally met. They agreed, the focus had to shift from finding lost and abandoned and unclaimed children, to finding the next generation, the descendants of the lost and abandoned who hadn't displayed powers. People who had married others like them, produced children who might be Gifted, and had helped them hide their Gifts.

Other members of Hoax got to work doing research. They dug into the few records of Neighborlee Children's Home that had gone public, following up on the lost children who had grown up normal, who had been adopted or who had graduated and gone out into the world. Where they had gone, what they had done with their lives.

Jane dove into her own research, now that she had taken care of the big, time-consuming tasks like planning how to renovate the inside of her new building, ordering cabinets and display cases, and creating her own sanctum in the apartment on the third floor that was three times larger than her current apartment. She calculated how much more space she would have and researched new items to add to her spa's inventory. That was the fun part. Then she programmed her computer's search engine to flag any stories that appeared on the Web dealing with Neighborlee, any police news, TV broadcasts, following up on personalities. Digging further on news in the town and surrounding area kept her busy in the evenings and helped her ignore the constantly fluctuating feelings about the Ghost. Honestly, when was Fendersburg going to accept the fact the Ghost was gone, and nothing they could do or say would bring him back?

She studied the major businesses in Neighborlee, the community leaders, and town stories and legends. Jane learned the *Tattler* had been bought at Thanksgiving by Sheridan Communications. That necessitated a quick trip to the Sanctum to confer with Demetrius and Beau, resulting in two researchers being assigned to dig into the Sheridan family. The family patriarch had been a graduate of Neighborlee Children's Home, a lost child. Even more important, he had had several close calls with Demetrius and Beauregard in the past. Whether he was friend or foe was uncertain, but the Hoax family was sure he wasn't allied with the Rivals. Not like the resident Neighborlee nasties, the Grandstone family.

The research into the graduates of Neighborlee Children's Home ran into a roadblock. Only the records of the last ten or so years had been computerized. Everything earlier was waiting to be uploaded, and it wasn't a priority. Getting physical access to the older records would have to be added to Jane's list of tasks once she moved to town and became accepted.

"It just strikes me as odd, you know?" she told Katie during a quick dinner visit spent in speculating. "If I didn't know better, I'd think someone is hiding the information, protecting it, maybe ..."

"Maybe someone is keeping important information like that from leaving the town boundaries?" Katie suggested.

"Maybe. Who knows?" She looked around her apartment,

caught somewhere between packing and unpacking. She had been too optimistic, jumping the gun and packing before all the delays with the building hit. When she needed things for daily living, she had started unpacking. Every time she got a bit of news of progress from the landlord, she started packing again, but when there was another delay, she unpacked a little bit.

Her tiny electric ceramic Christmas tree sat on the mantle of the electric fireplace. A wreath lay on the floor where she was in the middle of unwinding a strand of multi-colored lights and replacing them with tiny faceted red and gold ball ornaments. At least her shop was decorated for Christmas.

The plan now was to go through the Christmas shopping season, and then have a post-holiday sale like she always did, but sell everything. Make no effort to re-stock. Empty out her shop as much as possible. And hope her new landlord was right with his latest estimate, and she could start moving in after Christmas.

Two days later, the landlord called from Neighborlee, saying the building inspector had approved the renovations and repairs and final inspections would take place after New Year's. She could start planning to move in January. Jane sent him a check for a security deposit.

The following Monday, she put her *Going out of Business* sign in the window of Lazy Days Spa, in among the Christmas decorations and day's special signs. No one remarked on it. They were too busy exclaiming over the Christmas tree designs and other fingernail art. They had to get a massage right that moment. Christmas shopping was wearing them down. What were those delicious aromas coming from those amazing candles? Jane didn't know if her extended holiday hours were a blessing or a curse. How much more obliviousness from Fendersburg could she take?

She let out a shriek of utter relief when she retreated to her apartment, and collapsed on her couch, in the dark, to listen to Christmas carols. She had survived her first day of Going out of Business.

Two minutes later, buyer's remorse struck.

If her life was a horror film, or a farce, this was the point where all the bad news would start rolling in. She would find out that Neighborlee had an insane asylum at the north end of town and a federal prison at the south end, and despite the renovations and repairs and the building inspector's certification, her building was prone to gas leaks, stubborn plumbing, ghosts, and had lost six tenants in the last four months.

"No. It's going to work out. I've earned it," she told herself repeatedly.

She certainly couldn't stay in Fendersburg. Even if no one noticed her *Going out of Business* sign, she couldn't, wouldn't turn back now. Learning to be blind and deaf to the regularly occurring minor catastrophes all around her had been painful. Letting Timmy Higgs suffer for his nastiness and refusing to pick up after irresponsible people was easy enough. Refraining from tripping shoplifters and chasing after runaway baby carriages was not. So she didn't. She could still manage such rescues without anyone guessing.

The fact that the accident and crime rate continued to trickle downwards rather pointed out she wasn't needed after all. She should have quit being the Ghost years ago.

Time to move on.

Things continued moving in the right direction. Her shelves and inventory emptied out. Maybe people weren't oblivious so much as conniving. No one mentioned her *Going out of Business* signs, but every time she marked something "on sale," it sold out that day. It was like her regular customers were stocking up against famine. Jane considered the possibility that she would have little old stock to move into her new shop in Neighborlee. She could start from scratch. That was both good and bad.

The *Tattler* came in the mail the day after each issue came out, and the Christmas day issue proved more than interesting. A story featuring the *Tattler*'s copy editor and advice columnist, Lanie Zephyr, was tucked into the bottom of the fourth page. The three boys who had been involved in the accident that broke her back had come back to Neighborlee to harass her. One of the young men was clearly out of his mind and raving when the police captured him. He claimed Lanie could fly. He claimed many people in Neighborlee were freaks, dangerous, and needed to be wiped out for the safety of the whole world.

Jane wasn't sure what she was thinking, what she feared, what she suspected. So she listened when instinct said to take this to the Sanctum. Face-to-face This wasn't something to handle on the phone. She was fidgety and headachy by the time she could close the spa and head home. She made sure the curtains were closed in her apartment, then activated the Ghost field, and fled so fast, it wasn't fully engaged as she went through the ceiling. Jane ignored the scratches and flew fast enough she made her ears pop.

When she reached the Sanctum, she discovered her teachers were also following developments in Neighborlee, and her suspicions were well-founded. Beau had left that morning with a team, to deal with the three boys. Demetrius put into words what had been crystalizing in Jane's mind: Rivals were likely involved in the attack. Lanie Zephyr was now a person of interest, a possible Gifted, since she was also a lost child. Jane was just settling down, relaxing enough to talk about the progress of setting up her new spa, when Beau called. The boy who had been caught attacking Lanie had been taken from police custody, and it appeared the military officials who took him weren't any such thing.

"We might just have proof that boy we let go is involved in handling things," Demetrius murmured after hanging up and giving Jane that much information. His gaze was distant for a few seconds and his lips pressed into a flat white line.

"Meaning?"

"Boy." He snorted and his lips twitched. "He's a colonel, grown old in honorable service. Meaning … chances are good, if he's the intelligent, responsible man we've glimpsed over the years, his next step is to get those other two boys to safety. But he doesn't know what he's up against. Beau is getting his team into position to get those two boys out of there. Maybe if they come up against the Rivals, we can get some clues to track down the other boy before they take him too far away and he vanishes permanently."

"I'm going." She put down the plate with the enormous slice of peanut butter cheesecake she had been nibbling while Demetrius was on the phone with Beau.

"Of course you are. Neighborlee is your home now. You'll never fully retire from being the Ghost." He dredged up a weary smile for her. "You've always made us proud, Cookie." He fluttered his fingers at the ceiling. "Go home."

She jumped as she activated the Ghost field.

"I'll try to send some backup," Demetrius called as she rose to the ceiling.

Backup, Jane learned, an hour into flight, meant Katie. Her friend called her, making her glad she had had the sense to bring her cell phone with her when she flew to the Sanctum. The phone connection was full of static and whistling, thanks to their two opposing energy fields conflicting and interfering with the signal. Jane gave her the address of the Spindelmutter building as their meeting place, and she laughed when she thought about it later. She wanted to show off her new place to her big sister.

Jane got to the building before Katie and went inside. She stayed in Ghost phase, sticking her head out through the brick wall into the alley next to the building from time to time. When Katie showed up, rainbow shimmers swirling around her as she slowed to a stop, Jane said her name to get her attention. She caught hold of her hand, and as soon as the Ghost field enveloped her, pulled her through the wall into the darkness inside the building.

Katie filled her in on the situation. Col. Hayward was taking the two remaining boys away to safety. An older member of the team, Macaroni, had tapped into the colonel's phone and learned he was taking the boys tonight. That was his talent, tapping into all sorts of communication channels by "tuning in" to the signals. His real name had been lost decades ago in favor of his nickname, Macaroni being a twisting of Marconi, radio telegraphy pioneer.

Beau had his team in place, at strategic spots along the different routes out of town, watching for Rivals lying in wait. Katie had gone out to the command post in the quarries, checked in with Beau, picked up food for the teams, delivered it, and finally came to the shop to meet up with Jane.

"Show-off," Jane muttered. That earned a grin from her friend. "So, what do we do?"

"Wait to be backup and hope we're not needed. And you can tell me what your plans are for this place." Katie gestured around. "Start at the top?"

"Race you." Jane engaged the Ghost field and leaped for the ceiling.

"No fair! I don't know where the stairs are." Katie muffled her laughter and turned into a blur of rainbow streaks as she zipped to the nearest door.

Jane just barely beat her, turning solid again and settling on the floor of the open space that would soon be her apartment, just as

Katie hit the door of the stairs. Before she could say anything, Jane grabbed her hand, enveloped her in the field, and took them both straight up through the skylight to the roof. They had a great view of the town. Most of the stores were only two stories high. A handful of buildings went as tall as six stories, and most of them were either office or apartment buildings. Jane pointed out what she remembered of the geography, orienting herself to the layout of the town and the important features: the park system, the quarries, the college, and Divine's Emporium. She saw a single light, soft, small, like it slipped through a gap in a curtain or blinds. The rest of the building was dark, and she imagined Angela sitting up late to read. Maybe aware something was happening in the darkness below her in the park.

"Nice." Katie turned from surveying the landscape filled with lovely old buildings full of character, most of them built of brick or Neighborlee-quarried sandstone. "Any plans for your apartment?"

When they had worked their way down to the first floor, Katie stepped away to call Beau and check in with him. Jane walked toward the back wall, trying to understand the itchy sensation whispering up her back. She felt like she was being watched. That was impossible, because she had disengaged the rudimentary alarm system while she was still in Ghost phase, and no one could know she and Katie were inside. Yet she still had that sensation of attention focused on her. The same sense of being watched had driven her to wish herself invisible, back when she was a child in the orphanage and had to deal with bullies. Jane didn't like the idea of feeling threatened here in Neighborlee. Yet as she thought about it, she decided she didn't feel threatened, so much as just being watched. With interest. Curiosity?

"Oh, heck." Katie lowered her phone. "They're going down the one route Beau didn't anticipate. He's got to move people —"

"I can get us there without anyone knowing. Where?"

"Through the park. You go ahead." She raised the phone back to her ear. "I'll meet you there."

Jane was up and out of the building and nearly laughed when she realized she was facing east and not west, toward the park. She arched higher as she turned around. The height let her see the spots of light from vehicles. She saw what had to be the car with the colonel, so tiny and alone in the darkness of the park road. A light popped into existence, seeming to leap out of the thick darkness, aiming toward the first light. Jane pulled out her phone and dove. She called Katie. Busy signal. She called Beau, half-expecting the same, because wouldn't he still be on the phone with Katie? But her mentor answered on the first ring.

"They're being attacked. Park road," she blurted as she hurtled toward the spot where the two vehicles had met. The picture resolved as she got close enough to see.

A sedan sat halfway down into a ditch. A dark van disgorged men in HAZMAT suits, who waded through a dissipating cloud that enveloped the car. Jane gritted her teeth, knowing that chalky smell and flinching away from it, despite the Ghost field protecting her. Definitely, the Rivals were here, attacking.

"Going in," she told Beau, and hung up. Her phone pinged and a text from Katie showed up.

Incoming.

Jane grinned and turned to look for the rainbow shimmer with icy sparks of energy that was Katie at her fastest and most furious.

She dove at the men hauling the two boys out of the car. Knocked them off their feet. Grabbed the boys. Flew them away. Almost too easy — the boys were unconscious. Jane took them to Beau at the command post.

When she returned, Katie was taunting the Rivals. Running in circles at hyper speed drove away the last of the tranquilizer gas, protected her, and made her nearly invisible to the enemy. She ran from one man to the other, leading with her shoulder, hitting them like a linebacker and knocking them off their feet. It was a classic tactic to frustrate and distract the enemy until the heavy hitters in Hoax showed up to handle them.

Jane found Col. Hayward, sprawled on the side of the road where his captors had dropped him, and flew him away. She saw flashing lights heading down the park road from the town hall complex, and lights coming from the park ranger station west and south. Lights had come on in some of the houses sitting on the elevation looking down into the Metroparks and quarries. The ruckus had been enough to wake some people. Jane guessed one of them had called the police. She told Beau what she had seen as she deposited the colonel into the van with the two sleeping boys.

"Time for a strategic retreat," he said, nodding, and tapped the screen of his phone. It flashed, signaling the team.

"Did we capture any of them?" she had to ask.

"Next time. For now, I will focus on being happy we frustrated them so badly, and stole their prey from them."

"What about the boy they took?"

"We can only hope that what we do learn will help us track them down. Phoebe is our best hope for getting into their minds and unraveling what was done to them, perhaps finding some clues to lead us to the Rivals' headquarters."

"But what are our chances you'll get there and find out they've moved on to some new place?"

"Then, Cookie, we will be satisfied with knowing we inconvenienced them and took yet another lair from them. Consider," he said, raising one finger to silence her protest, "that in all the years of this war they started, we have kept our home secure, and yet we have driven them out of a good dozen lairs."

"That just means they have a lot of baskets, but we have only one for our eggs." The moment those words left her lips, Jane regretted it. "Beau—"

"No, you're quite right. And that is why your new mission is so vital. We need allies. Neighborlee is a place of wonder, mystery and possibly danger. More than our own anonymity, we must protect it. It is high time the Gifted go home, contact those who remain, and we join forces." A wintry little smile twisted his lips. "And at the very least convince those who stand at the gates that we are not the enemy."

Jane tried to feel some satisfaction with the results of the evening, as Beau had said. It was hard. The Rivals fled before the rangers and police showed up. She had to wait for Phoebe to return from Denmark before they could learn anything from Hayward and the two rescued boys. Amelia kept all three in a twilight state, using a variant of the Rivals' tranquilizer gas with the nasty psychotropic elements removed.

Soon, Hoax learned that Toby and Steve had been under the influence of the Rivals for a little less than a year. They knew very little, as most of their stay and their training had taken place in a fog. That news was encouraging. It meant the Rivals didn't have anyone with equivalent talents to Phoebe's. They depended on drugs and psychological conditioning to meet their goals. The two boys from Neighborlee would be taken care of, healed, and protected. Part of Jane's mission in town now included watching over the Malone and Muldoon families to protect them from the Rivals trying to find the boys. If necessary, Hoax would make both families vanish, and take them to where their sons were living in hiding.

Colonel Hayward proved to be an entirely different kind of nut to crack, in Demetrius' words. Whether it was his military training or some minor Gift of his own, he was resistant to Phoebe's mental probing. They kept him in a twilight state, asking about Neighborlee, Lanie Zephyr, and his connections with the town. It took several hours to convince him he was dreaming, and even then his mental discipline protected much of his unconscious mind.

There was no surprise to learn that Col. Franklin Hayward was in contact with Angela and made regular visits to Neighborlee and Divine's Emporium. He had particularly strong protective feelings toward Lanie Zephyr and several of her friends, toward the Longfellow family, and especially their oldest granddaughter, Athena.

Most important of all was the tantalizing snippet of information that Angela led a small group of people who called themselves the guardians of Neighborlee.

"It's just what we had been hoping for, and yes, I must admit, fearing a little," Beau admitted later to Jane. "Well entrenched defensive forces. Thanks to mistakes we have made over the years, and our own paranoia, unwilling to trust anyone ... we may have built up some rather thick, hard walls that we need to tear down before we can form an alliance. We can only pray that time is not working against us, and doomsday is still far off on the horizon."

Col. Hayward was left in his twilight state, on the front porch of Divine's Emporium, carrying a message to prepare the way for that alliance. Jane needed to establish herself in Neighborlee and work her way into Angela's confidence before Hoax would make the next move. Meanwhile, they would focus on healing the minds of Toby and Steve, and work on finding and freeing their friend, Jay Parker, from the clutches of the Rivals.

Chapter Six

Neighborlee wasn't even in another time zone, north of both the Sanctum and Fendersburg. Despite its proximity, the move felt like going into another hemisphere once Jane entered Cuyahoga County late in January to take care of the last bit of paperwork and do an official inspection of the building. It felt like one of those unseasonably warm days that could go straight through spring in three days, and summer would last until November. Jane had to laugh as she drove down the streets of Neighborlee to get to her new store and home. She had the driver's side window open, enjoying the warm breezes, and heard water running from melting snow. Her realtor, Debbi, said to park in the little lot behind the building, accessible through the narrow alleys that ran between every three buildings in the long strip of shops. She would be waiting inside. Jane saw her standing in one of the big show windows, tearing down the thick brown paper, as she drove up.

The Spindelmutter building looked incredible. The power washing treatment had brightened up the brickwork, changing it from drab brown to a muted red. She hadn't even noticed the name engraved in gray granite across the middle of the second floor, right under the long strip of windows, because the building had been so grimy. Now the name stood out in proud glory. Jane felt a little breathless with anticipation as she drove down the alley next to the building and parked in the little lot.

All this was hers now. If the spa succeeded, maybe in a few years she could buy the building, instead of just renting.

If the spa succeeded and her mission succeeded.

If, if, if...

The crew Debbi had hired on Jane's request had been doing a lot of scrubbing and hauling away of unnecessary debris. Jane was surprised how much bigger the building looked without the empty, broken display cases and wire on the walls and empty crates and cardboard boxes. The bright winter sunshine spilling inside helped her firm up her ideas for painting. They started the tour with the basement, where Debbi showed her the repairs to the foundation that had been required by the new zoning codes and the building department. When they walked around the main floor, they threw ideas back and forth for things like movable display tables or a grid to hang from the ceiling so Jane could attach chains and poles for instant clothes racks. The pseudo-cobblestone flooring was perfect just as it was.

She wrote down the names of various local handyman businesses, along with Debbi's assessment of their reliability, ease of working with them and how busy one or the other might be at this time of the year. Debbi was one of those people with her finger on the pulse of all the businesses. She certainly seemed to know what everybody was doing.

They went up to the second floor, which had been used as a small workshop and storage for the previous several tenants. Jane mulled the research she had done, still undecided about the cost of installing a small elevator as opposed to a ramp to increase accessibility. Lanie Zephyr was a big part of her mission, and if the physically handicapped couldn't get upstairs, that would limit what she could offer. When they reached the third floor, her apartment, she reveled again in the sight of that skylight and the open spaces, lots of cupboards and closets. She was going to have fun decorating.

The dishes and other housewares she had seen on sale at Divine's Emporium came to mind. Divine's would be the first stop she made, to shop, and let Angela know she had come back.

She bit her tongue to stay silent, to avoid a slipup when Debbi showed her one of the four doors in a row opened onto the stairway up to the flat roof. Jane certainly couldn't admit she had done some exploring already. She imagined coming up here to stargaze, or maybe even sunbathe on her days off. Her plans included long trays for gardening, flowers as well as vegetables.

On the roof, Debbi pointed out the places where a cabana and wading pool and deck chairs had been set up in the past. It was like a tiny private country club up here, where one could gaze down on the streets of Neighborlee.

When they headed downstairs again, she delayed to take some pictures with her phone and note down dimensions, in preparation for her first big shopping trip. Paint, borders, throw rugs, other items for decorating. Debbi headed down ahead of her and said she would pull out the last paperwork to be signed. In a few hours, everything would be finalized and official, and the Spindelmutter building would be all hers.

Jane made the first item on her list contacting the handyman companies, to have them look around the building and give her estimates for both the apartment and the spa. She started down the stairs, then hesitated, one foot raised. A thin shiver washed over her, the hint of a tingle of Gifted energy in her fingertips. Her stomach clenched in anticipation and she held her breath for a few steps as she resumed walking. Someone within close proximity had used his or her Gift, just for a moment. It wouldn't do to go tearing down the stairs to try to see who had been walking by her front window, or even go into Ghost phase and fly out through the wall. Not yet. Her plan was to fit into the town, become accepted by residents, so when she started asking questions, people would answer them honestly and openly. They would be talking to one of their own, not an outsider or newcomer.

"Hey, Deb, what's up?" a woman was saying as Jane made the turn at the second floor landing. "I thought maybe someone had broken in when I saw the paper out of the windows."

"Oh, hey, Lanie," Debbi responded, accompanied by the sound of papers shuffling across the one remaining display case/cabinet Jane had decided to keep.

Jane nearly stumbled on the next step. Lanie? As in …? How many Lanies could there be in one small town? She took a few deep, slow breaths, then continued down the stairs.

"So, is somebody thinking about setting up shop here?" Lanie asked.

"It's perfect," Jane said, as she reached the ground floor and stepped out of the stairwell. *Yes!* She fought to keep a pleasant expression and not reveal her relief mixed with excitement, when she saw the dark-haired woman in the wheelchair.

Had she just been given proof that Lanie Zephyr was a Gifted? Jane guessed that flicker of Gifted energy was from her getting her wheelchair up the shallow step in the recessed doorway, and down the two shallow steps inside the building. She made a mental note to have the handyman deal with that before everything else. How had they managed to ignored the ADA requirements before this?

"Jane, this is Lanie Zephyr. She works at the *Tattler*," Debbi said. "Lanie, Jane is opening up a spa."

"Yes!" Lanie let out a growled sort of shout and made a downward "cha-ching" pump.

Jane had all she could do not to burst out laughing. She recognized Lanie from last summer when she came to visit Neighborlee. What were the chances? She hoped they could be friends, and her mission for Hoax wouldn't make things awkward.

"You have no idea how much we need a place like yours in town," Lanie continued.

"You don't even know what kind of spa she's setting up," Debbi said, laughing.

"Hey, as long as the massage rooms are wheelchair accessible, I don't care. And you have those detox masque things and aromatherapy candles and oils and stuff? And you do bridal party packages?" She pressed her hands together like she was praying.

"Even if I didn't have them at my old store, I'd bring them here," Jane promised. "You're the bride?"

"I'm crazy, but I'm not totally insane. Nope, two of my really good friends got engaged at New Year's, and I want a super splendiferous gift, and a spa day would be perfect. So I take it that means you do offer them?"

"As soon as I get set up." Jane nodded. She tipped her head back and looked around the big, open room with the brick walls and vaulted ceilings with fancy gingerbread cornices and all the woodwork around the windows. "This place is perfect. And best of all, I can live right over the shop."

"You know, a tearoom where you sell candles and loose tea and other stuff like that, where people can have book clubs and meetings and stuff would be really good for the second floor," Lanie offered.

For a moment, Jane couldn't breathe. It was like Lanie had looked into her mind. Still, she knew from experience no matter how skilled the one who initiated mental communication, it was impossible to do so without a slight ache, or a sensation that metaphorical ears would pop from changing air pressure. Jane had felt none of the indicators, so Lanie couldn't have been reading her mind. No, this was one of those "coincidences" that would turn out not to be a coincidence, but fate.

Thanks, God.

"I've always wanted to do something like that," she admitted, "but my old place was too small. And the people in the town weren't...of the right mentality for that kind of thing, if you know what I mean." Jane offered a smile that felt somewhat uncertain. The last thing she wanted to do was even think of, much less speak about, Fendersburg. She didn't want even the slightest hint of that loony bin to contaminate her new life, new home, and new friendships.

"Lanie, can I hire you to talk to some people I'm having come look at the empty unit in the Dexter building next week?" Debbi said. "If Jane hadn't already signed the lease, I think you could have talked her into it."

"Probably," Jane said, nodding.

A muffled sound like an angry cat got a flinch and a grin from Lanie, and she pressed one hand over her belly. "Uh, sorry, I was on my way out to pick up lunch. I should get going and get back to work. I'm at the *Tattler*. If you want a guided tour of town, want to meet up with people and find out what's going on, stop on by."

"That's great. Where are you going for lunch? That'd be a good place to start getting to know the town," Jane said.

Of course, that turned into another half hour of talking. Debbi and Lanie made recommendations for where Jane should get meals while her apartment was being renovated, where she could get supplies for her business, the best place to post flyers advertising the grand opening, that sort of thing. And of course, Lanie wanted to know all Jane's plans for the building. From her widening grin, Lanie approved of everything Jane decided to retain, plus the innovations she wanted to try. The spa was going to be a hit.

Lanie invited Jane to the next game of her wheelchair basketball team, but Jane had go back to Fendersburg to finish packing. She was more disappointed than she thought possible. When Lanie asked where she was from, Jane had hedged by saying it wasn't worth talking about, and she was glad to put the lazy, spoiled town behind her. Maybe that was too much information. She made a mental note to herself not to talk about Fendersburg in the future, even when people asked.

"Okay, so you were in a place that sounds like the armpit of the nation," Lanie said. That earned a sigh from Debbi, which she responded to with a flick of her tongue sticking out, then a grin.

"Other than the fact you're intelligent and sensitive, why exactly pick Neighborlee when you managed to escape?"

Jane wanted to tell her. For just a second, the urge to say she was one of the children who had been found abandoned outside town and she had come back to find out what happened to all the others, and their descendants, was strong enough to burn her lips. She held it back and glanced away while searching for answers. Even if Lanie was Gifted and likely involved in the group Col. Hayward had called guardians, such a confession wasn't something to blurt out in the open, less than half an hour after meeting her. Plus there was Debbi to consider. She was what some members of Hoax referred to as a "mundane." Many residents of Neighborlee seemed totally oblivious to the strange and wonderful aspects of the town. Debbi might decide Jane was dangerous, or she would write her off as a lunatic. It wasn't wise to hack off a realtor.

"My guardians, my backers, actually, recommended I set up shop here," Jane said. "They say I'm a perfect fit for the town, and I'm needed here. The old farts have never been wrong before," she added with a shrug and a smile. "You'd have to meet Demetrius and Beauregard to really understand what I mean. Not that they smell bad, but..." Jane shrugged again and all three laughed together.

~~~~~

Jane planned to take her time setting up shop in Neighborlee. She would concentrate on her apartment, first, and get to know the whole town, get a sense of its lifeblood and its people before she opened up for business. In a sense, this was the vacation she had never taken, practically from the day she woke up and realized she wasn't going through adolescent anguish, she really was a freak of nature. From the moment she realized she could hover and affect the density of objects around her, she had wanted to use those powers to help others. Starting with the girls in her cottage, she branched out to her schoolmates, helping them stand up against bullies or get out of jams. Then Demetrius and Beau had found her, finagled official paperwork to get custody, and took her away to the Sanctum.

She reveled in the quiet from the first day she officially moved in. For two solid days, she stayed indoors, painting the walls and refinishing the floors. She went to bed when she felt tired and slept until she felt like getting up. She took her time, constantly modifying her plans to indulge her taste for eclectic combinations. Her landlord had given her complete freedom to do whatever her little heart desired to renovate the building, from cellar to roof — as long as it was reversible when she moved out. If she moved out.

Jane targeted used furniture and secondhand stores to search, to outfit the tearoom on the second floor and take advantage of all the open space in her apartment. She planned to refinish furniture on the second floor while the handyman, when she hired one, took care of the main floor. She would refinish until she got woozy from fumes. Cherry stain and black and red lacquer. Futons and lots of open shelves. Steamer trunks for tables. Lamps hanging on chains from hooks in the ceiling. Rag rugs on plain wooden boards.

Once the painting was done, and before she started her whirlwind shopping tour, she went walking, getting to know her town. The weather was pleasant, but there was no guarantee that the unseasonably balmy weather would linger. Best bet was to get out and about now. First was a long walk up her own street.

El Greco's Bakery exuded aromas that threatened to put her into a trance. Jane guessed she gained four pounds just inhaling the aromas coming through the front door. She saved the bakery for her return trip.

Benjamin's was a dime store. A friendly sign painted in bright rainbow colors and surrounded by balloons admitted that with the current economy, very little in the store was sold for a dime. The sign invited shoppers to come in and explore the dime special bins for that week, guaranteed to be a massive savings and a delightful surprise. Jane lost nearly an hour there.

After that was Goody's, the office supply store. They had a special on personalized, self-inking rubber stamps and receipt books. Jane placed an order.

Her first twinge of second thoughts came as she walked out the door. What were the chances, really, that every store she looked at had something she needed or wanted? Coincidences just didn't happen. She knew all about manipulating circumstances so people didn't know they were being helped. She had earned top grades from Beau in that class. And then she had been assigned to Fendersburg, with orders to make it obvious someone with Gifts was operating there, to draw the attention of the Rivals. Look how that plan had turned out.

Neighborlee's guardians certainly seemed good at hiding their tracks. Maybe the paucity of Gifted children awakening to their Gifts wasn't because no more were arriving in Neighborlee. Maybe the guardians were that good, sensitive enough to detect awakening Gifts and keep those children from making mistakes and getting snatched by the Rivals or Hoax.

"I am going to think myself into knots," she muttered, while standing in front of the alley between Goody's and Fresher Folks Grocery.

The sooner she made friends with Lanie and earned Angela's approval, the sooner she could be admitted to the secrets of Neighborlee and start working on that alliance Beau had mentioned in the note left with Col. Hayward.

A momentary shiver curled around her from the inside working its way out. Jane glanced in both directions down the sidewalk. No one seemed to be watching her. Then she looked up, in case those people she had seen flying in the park happened to be doing a mid-day surveillance flight. Jay Parker had accused Lanie of being able to fly, so maybe she was one of the three Jane had glimpsed that night? It made sense.

No one in the sky. No one watching her. But just because she couldn't see someone studying her didn't mean the sensation of being watched was just in her imagination. If she could go invisible, so could others. Maybe that was how Neighborlee's guardians managed to do their work. The sensation that someone might be standing just a few feet away, maybe smirking, reading the tiny physical reactions she couldn't fight, maybe laughing at her … it made her want to go Ghost. Her years of training, preventing observation and suspicion, fought hard with the panic. She was the Ghost. She wasn't allowed to panic.

"Not the Ghost anymore." She glanced upward once more and wondered if she should be looking downward. After all, who would think of the town's guardians traveling through the water pipes and sewage system? If she could phase out and walk through walls, then other people could, too. Walking around underneath the town, able to see up through foundations and pipes, would make guarding it much easier. The guard would never be noticed or suspected, or worry about rain, snow, or any other bad weather.

The thought of someone able to look up at her from below her feet gave Jane a few shivers of the oogies. She was not wearing a skirt until she could determine if there was someone looking up.

"Get a grip!" She flinched, looked around again, and then a shaky little laugh escaped her.

How long had it been since she had been this shaky, frozen to one place, her mind spinning? Not since the first time she phased through a wall to escape a couple bullies at the orphanage. A few boys had made it their duty to patrol and keep the bullies from picking on the smaller children, but they couldn't be everywhere at once. Not even Kurt, whom Jane had adored from afar. There were two girls he hung around with constantly, and she hadn't worked up the courage to approach them and ask if she could join their group before Demetrius and Beau had swept her away. Jane never even got close enough to see if Kurt's eyes were the same stormy gray when he smiled as when he was furious and throwing the bullies right and left.

Jane knew better than to stand there in front of the alley and panic. Especially if someone was watching. She tossed her head and got moving. Nothing and no one would spoil her day of exploration and freedom. Besides, Katie hoped to visit tonight or tomorrow and see her new home in the daylight. If she was showing up tonight, Jane didn't want to be late getting back home.

Katie wasn't as sensitive to the signals of the presence and activity of Gifted as Jane was. That didn't mean Jane couldn't bounce ideas and suspicions and "supposes" off her.

Jane didn't enjoy wandering the aisles of Fresher Folks as much as she had the previous stores. She loaded up on ingredients for salads, fresh-baked bread, and pomegranates. She adored pomegranates, but usually they were out of season when she really wanted them. Like right now.

Another sign of someone manipulating the situation on her behalf? Jane told herself she didn't care.

By five that afternoon, she had seen almost all of downtown Neighborlee. Her arms would have ached from the weight of all her purchases if she hadn't changed their density to make them just slightly heavier than air. To keep everything together, safe from an errant gust of wind, she had invested in an enormous net shopping bag. Jane had gone from one end of the center of town to the other, and all the offshoot streets. A number of the people she encountered recognized her from seeing her haul boxes and bags from the moving truck into the main room of the shop. Anyone who asked, she took the time to stop and answer questions. She had been delighted with their friendliness and their interest in the spa.

She had turned around, ready to re-walk her path and go home, when she glimpsed something out of the corner of her eye. Even as she kept turning, a sensation like warmth and welcome and a tiny twinge of guilt, as if she had ignored something important, washed over her. Turning slowly, she tried to get back into the same position where that flash, that bit of sparkle and color had caught her attention.

Between two buildings, she saw the peaked roofs, gold weathervane, and the gold and olive walls of Divine's Emporium.

Definitely, that was guilt she felt. She should have visited Angela and told her the good news the moment she signed the papers to rent the Spindelmutter building. She should have stopped in the day she arrived in town behind the moving truck. Angela had the right to know, since she had made the suggestion. Maybe that was the niggling sensation of something not being quite right that had hovered at the edges of her mind. That sense that she wouldn't feel quite at home until she stopped in and reconnected with Angela.

"Divine's it is." She checked her watch. She had time before Katie showed up. Plenty of time to put away the spoils of her shopping trip and create a feast.

A sigh of satisfaction and the sense of something settling into its proper spot came over her as she turned the last corner and saw the Victorian house with its peaked roofs, ornamental gingerbread and wrap-around porch. Angela had left the Christmas lights up and they twinkled green and gold, creating a sense of liveliness and color against the lingering snow and the clouds beginning to fill up the sky.

Divine's Emporium. A bit of everything and just what you need, proclaimed the sign on the fence next to the open gate.

Jane considered the bag hanging over her shoulder and the bags clutched in her other hand, and laughed. If she didn't have everything she needed by now, she was in serious trouble.

She glanced up again, and froze as her gaze met and was

caught in the deep blue gaze of Angela, standing only ten feet away, on the other side of the fence. Jane had heard no footsteps, no door opening, no brushing of that long, royal blue hooded cape dragging on the snow. It was as if the woman had simply appeared out of nowhere.

"Welcome home," Angela said.

"I'm sorry."

Angela beckoned. Jane scurried to follow her up the neatly shoveled flagstone path to the front door.

"Sorry for what?" She laughed.

"I should have told you when I signed the lease. I should have stopped in the minute I got back to town. Everything's just been so...crazy," she ended on a sigh, as she stepped through the door into the cinnamon-and-pine-scented warmth of the shop.

Had the door swung open just before Angela stepped onto the porch? Maybe she had one of those sensors, to open it for her?

"Jane, no need to apologize. If you had had time to remember, you would have come. Not like some people who think about something they have to do a dozen times, and a dozen times put it off for later. Here, put those bags down and have something warm to drink." Angela shed her cloak and gestured toward the little bistro tables in the corner of the main room. "Let me see... If I remember correctly, we had dark chocolate cocoa with peppermint whipped cream, the day you walloped Stewart McCavity for taking Stephanie Tubbs' doll. To celebrate you coming home, let's see if I can recreate that recipe again. How does that sound?"

"That sounds great," Jane murmured. She sank into a chair without really paying attention.

As if it were yesterday, she saw Stewart leap a fence and snatch Stephanie's doll from her arms as she and Jane walked home from school. Jane had had permission to stay overnight with Stephanie, and they'd been laughing and making plans. Stephanie had brought the new doll to school for show-and-tell. Stewart held the doll by its curls as he raced away, across the street, and swung it toward the big old lightning-struck oak tree. He laughed and promised Stephanie the pieces when he was done.

Jane could still feel the tingle of energy and anger jolting through her limbs in response to Stephanie's shrieks. Something took over as she leaped the street in one bound, snatched the doll with one hand and smashed her other fist into Stewart's nose. He had stumbled backwards so fast and hard, he bounced off the trunk of the tree. He had shrieked, an octave higher than Stephanie. The sight of his blood had terrified Jane, so she grabbed Stephanie's hand and the two of them just ran and ran, until they ended up at Divine's Emporium. Angela had comforted them, before sending Stephanie to choose a dress for her doll. Then she held Jane close and told her she had done a good thing protecting her friend and standing against the bully. However, she had to learn to use her strengths and skills for good, or she would be a worse bully than Stewart. They had sat around the table in Angela's apartment upstairs and drank hot chocolate and ate chocolate sandwich cookies until Mrs. Silvestri came to drive them to Stephanie's house, where she lived with her grandparents.

In the time it took to remember, Angela had created the hot chocolate. Jane couldn't be sure, but she thought she used the same big green glass mugs, with a green and red-striped candy cane to stir the thick, creamy mixture. They sat and sipped and talked about what was going on in town. Jane was fascinated when Angela related that yes, the newspaper reports were true, some of the town's "rascals," as she called them, had been badly influenced by their time in the military. They had twisted around the guilt they felt for putting their high school teacher in a wheelchair, and had given Lanie Zephyr a hard time just before Christmas. Then she went on to relate the oddness that had taken place at the New Year's Eve lock-in party at Eden, the community center. Town officials were blaming a gas leak and hallucinogenic drugs slipped into some of the refreshments.

Angela sat back and toyed with her candy cane in her empty mug. "That's all behind us and we're in a new year. So, what have you been up to? How is the shop coming along? Debbi Kunardi isn't a gossip by any means, so when she's excited enough to talk about a new business coming to town, people know it's solid fact. I know a dozen people who can't wait to get a massage or facial."

"Oh, I'm still a long way away from getting the renovations done." Jane shrugged and cradled her mug, with a few inches of cooling chocolate in the bottom. Before she quite knew it, she had told Angela her plans for furniture shopping over the next few days and contacting the handyman businesses Debbi had recommended.

She ended with a list of the shops she had visited, and the fun she had today shopping and getting to know the town.

It was on the tip of her tongue to blurt what she had seen last summer, when she was flying over the town. Would that make a good opening for revealing what Beau and Demetrius and the rest of the Council suspected about, hoped was true, in Neighborlee? Or start by saying she saw people flying because she was flying too?

Beau had counseled her to take her time. Demetrius advised she become part of the town, reconnect with the people who had known her, and gain their trust before dropping the implications, dangers and revelations on Angela and the guardians.

"You've had a long, wearying day," Angela said, "and you have things to do to get ready for your friend to visit." She stood, and Jane realized she was on her feet, putting the mug down on the table. "Go on home and relax. You're going to be busy once your spa opens. Neighborlee has been waiting a long time for you, and you're needed. And being needed takes up a lot of time and energy." She smiled impishly, eyes sparkling.

"Can't be anywhere near as exhausting as the town I just left," Jane said, grinning back.

"Well, there's needed and there's appreciated. Be sure, you'll be appreciated, no matter what you do here." Angela handed over her coat and patted her arm. "Mind if I send a few girls your way who might be needing jobs along with their beauty treatments?"

"I don't know. It depends on how busy I get."

"Just some high school girls, orphanage girls, who need weekend and after school jobs. Minding the front desk, answering the phone, letting you run errands before the stores close. You've heard people joke about rolling up the streets at closing time? In Neighborlee, that's just about the way of it." She nodded, looking somber and serious...until she winked.

"So I should do my running during the day. Sounds good." Jane sighed. "Sounds like just my kind of town. Thanks. And yes, do send the girls." She silently added, *Especially if they're orphanage girls,* as she picked up her bags and turned to leave.

Jane smiled as she walked home, feeling the last residue of tension from her Fendersburg days sliding off her shoulders with every step. She was home, in Neighborlee.

A pickup truck rumbled past as she paused on the doorstep of her building to pull her keys from her pocket. Jane glanced over her shoulder at the wide-shouldered, sandy-haired hunk with the five o'clock shadow, and deep, wide-set, gray eyes. He had a whimsical multi-colored scarf wrapped around his neck, and wore a black jacket. Their gazes met and one corner of his mouth quirked up in a smile. He nodded as his truck continued past the shop. Jane felt something go melty-soft in her stomach.

Halfway up the stairs, Jane stumbled when it occurred to her that she *hadn't* told Angela Katie was coming to visit tonight. Or had she? Now she couldn't remember.

"Weird." Then a giggle escaped her, surprising her as she lifted a foot to continue up the stairs. In Neighborlee, *weird* had a totally different connotation. A good connotation.

Definitely good, she decided, as she emptied out her bags and put away all the provisions she had bought, and found a note tucked in her purse in unfamiliar, clear handwriting that just looked like it had to be Angela's. She recommended Jane start with the best handyman in town, and provided his name and phone number and email.

Kurt Hanson. The silvery-blue ink seemed to sparkle, just a little bit, as Jane stared at the name and wondered, hoped, this was the same Kurt Hanson who had been her hero in the orphanage. Sandy hair and gray eyes and a talent for gizmos.

Somehow, though, she couldn't get herself to make that call to Kurt to ask him to come over and look at the shop and talk about the renovations. Not tonight, anyway.

Chapter Seven

"Weird. And how come the Old Poops didn't pick up on the whole brouhaha at New Year's?" Katie sat back from her notebook computer, after half an hour of searching for news on the events at Neighborlee's community center.

"Well, considering how everybody seems to have worked together to keep it quiet? Not like all the witnesses and the noise when Lanie was attacked at Christmas." Despite her words, Jane had to admit this was all suspicious. There had been newspaper articles and mention of events on broadcasts, but everything had died away quickly and the rest of the world seemed to have forgotten about the events of New Year's Eve, including the death of a Grandstone. Now that she thought about it, Jane found the quiet handling of the events of New Year's Eve even more suspicious, because the Grandstones *weren't* raising an unholy racket, threatening to sue everyone and their lawyers.

Jane remembered the three bully Grandstone cousins who made a point of picking on any orphanage children who wouldn't be their followers. Why weren't they suing over the death? What had happened and how were they involved?

For a few seconds, she felt as if something whispered in the back of her mind. She caught a whiff of damp and stone, and the lights dimmed. Or did they? Maybe she was just tired.

"Maybe that's something I need to investigate, along with making a place for myself."

"Probably. Anyway, I did a few circuits through town before I came up here. Very different in daylight," Katie added with a grin. "I really like it. There's this feeling. Welcoming, like you said. I could almost envy you. Maybe if things work out for you, and you figure out what's up and we make that alliance, this would be a good place to settle. It's not like I have to be in the center of the country to do my job." She shut her notebook with a decisive click and slid it off her lap, to rest on the rag rug next to her.

She raised her arms above her head and stretched luxuriously. "Got to admit, I thought you were crazy when you said you were moving here. I mean, who really wants to go back to the town where you were dumped like month-old garbage, right?"

"We were all dumped. Not a one of us ever had parents who admitted to ownership." Jane shrugged and made a mental note to go over to the orphanage and see if she could check her own records. It would be a good starting place.

"I mean, it's like we were all whipped up in test tubes in some hidden laboratory, and the eggheads who made us didn't know anything about raising kids, so they dumped us."

Jane sighed. "Just mysterious circumstances. That's all they ever write on our records."

"Who the heck cares?" Katie slouched a little lower in her nest of floor pillows. "You know, I can really see it. The change. You look happier."

"Who wouldn't be?"

"This place agrees with you. I can't wait to go do more exploring in the morning."

Jane reached up, flicked her wrist, and a bundle of folded papers slid into her grasp from the other side of the room. "Here's the map I made up for you, and a shopping list. Could you pick up the stamps and other things I ordered, while you're out gallivanting? I have to take a few deliveries tomorrow, and I have no idea when the trucks will get here." She tossed the papers to Katie. "Do you mind doing your exploring on your own? At least for the morning?"

"No problemo."

~~~~~

"Problemo." Katie soft-stomped her way into the spa at quarter after eleven the next morning and slouched into the only chair.

"Like what?" Jane glanced up from inventorying the contents of the last delivery box. She frowned as her gaze slid over the boxes and bags Katie had brought back with her. "Looks like you found and got everything I asked you to."

"No Divine's Emporium. Just an empty lot where you said it would be and where the map said it would be."

"What?" Jane was about to accuse Katie of teasing her, but that little crease right between her eyes was a dead giveaway. Her friend looked a little troubled, not playing games with her.

Maybe Katie had just gotten herself turned around and misread the map. The problem was, there were only a few dead-end streets looking down over the slopes into the Metroparks. How could Katie mistake one street for another, especially with street signs to guide her? Jane decided now was a good time to take a break for lunch, walk with Katie down to Hunky & Dory's, and then walk out to Divine's while the weather was still nice and calm. All her deliveries had come in ahead of schedule, leaving her free for the rest of the day. She shoved all the boxes behind the one remaining counter, so no one walking by on the street would see them and made sure all the lights were off and the doors locked.

It occurred to her that it was a good thing she hadn't called to make that appointment. What if Kurt had been here, assessing the shop for renovations, when Katie walked in and announced Divine's Emporium didn't exist? Jane knew the shop was there. So why couldn't Katie find it?

"Weirder and weirder," she murmured as the two of them hurried down the cleared sidewalks.

"Curiouser and curiouser. Down the rabbit hole, Alice?" Katie murmured back. Then she laughed.

Divine's was exactly where it should be. If not for the open-mouthed amazement and slightly glazed look in Katie's eyes, Jane would have accused her friend of trying to play a joke on her. She led the way, up the sidewalk to the gate and then to the porch. Katie didn't hang back, but she didn't leap ahead and blaze the trail, like she usually did.

"Back so soon?" Angela called from behind the counter the moment the door swung open. Four strings of copper and silver bells chimed sweetly.

"What a cool place!" Katie crowed, and immediately darted away, out of sight beyond the shelves.

"My friend is here for the day, just to make sure I'm settled in all right," Jane explained. She sauntered over to the counter and leaned against it. "She couldn't find your place, when she was out exploring alone, so I thought I'd bring her over to show the way."

"Now how in the world could such a big house get lost in such a little town?" Angela muffled her chuckle behind her hand. Her eyes sparkled with mischief.

"That's what I thought." She shrugged. "Do you have—"

Her mouth dropped open and she ran out of words when

Angela shoved a double-sized mug across the counter to her. Whipped cream and a sprinkling of cinnamon swayed slightly on top of the creamy brown, steaming concoction.

"Chai, extra spicy, with genuine whipped cream," Angela said. "You said it was your favorite, when you were in yesterday."

Fighting back a shiver, Jane went on her tiptoes and looked over and behind the counter. She felt a little throb of disappointment when she saw the two-burner coffee machine, a little espresso machine, a refrigerator, some short shelves with glasses and mugs, and a shelf full of flavoring syrups. That was an awful lot to cram in behind the counter. The space just didn't look that large, from the other side of the counter. Somehow, Jane had expected to find nothing except maybe a shimmering spot on the wall where Angela pulled out all sorts of wonders, made to order.

"Yeah, it is," she murmured, and cradled the enormous mug in both hands. "This place... There's more to this place than I thought."

"What does your friend like?"

"Mocha with a big splash of vanilla syrup, and chocolate sprinkles."

"Coming right up."

Katie joined them at the same moment Angela set her mug on the counter, smiled and slid it along the counter to her. She picked it up with a grin and nod of thanks and took a long gulp before launching into raptures about the shop.

"This is a fantastic town. You are so lucky," Katie said for what seemed like the twentieth time, after they had left Divine's and brought their lunch back to the spa.

Jane nodded, not really hearing. She tried to untangle the niggling suspicion she had missed something very obvious when they went into Divine's — but she couldn't remember what.

~~~~~

The snow resumed, falling thick and fast, within minutes after Katie left that afternoon. Jane let the falling snow mesmerize her while she curled up directly underneath the skylight, wrapped in a thick blanket, and sipped hot chocolate. She didn't feel like doing anything — not running around looking at used furniture, not checking out home renovation supply stores. When Angela called and invited her to come out for the evening, Jane almost said she didn't want to go anywhere or do anything. She knew better than to refuse the invitation, and offered to pick up Angela.

They ended up at a comedy club in Broadview Heights, where Lanie Zephyr was one of the headline acts. It was like theater-in-the-round, with the main body of the stage sticking out like a wide runway. They found seats at a table to the far right of the stage.

Something prickled against Jane's fingertips and her sense of power at work tugged her attention to the stage. She caught a twitch in the curtain, maybe indicating someone had been looking out at the audience. Then the waitress came to take their order and she couldn't keep staring at the curtain without someone noticing.

The first hour was essentially amateur night, giving local comedians and up-and-comers ten minutes to show they had the right stuff. Some barely had five minutes of good material.

The hopefuls were followed by two comedians who were as different as night and day, in terms of physique and subject matter. Angela pulled an iPod out of her purse and offered to share the earbuds with Jane as the first, a skinny young man with a straggly, long beard that looked like dirty spaghetti, stepped out from behind the curtain. Jane hesitated, and then decided it was wise to trust Angela. She didn't think about the oddness of trying to block out the comedy routine with an earbud in only one ear, or the unsanitary aspect of using someone else's earbuds, until she went home that night.

The fact that the music filling her head was recognizable as the soundtrack from *How to Train Your Dragon* amused her. Then she realized that she only heard the comedian's voice as muffled "wah-wah-whoa," reminiscent of the old "Peanuts" holiday specials when adults talked. Unfortunately, she could read lips, and every third word out of the man's mouth was filth. Jane shuddered and turned her gaze to the menu printed on the surface of the table.

"Thanks," she whispered, when potty-mouth left the stage to a smattering of applause, and gave the earbuds back.

The next comedian came out, a pudgy, olive-skinned woman with red-dyed hair, violet eyes that had to be contacts, and an inch of silver in the roots of her hair.

"Yeah, thanks," a man whispered, settling at the table directly behind them. "It's a good thing I got tied up behind stage helping Lanie and missed most of that. You were supposed to rescue *me* from the Septic Tank that Ate Cleveland."

"You're a big boy," Angela said, laughter making her whispered voice musical. "Jane's the new girl. Since you weren't around to rescue her, like when you were children, I had to." She winked at Jane. "Not that Jane needs you to rescue her that much."

Jane shivered. A momentary whisper of Gifted energy, there and gone, barely disturbed the roots of her hair. She turned around to look at the man behind them. The comedienne on stage was still getting settled, making the audience laugh as she fumbled with the stool. It was almost a juggling act, balancing it on one leg for a few seconds. She acted totally stunned, as if she didn't want it to do that.

"Hey," he said, as she stared into the gray eyes of the man she had seen in the truck: sandy hair, black leather jacket, multi-colored striped scarf. "Welcome to town. You're the Jane taking over the Spindelmutter building?" He held out his hand to shake.

Jane felt nothing but callouses and warmth and strength in his hand. She didn't know whether to be relieved or disappointed when she didn't feel that energy flicker. Could it be coming from the comedienne, who had just made her stool do a somersault?

"Ah—um—yeah, I am." She released his hand. Did he tighten his grip for a moment, like he didn't want to let go? "You are?"

"Kurt." He grinned. "Sorry. Kurt Hanson. When did I rescue Jane when we were kids?"

"Jane was at NCH with you and Felicity, a year or two behind," Angela said. "Don't tell me you don't remember her: quiet, almost a talent for making herself invisible when she wanted to be." Eyes sparkling, she pressed a finger to her lips for silence. The comedienne took her seat and shouted a greeting to the audience.

Jane faced forward, focusing on the comedienne to fight off the sensation that Kurt was staring holes into her.

Kurt Hanson. *Her* Kurt Hanson, from the orphanage? The same Kurt Hanson Angela had recommended to handle her renovations?

Okay. Might be good. Might be bad. Might be a total disaster.

Angela was a schemer and manipulator and knew far more than she ever let on.

But maybe that was comforting? With so much uncertainty, it was nice to know *someone* had a better idea of what was going on. The question was if Angela cared to share that information with them. Jane's gut instinct said she couldn't badger her for answers. Angela's information would have to come in its own good time.

While she mused over the possibilities and problems and new challenges ahead of her, the comedienne went through her routine. Jane caught enough of it to appreciate the fact her humor was intelligent and based on irony, not filth. The laughter was consistent throughout the routine and the comedienne got near-deafening applause as she skipped off the stage.

A man built like a bouncer came out onto the stage and announced the first headliner: home-grown comedienne Lanie Zephyr.

Jane's fingertips tingled as Lanie rolled out onto the stage. The wheelchair moved with a steady speed, yet she didn't touch her wheels. Okay, Lanie had Gifts. Enough to move her wheelchair, but not enough to heal the injuries that put her in the chair. Jane writhed a little bit as her overactive imagination filled in just how bad that injury had to be.

"Hey, is everybody looking forward to Valentine's Day? Coming up fast. Do you have somebody special to give a fantastic gift?" Lanie looked around, not really meeting anyone's gaze. "Warning. Forget that gift, and you'll pay for it for the next three months."

She looked wide-eyed in surprise as groans and muttered comments rippled through the room. "Now, I'm a traditionalist. I believe in celebrating Valentine's Day the Italian way. I go to a Chicago garage and I shoot someone."

For two seconds, Jane thought no one got it, and she was afraid to laugh aloud. There was enough light to see the expressions around her and reveal the mental process as people figured out what Lanie meant. Then laughter roared through the room. From the looks some girls gave their guys, maybe they thought shooting someone was a good idea.

If only Jane had someone to be angry with, for forgetting her at Valentine's Day. She had the most awful urge to look at Kurt. It hurt her neck not to turn her head. From the corner of her eye, she caught him looking at her. Why was he looking at her? Was he still trying to remember her from Neighborlee Children's Home?

"Yeah, romance is a big problem," Lanie continued, once the laughter died down. "I say the movie *Love Story* got it completely wrong. Love means *always* having to say you're sorry!"

A few boos came along with the laughter, but they sounded

good-natured to Jane.

"But I'm a fine one to talk. Like I know anything about romance? If the statement *unlucky at love, lucky at cards* were true, I would be a star on the Poker Channel. I could give Bret and Bart *and* Beau Maverick a run for their money." Lanie scowled at the people directly in front of her. "You know, the old TV show, *Maverick?*"

Jane sat back and relaxed, marveling at how Lanie managed to slide back and forth between astonishment and disgust, mocking people who didn't belong together and made the mistake of getting married, while somehow giving people something to think about. There was a fine line between viciousness and knife-sharp, intelligent humor. She rode that line with style.

Lanie glanced to the right, and Jane caught movement from the corner of her eye, by the side door. Her inner sense of time said Lanie had been on the stage twenty-five minutes. Angela said she had a half-hour show. She had probably gotten the five-minute warning.

"Getting back to Valentine's Day..." Lanie looked around the room, frowning as if deep in thought. "Men think they are smarter than women, and women think they are smarter than men... But you know what? I think hormones make idiots of us all."

Jane grinned, hearing laughter that certainly sounded like it came from both sides of the gender wars.

"Hey, equal opportunity harassment, you know? I'm all for equal opportunity, equal access, leveling the playing field. Because it's dang hard going for a touchdown when your front wheels keep getting stuck in ruts, y'know?" Lanie pivoted back on her main wheels and waggled the footrests. That got snorts of laughter.

"Now let's get serious here for a few seconds, okay? I have some deep, world-shaking questions that have been sticking in the back of my mind for a while. Maybe you can give me an answer." She wheeled to the front of the stage and leaned forward, as if she would whisper to the front couple of tables. "I really need to know. Where is *Old* Zealand?"

That got her some wide-eyed, confused looks, and then some giggles.

"Just how grateful is Gerry Garcia now? And the most important question of all: If you eat Captain Crunch, does that make you a cereal killer? Or a cannibal?"

Lanie spun her chair around and zipped back to the curtain, accompanied by applause that almost shook the lights.

"You two need to talk," Angela said, and turned to include Kurt. "Jane has been busy with her apartment, but now she needs to get to work on the spa. You're at the top of my list of recommendations, but if you want to stay there, you should discuss what she wants right away. We already have people lining up for appointments, Jane. Not good to keep them waiting."

"Lining up?" Jane closed her mouth before demanding to know how anybody could know what she had to offer when her first advertisement hadn't run yet. She suspected between the ladies at the *Tattler* who were setting up her first ad, the people she had talked to in town, and Angela working her own magic, her opening day was going to be a blow-out success.

"Sounds good," Kurt said. That little crinkle between his eyes made her think he was still trying to place her from the orphanage.

Maybe her attempts to be invisible had been more successful than she thought. Even when Kurt rescued her from the bullies, she wasn't memorable. She shook herself free from those thoughts and focused on talking business. Before Lanie rolled up to join them at the table, she and Kurt made arrangements for him to come by and look over the shop in the morning.

~~~~~

Jane's apartment was decorated to her satisfaction, Spartan and open and clean, with warm colors on the walls and a pale blue ceiling streaked with swirls of clouds and even a few rainbow streaks near the windows, where she had strings of crystals to catch and fracture the light into more rainbows. She was especially pleased with the wide, low counters and open wire racks to hold her dishes and pots and pans. All her herbs had made the transition from Fendersburg without a single wilted leaf or broken stem, and she looked forward to creating a rooftop garden in the spring.

With her nest arranged, time to focus on her shop. With the brown paper out of the picture window, anybody walking by could see just what was going on. That would be good, free PR. She might even unlock the front door, so the curious could come in. As long as they understood she wasn't open for business yet.

Several times in the last week, Jane had awakened in the

middle of the night, heart pounding, expecting to find her blissfully quiet life was only a dream. In the morning she would go to her shop in Fendersburg and find Otis Conroy waiting for her with an engagement ring and the announcement already in the newspaper.

If she didn't dream about Otis imprisoning her in Fendersburg, she awoke from dreams of a voice calling her, whispering in words she couldn't quite make out. She woke with her heart pounding even faster than the other dreams, a chill in the air around her bed, and oddly, a fading aroma of dampness and stone. She had that dream twice the night of her visit to the comedy club, and told herself to be grateful that Kurt was coming over in the morning to see about the renovations. No more hanging on the edge of the abyss, with a to-do list a mile long and no forward momentum.

~~~~~

Kurt showed up ten minutes early the next morning. Jane was eager to get to work, so she was dressed and waiting and had a pot of coffee and muffins from Hunky & Dory's waiting.

He was business-like and genuinely interested in what she planned for the shop. He approved of the preliminary work she had done, stripping paint and badly done, flimsy paneling from the walls upstairs, pulling up worn institutional carpeting, and uncovering hardwood flooring. He liked her tearoom idea for the second floor and the sketches of floor plan ideas. When she asked about installing an elevator for easier accessibility, he laughed in a nice way and pushed aside what she thought was just badly installed drywall to reveal a small elevator, very old design, more for cargo than people, that went to all three floors. Kurt then revealed he had helped with several phases of renovations in the Spindelmutter building, starting in high school, and knew her building better than she did. His few suggestions expanded on what she wanted to do. Essentially, he approved of her plans, which made her feel so much steadier about them.

Should she be worried that his opinion mattered? Or was this just a holdover from the days when he had been her elementary school hero?

Over the next week, they worked together well, but didn't work *together*. Half the time, she was out, picking up furniture and equipment and supplies. When she was in the shop, refinishing or assembling shelving or unpacking more merchandise, Kurt was out, taking care of other jobs. During the short periods when they were in the shop together, she constantly turned around and found him watching her.

It wasn't the "checking out the goods" look she was used to in Fendersburg. She had developed a thick skin from warding off Otis and his idea of suave. Kurt didn't frown when he watched her, like something about her bothered or irritated him. The momentary blankness in his gaze made her think he was concentrating so hard he didn't realize he had been caught. What could he be concentrating on?

Kurt joked about having an unofficial date after he followed her all the way over to the community center, Eden one evening. Both were going to the grand re-opening. The building had been partially closed down, limited access, during the cleanup and investigation after New Year's Eve. As the investigators had cleared each room, the building had been gradually opened for use. After all, there were vital town functions that couldn't be shut off during the winter, when the town's youth and the seniors depended on indoor activities. A daycare center also worked out of Eden.

Jane had taken breaks from the renovation to assemble goody packets to give away and promote the spa. Such things as tea light samples of aromatherapy candles, tea bags, and foil packets of scented hand cream.

According to Gina, the director of Eden, about four times the usual number of patrons came to the grand re-opening festivities, just from curiosity. People wanted to see where Pamelia fell through the ceiling and Sylvia's body was found. So Jane gave away everything she brought with her and got a lot of good publicity and generated interest outside the boundaries of the town for her own grand opening. It was also a good way to meet most of the residents of Neighborlee, and make connections with a growing number of people she remembered, if only vaguely.

Four days before the spa's grand opening day, Jane walked down the street to the *Neighborlee Tattler* to pay for the ad she had discussed with the advertising department more than two weeks before. She spent nearly an hour, sitting with Martha and Myrtle, elderly twin sisters who handled advertising, talking about her shop and her plans for the future. She signed up to have a rack inside the front door of the spa to dispense papers, which gave her an automatic discount on all future advertising. The sisters made her feel like she had been adopted, and served her quite possibly the best coffee cheesecake she had ever tasted.

Assured that she had made two more friends, Jane continued down the street. If everything went as Martha assured her, she would be too busy to explore her new home for at least a month after opening day. Better to get it done now, while she had time.

Kurt was finalizing the lighting for the shop today, and Jane wanted to avoid the feeling of his gaze resting on her. With the threat of another storm approaching town, this might be the last day of nice walking weather she would have. A stop at Hunky & Dory's, then the bakery, then a visit at Divine's Emporium. After that, she would follow the inclinations as they hit.

~~~~~

Penny Miller was waiting in front of the door when Jane came downstairs Saturday morning for her first day of business. With her red hair in ponytails, her freckled face free of makeup, in faded jeans and a navy WBC sweatshirt, she was a picture of wholesomeness Jane didn't quite trust at first glance.

"Miss Angela sent me," the girl said before Jane could ask what she wanted. She handed over a business card with Divine's Emporium written out in calligraphy, the D and E oversized and surrounded with big swoops and curls until they were almost illegible. On the back, Angela had written an introduction and recommendation for the girl.

Penny, age fourteen, lived in Cherry Cottage at Neighborlee Children's Home. Just like Jane had, when Demetrius and Beau had found her.

"Well, if Angela vouches for you..." Jane shook off the suspicion things were just a little too convenient. This was Neighborlee, after all. She had agreed Angela could send over girls who needed work. "Think you can handle the phone and the appointment book?"

The girl's big grin was reward enough for Jane.

Ten minutes later, as people streamed into the spa like bees drawn by the honey of her "Grand Opening" sign, Jane was grateful. Penny greeted everybody as "sir" or "ma'am," and whispered bits of information about each person before they approached Jane with a question. The girl listened avidly as Jane explained the properties and benefits of her massage oil and facial mud, mousse and gel, hypoallergenic makeup and herbal teas. When Jane was busy with her first chair massage of the day, she heard Penny repeating everything she had heard, word for word, even using the same inflections. The girl even handled several sales without asking for help.

Before she quite knew it, Jane looked up from her fifth chair massage and realized it was past noon. The traffic had slowed down to a steady trickle. Three people wandered around the shop, reading the signs in front of the makeup and health food racks. Four more were watching the last massage and wanted to make appointments for table massages next week. Jane gestured for them to wait a moment, pulled her tips out of the appropriately labeled stained glass bowl, and beckoned for Penny.

"Where's your favorite place for lunch?" She shoved the handful of bills into the girl's hand. "Get double of the best thing on the menu. We've earned a celebration." She winked at Penny, who grinned, snagged her parka from the row of hooks by the door, and dashed out, ponytails flying.

Jane said a silent prayer of thanks for Angela's help and her smart choice in sending Penny, and turned back to her customers.

"That Penny's a good girl. Glad you hired her. She deserves a break," Mrs. McGuillicutty said, nodding.

"I think I'm going to miss her on Monday when she's back in school," Jane said with a sigh. "I almost feel guilty wanting her to put in a couple hours after school, but she's such a big help already."

"Thea Alcott does a good job with all her girls at the home. Now, this brochure says massage is good for the lymph system. What all is a lymph system?"

When Penny returned with their lunch, most of the customers had made their purchases or appointments, or both. Jane rang up the last sale, watched a college girl walk out the door, and dropped down onto her stool behind the counter with a gasp and a chuckle.

"One fifteen and I have to restock. Who would have thought it?" She took a quick glance through her inventory program in the computer and scribbled notes on the stock items that were flashing, to pull the items from the storage room, and then turned to Penny. "Okay, I hope you brought a feast. We earned it."

Penny had brought salad wraps full of chunks of freshly grilled spiced chicken, fruit-flavored seltzer, and potato salad. Jane had expected triple-decker burgers, extra-large shakes and greasy fries or onion rings. Maybe this kid wasn't as normal as she looked. What teenager ate sensibly?

"Great choice. I'm not paying you nearly enough, which means you're getting a raise," she said, before taking a huge bite of the wrap. Jane moaned as spices filled her mouth and she crunched through the lettuce and bean sprouts, peanuts, cabbage and carrots.

"Um, Miss Wilson, how much are you paying me?" Penny asked in nearly a whisper.

"Well, let's see...employee discount of forty percent. First look at all the clothes we get in." Jane laughed when the girl's eyes lit up. She thought she had seen Penny give longing glances at the workout clothes, the leggings and wraparound skirts, shawls and vests. "All your meals while you're working. And $10 an hour."

Penny choked on her mouthful of seltzer.

"Not enough?" Jane handed her a napkin.

"I'm just a kid, and not full-time or anything, and that's more than the minimum wage."

"You're worth it. Already, I don't know how I'll manage when you're in school."

Jane loved that bright smile the girl gave her, and the certainty she could trust her and be trusted by her. She vowed she'd make sure her new assistant had all the help she could give. This early, she didn't have the right to get involved in Penny's life, but as they became friends and she made a place for herself in the community, that would change.

Helping one teen find her path in life was far more worthwhile than babysitting the idiots in Fendersburg.

Chapter Eight

Lanie came by the spa at the end of the day. She glided up the new ramp Kurt had installed on one side of the shallow step of the front door as Penny was scurrying to leave. She had to be back at NCH for some activity that evening. Jane didn't know what, only that Penny was excited about it. She looked up from the crate of loofah pads she was unpacking for a display on a shallow-shelved display rack she had just assembled. Penny and Lanie exchanged grins and comments. It didn't surprise her that Lanie knew the girl. Probably she was involved in the mentoring program at the orphanage.

Then Jane felt that tickle of Gifted energy at work. She blinked. Was that just a momentary flicker of multi-colored light, swirling around the wheels of Lanie's chair as she slowly bumped over the threshold and down the short ramp into the shop? The light was too brief to be absolutely sure, but all the bits and pieces were adding up. Lanie had to be one of the three people Jane had seen fly last summer. She seemed to be close to Kurt, so Jane suspected she was one of the two girls he had spent so much time with when they were children. Could he be part of the trio of flyers? He did seem to be close to Angela, who led the guardians.

"Hi, Lanie." Jane slid a handful of loofah pads, some with wooden handles and some with ropes, onto the closest shelf. "Angela sent Penny over. She's been incredible."

"Yeah, Penny's a good kid. She's had it really rough." Lanie looked around. "Where's that appointment book? If I hadn't been scared of driving you out of town, I would have called dibs on massages the first time I saw you in here."

Jane laughed. She gestured over at the main counter. Her computer was currently open to her inventory program, to place re-stock orders with several different suppliers. After just one day. This was a wonderful start to her new life.

"Give me a sec." She bent down and brought up another armload of loofahs, emptied the box onto the bottom shelf, and kicked the box toward the cellar door. Arranging could be done later. "So," she said as she walked over to the counter behind Lanie, "what's Penny's story? Is she another...well, another lost puppy?"

"Wellington calls us the Lost Boys. Still can't get him to settle on Peter Pan or that weird vampire movie."

"Wellington? You mean the mayor?" Jane nearly missed her stool, hitching her hip up to sit down. "Okay, I know there's a high percentage of abandoned kids, but the mayor too?"

"Lots of people who stayed in Neighborlee were abandoned kids found in the surrounding countryside. The ones who belong can't think of living anywhere else. The ones who don't belong take off as soon as they graduate."

"Uh huh. Who else?" Jane shook her head. "That doesn't really matter, does it? What's Penny's story?"

"Harder luck than some of us. I think it's easier having no answers, rather than knowing you belong to someone, but they're not really sure they can take you." She grinned as Jane showed her the physical appointment book, and pretended to keep it just out of her reach.

Jane half-wanted Lanie to use that flicker of Gifted energy again, maybe try to tug the appointment book from her hands. She wanted a confrontation, wanted it all to come out into the open. She knew better, though, than to think it would be so easy to get the biggest part of her assignment over with. She wouldn't be ending the day by driving to the Sanctum with Lanie and Angela for a meeting with Demetrius and Beau.

"Okay, Penny isn't a Lost Kid." Lanie slouched a little in her wheelchair. "Her mother was killed by a drunk driver when she was ten. Her father basically lost it and abandoned her. He didn't really fit into Neighborlee, but he was in love with Sheila and that sort of ... I don't know ... made a place for him here. Well, whatever it was, he lost it when Sheila died. Anyway, Penny had friends at NCH and asked to go there, instead of to some distant relatives in France. What kid wouldn't want to go to France?"

"A kid who knows where she belongs," Jane murmured.

Lanie wanted to hear about all the little things Jane still had to do with the shop. She liked the bare bones of the tearoom on the second floor. Jane was considering putting a sauna on the second floor with the tearoom.

Kurt showed up half an hour sooner than Jane expected him,

to get to work on the shelves she wanted to install in the corners of the elevator, for displays. He volunteered to run down the street to get dinner for the three of them, and they talked and threw ideas back and forth for the shop.

The next step, after installing the shelves and more display racks to hang from the ceiling, was for Kurt to expand the display area in the bay windows on either side of the door. He wasn't up to painting the old-fashioned gold and black-edged lettering Jane wanted in the window, to replace the vinyl sign she was using now, but he had lined up the person to handle it for her. After that would be the sauna upstairs, and stations for freelancers to come in and handle the manicures and pedicures, and another massage chair station. Jane was more than willing to share the wealth of customers who wanted pampering.

"Next time, we have to get Felicity," Lanie said, as she and Kurt were preparing to leave. It was nearly ten, and Jane was grateful they weren't going to make a long evening of it. She had dozens of ideas for the shop, confirmation that her ideas would be a hit in Neighborlee, but she was exhausted from her first day of business.

"Felicity?" Jane asked.

"Our third musketeer," Kurt said. "She got engaged at New Year's, so she spends more time with Jake than us. But yeah, she definitely needs to meet you," he added, his voice softening.

Again, that assessing, almost emotionless expression. Jane shivered, feeling as if Kurt were trying to see through her, trying to tap into her thoughts, waiting for her to do ... something. Just like, she realized, she waited for him to do something.

What if she simply turned on the Ghost field and showed her new friends what she could do? Would they accept her or be frightened?

~~~~~

By the end of the next week, the flood of customers had decreased to manageable levels, and the nice people of Neighborlee helped by spreading news of her shop with word-of-mouth. Jane had at least two table massages a day, and at least five short stints in the chair. More important, Penny had relaxed enough to drop the "Miss" and call Jane by name.

Her most important function was introducing Jane to the people of Neighborlee. She had stories about everyone who came into the shop, giving insight into their hobbies and families and pasts. That helped Jane make suggestions when someone wanted help in selecting makeup or finding a tonic or picking out a gift.

By this time, Kurt was close to finishing all the little adaptations and tweaks to make the shop what she had envisioned. Jane caught herself trying to come up with new projects, just to have him come into the shop. So when Kurt walked into the shop Friday afternoon, she flinched a little and felt guilty, because she had been thinking about him a little too much.

For a moment she had the strangest feeling he didn't see her, but was surveying the surroundings like it was foreign territory. The silence rang like one of those enormous gongs in an MGM classic movie set in the jungle or the Orient.

"Can I help you, sir?" Jane joked, to push down the creepy-crawly sensation that made the fine hairs stand up on her arms and on the back of her neck. She stepped out from behind the counter. Just the physical action of approaching him, rather than feeling like she was hiding behind the counter, should help her.

For a few seconds, it seemed like Kurt didn't hear her. He continued looking around, taking in the display racks of cosmetics and teas. Clothes and health food and jewelry. The lounging corner with the bucket chairs and magazines to browse, and a pot of Indian spice tea perfuming the air.

From his faded denim shirt with the rolled-up sleeves to his scuffed, sand-colored work boots, he was clean, simple and elemental. No glitz, no glamour, no hair gel. His afternoon stubble hinted at shades of cinnamon among the wheat. No jewelry or watch. His hands were clean and looked strong and sensitive.

Then he smiled at her. Just an upward tilt of the left side of his generous mouth, it hinted at a dimple, hidden among the stubble.

"Just checking things out. Sometimes I spend so much time on the little details, I don't get the big picture. You should hear the fuss people have been making about this place." He gestured with a tilt of his head to take in the contents of the spa.

Fuss? Should she be insulted?

"Yeah," he continued, voice softer, "this'll be great, if you decide to stick around."

"*If* I stick around? Excuse me, but I don't put this much effort into a new place if I'm not planning on staying long-term." She decided to take his words as a joke. Otherwise, that sense of being assessed and turned inside out would make her shiver right out of her skin. When her Ghost field had first awakened, sometimes she had needed to phase out and fly, as far and as fast as she could, to try to outfly the feeling. Kurt made her feel uneasy, needing-to-run, just for a few seconds.

"Hmm, yeah. We make plans, don't we? When they don't work out, instead of fixing, it's easier to leave."

"You maybe, but not me." Jane almost choked, thinking immediately of how she had finally, after much grumbling, shaken herself free of Fendersburg.

"But see, me, I'm the Handyman. That's what people call me." He snorted. "Lanie and Felicity tease me that should be my superhero name." His eyes narrowed a moment when Jane flinched at "superhero." "I guess, growing up where we did, some of us feel responsible. Make things right. Repairs. Put them back the way they should be. Track down trouble, things that don't feel right, vibrations that are out of synch. That sort of thing."

Had he decided *she* was trouble? That she didn't fit? Was that what all those unreadable, assessing looks over the last two weeks meant? Did he have the ability to sense when Gifted people came into town and used their Gifts?

Friend or foe? she demanded, not really expecting him to hear. Few ever did, except in her dreams.

Friend.

His voice reverberated in her mind. Both of them jumped back two steps, and she suspected her eyes were as wide as his.

That's not supposed to happen.

Tell me about it! How can you — I knew I felt something — I've never been able to hear anybody in my head before. How did you do that?

"Heck if I know," she said aloud. "Usually when I hear someone's mind in my head, it hurts and they're doing all the work." She reached up to press her index fingers against her temples, but the expected throbbing wasn't there.

"Okay, so... You're used to people with powers. So I wasn't imagining there was something about you." He nodded, taking a step closer, and lowering his voice. "You thought I was serious for a second, when I said my superhero name was Handyman. That means you've got one, maybe?"

"Hardly." Nothing in the world was going to get her to admit she was called the Ghost by people with entitlement attitudes. "We're all just ordinary folks here."

"I think that's wrong on a lot of counts." He smiled, but that wasn't the relaxed look she wanted.

"Look, whatever you think is going on—"

"Still trying to figure that out."

"It's supposed to be clear tonight, not much wind. A good night for flying, you think?" She had the pleasure of watching him flush, then his eyes widened.

"What do you mean by flying?"

"What do you think you're doing? The air's vibrating like..." She shrugged. What she wouldn't give for him to be sitting down, so she could use her Ghost field and take apart the chair, just like she did to Otis. Knock some humility and cooperation into him.

"Yeah, it is. Vibrating." Kurt took a step back and looked around. "You're going kind of...transparent?"

"No I'm—" Jane held up her hand and swallowed hard, stunned to see the opacity of her hand varied, rippling, transparent in a few spots and then solid again. She hadn't lost control of the Ghost field since she first awoke to her Gift. She took a deep breath and focused. The tingling in her fingertips faded and her hand went back to normal.

"That's kind of interesting." He looked thoughtful.

"What did you do to me?"

"Me? Do to you?" He stopped, his mouth open, like he had been about to contradict her and then thought better of it. "You mean you don't usually fade out like that?"

"What does it mean, being the Handyman? What's your Gift?"

"Gift?" He snorted. "If it was a gift, sometimes I'd like to give it back. Like I said, I fix things. When Lanie broke her back, she couldn't—" He flushed and looked away. "Nobody knocks me off my cool like this. Is that your-- What do you call it? Gift? You frustrate people into saying things they shouldn't? You're walking truth serum?"

Jane took a few slow breaths, studying him. This was all wrong. This wasn't the confrontation she had anticipated. Shouldn't they both be pleased to have a few theories confirmed?

"There are three of you who fly, aren't there? Lanie flies—or used to fly? She broke her back and lost the ability. But you, being the Handyman, you can fix other people's Gifts. Or at least influence them," she whispered.

"Let me guess. You read minds?"

"There has to be something to read," she snapped, stung by the sneer in his voice. Why did someone so hunky have to be so nasty? "No." She sighed. "I don't read minds. I usually can't talk mind-to-mind, unless someone else initiates it. And the only reason I'm asking is that I was here last fall, checking things out—" She hesitated when that got a spark of interest in his eyes. "I was out checking things, and I saw three people get out of a truck down by the park and they linked arms and flew." She saw more interest. "August."

"Uh huh." He grinned, his lips stretched just a little too thin for genuine humor. "Thought I was going nuts for a few seconds. I'm kind of like the Geiger Counter. I can feel when something's going to happen. We thought Big Ugly was waking up way too early."

"Who's Big Ugly?"

"If you hang around long enough, you'll find out."

"Look, I'm not here to start trouble, or even looking for trouble. If there are more Gifted in this town—"

"Where do you learn to say things like that? Gifted?"

"I'm late! I'm sorry! We were goofing around in Yearbook—Oh, hey, Kurt!" Penny barreled in through the front door, peeling out of her parka as she babbled her excuses. As a matter of fact, she was only five minutes past her usual arrival time.

"Hey, Penny." Kurt glanced at Jane, then turned to watch Penny hurry to hang up her coat and scarf and jam her gloves into her pockets.

"Warning, warning!" Penny pulled three pieces of paper from her pocket and handed them to Jane. "My friends at school want to make appointments for their nails. They never thought about anybody doing their feet like you were showing me on Tuesday. And this." She handed over a piece of pink notebook paper. "Caroline does nail art, but not professional. She's got really steady hands, but she doesn't know where to get the really good polish like you've got, and she was thinking—"

"Of getting a job? Have her come in and show me what she can do." Jane was very conscious of Kurt watching her. She knew she would have given Penny's friend a chance even if he wasn't there, but it bothered her to sense him judging her.

"Hey, there are child labor laws." Kurt grinned when Penny squealed.

"Don't be a jerk." Penny rolled her eyes and punched him in the shoulder.

"That's what big brothers are for."

"Brother?" Jane wondered if she had missed out on something during their exchanges over the last two weeks. She couldn't see much similarity between them. He was old enough to be her legal guardian. If they were related, wouldn't she be living with him? What about the relatives in France?

"Kurt leads an engineers club at NCH," Penny said as she hurried to put the appointments in the book on the front counter. "He's big brother to everybody."

"Oh, okay. That's...nice," Jane said, unable to think of a word that would express her uncertain feelings. How could she express what she felt when she wasn't sure what she felt? It was like the Kurt she had gotten to know wasn't there anymore, like he had been only a mask, and now she was meeting the real Kurt. A "real" she didn't think she would like.

"The least I can do, considering I grew up there." His eyes narrowed again. "You were at NCH. That's something we haven't talked about, but Angela did say..." He sighed, and for a moment she had the strangest sense he was kicking himself for overlooking something. It made sense to her that when Angela pointed out anything, no matter how small, it was important. "Okay, when did you leave? If you graduated from there, I'd remember you."

"I didn't graduate. I was adopted. Kind of."

"Kind of? Either you were or you weren't."

"Kurt." Penny frowned at him. "Don't be a jerk. Was it a nice place where you went?"

"Yeah. Lots of people like me." Jane tipped her head slightly, widening her eyes, to get Kurt to understand. From the cocking of one eyebrow, he did.

"I think I'd like to hear more about this place. But I got to get back to work. Catch you later." He nodded to her, to Penny, turned neatly on one heel and strolled out the door.

"What is with the cute guys?" Penny said with a sigh, and

watched him walk down the street, until he left the frame of the window. "It's like being a hunk causes testosterone poisoning or something."

"You think he's cute? He's your big brother."

"Not like that. And he's way too old for me, anyway." She grinned. "Not for you, though."

"Ah... You know, I think I'd like to settle in more before I start looking at guys that way." Jane returned to the counter where she had been filling out resupply orders.

"Makes sense. But I have to warn you, he's pretty close with Lanie and Felicity. Sometimes when a guy is pals with some girls, it's hard to get — I don't know — romantic?"

"I'm not looking for romance, but I am looking for some new, good friends. Girlfriends. I definitely need to spend more time with Lanie. Come to think of it, she and Kurt both mentioned introducing me to Felicity, but she's been kind of busy with her fiancé, from what I heard. So, were they at the orphanage too?"

"Yeah, that's why they're big sisters. To pay back. People at Miss Lanie's church are always coming out and spending time with us, taking us canoeing or to movies and things, or summer camp. Neighborlee is the greatest place in the world to live."

"Definitely," Jane murmured.

She and Kurt needed to talk. She had learned so much from this little encounter but had a dozen new questions. The most important one was why he had waited until now to suddenly start an inquisition.

~~~~~

Hey, Hanson.

Jane felt for stirring in the mental atmosphere to get an idea where her suddenly unfriendly handyman might be hiding. She sometimes helped track down new Gifted because she had some sensitivity. From things Kurt had said, he had some sensitivity, too. The fact that he had heard her thoughts and she had been able to hear him in response, and it hadn't hurt ... Shouldn't that mean if she focused on him hard enough, he would hear her?

Just trying to analyze and understand what had happened that afternoon gave her a headache. Kurt Hanson — it just wasn't fair that a guy who had been her hero when she was a child was suddenly unfriendly. Like he thought they were enemies.

Get back on track, she silently scolded herself. *Hey, Hanson, I know you're there!* Whatever his powers, Kurt Hanson created no ripples in the mental atmosphere. *Tell all your Gifted friends and anybody else who might be listening, I am not here to cause trouble.*

Prove it. Kurt's mental voice sounded as if he were in the same room. Jane could have sworn she felt his breath on her neck.

She turned around quickly, scanning her apartment. Jane repressed an image of Kurt sitting on her new red plaid futon, watching her scurry around the room, trying to find him.

Just let me get on with my life. All I want is a normal, ordinary life.

Prove it, he repeated. Followed by a chuckle.

Just what do I have to prove? How?

You'll figure it out.

Figure what out?

Oh, just a heads up. My talent changes to suit whoever I'm concentrating on. I'm figuring out what you do, and I look forward to exploring it.

Jane had the awful feeling she would soon know what he meant. And she wouldn't like it.

~~~~~

Heads up! Kurt called an hour after she opened the spa the next morning.

Jane turned, expecting to see him come slamming through the front door. A hand waved at her, poking through a wall. Then all the screws holding up wooden display shelves of hair care products fell out of their holes and chimed to the floor.

She reacted without thinking, dashing across the spa at triple speed, and phased out, to throw a field around the shelves and keep them upright. Jane caught herself in a heartbeat and phased back in enough to be visible. She had people in the shop, after all. Her fingers flew, whipping the fallen screws back into place. It was hard work at half-phase, bringing beads of sweat to her face.

So this was what the Handyman did? He borrowed other people's talents, whether they were using them or not?

How could she fight against that?

Why did he think he had to use her Gift against her?

"Jane? Something wrong?" Penny asked, as the last four screws slammed back into their designated holes.

"Nope. Nothing." Jane tried to smile as she turned around and phased back completely. She shook inside, half from the strain and half in anger. Just what did Kurt think he was doing?

How could someone so ruggedly yummy be so juvenile?

At least he hadn't attacked the supports for the *glass* shelves of cosmetics and perfume. That would have been a disaster.

What was she doing, being *grateful* for his choice of targets?

I'm not giving up, she called to him, wherever the rat might be. *I wouldn't even think of asking. This is just the first salvo.*

Kurt didn't sound anything other than tired. Or was he bored? She wished he would gloat, just so she could hate him.

So this means war. She took a deep breath and cast a protective field around her shop. She had no idea if he could break the field, using her Gift against her. All she could do was try.

~~~~~

Deep in the caverns below Neighborlee, Native American paintings gleamed softly in the luminous glow of fungi. Stalactites dripped with soft chiming sounds. Something dark and somnolent on the other side of the dimensional barrier felt the diluted echo of Jane's sudden burst of power. Skin made of darkness rippled in response, like a horse shuddering off a pesky fly. Something began the slow rise toward waking.

~~~~~

When one kitten up a utility pole that afternoon didn't get Jane's sympathy or help, suddenly there were four, battling for a place to perch. Jane looked in every direction before phasing out and rising up to grab the kittens. No one saw her. On the way up, at least.

On the way down, Kurt zoomed in at her from nowhere, grabbed her arm, shoved her toward the ground and negated her invisibility. Then he let out a shout, so the people on the other side of the street turned to look as she tumbled six feet to the ground. He floated away, still out of phase, his silence more of a taunt than anything he could say.

Jane managed to pass off her tumble as having skidded on a patch of ice underneath the dusting of snow from last night.

She now knew the Handyman's strategy. She wouldn't think of him as Kurt Hanson any longer, because he was no longer a potential friend. He was the enemy who wanted to drive her out of Neighborlee by exposing her Gifts.

"That's what he thinks," she muttered, and cuddled the kittens as she walked back to the spa, her lunch forgotten, her appetite completely lost.

Penny cooed and sighed over the kittens. Jane knew the rules wouldn't allow pets at the orphanage, so she offered to keep one of the kittens at the spa, if Penny agreed to find homes for the others, and be responsible for food and the litter box. Jane had never felt so much like a hero, in all her years in Fendersburg, as she did that moment, looking into one teen's happy eyes.

That's not going to help you, Kurt said.

Jane didn't even bother looking for him. She finished pulling out money to send Penny to the grocery store for supplies.

She had the awful feeling she knew his tactics now. She imagined small disasters every time she ventured out of the spa. Or worse, whenever there were witnesses in the shop. Would he make her display window fall inward, all the caulking in the frame suddenly vanishing? Start fires in her shop? Would manhole covers vanish beneath her? Was he just testing her, or trying to drive her out of town? She couldn't imagine Kurt doing something that threatened the well-being of the people around her.

This was his town, his home. Why did he think she was a threat? What did he want from her?

Jane was drinking a soy and raspberry smoothie that Penny brought her at dinnertime. She choked and nearly spat pink all over her freshly washed counter when her thoughts solidified into one question: Would she fight for her place in Neighborlee, to the point of being the Ghost again?

~~~~~

Deep below Neighborlee, ripples of power expanded and soaked into the ground. The darkness awakened just a little more. The smell of extra-human energy stirred it like the smell of coffee stirred a man on vacation. The sleeping malevolence was content to continue drowsing a little longer ... but not much longer.

~~~~~

Jane decided the situation warranted doing more than living on double alertness. The only way to figure out what Kurt was up to, if he insisted on being cryptic, was to fight back.

But how?

While the Handyman could borrow her Ghost powers, she had

years of practice and "inside knowledge" at her disposal. That would be her advantage. She hoped.

First step: make her spa attack-proof by tightening up the defensive field. Not a strong one, and certainly not anything that would keep customers out or make her shop invisible. She had learned this trick utterly by accident, when she had realized just how different she was from the other orphans.

There had been a bully at the orphanage, a hanger-on of the Grandstones. They had him continue their tormenting activities when they couldn't follow their targets beyond the orphanage gates. He delighted in picking on anyone he could use to get ahead. The ones he could silence so the older boys who defended the younger children didn't find out and "talk sense" into him.

The smarter students, he made do his homework. The ones who were good at cleaning up the dishes or helping with the laundry or other chores had to do his chores for him.

When Jane refused to do his homework, he stole her homework. She learned, after wishing hard enough to give herself a headache, to surround her books, then her trunk in the dormitory with a field that made them both invisible. Having the trunk vanish got unwanted attention. She played with the protective field until it merely kept the bully from opening her trunk.

When he sabotaged her other belongings, she learned to surround everything she had with a field that stung him. Then she learned to adjust the field so only certain people were kept away. The first time the bully complained about electric shocks in Jane's room, she got the immense satisfaction of watching the bully get a long overdue scolding for even being in a girls' cottage.

After that, Jane had to watch her step outside the orphanage, because he was smart and never made the same mistake twice. She learned to become invisible soon after. Jane supposed she owed him something, for pushing her to test her Gift and find out what she could really do. Funny, she couldn't remember his name now.

What it came down to, though, was that she could protect her spa with a field that would keep anyone with Gifts from entering and yet let ordinary humans in. When Lanie and Angela came to visit, she would just deal with their questions then. They had proven themselves to be friendly. But how friendly were they if Kurt was on the attack? Didn't they work together?

What mattered now was dealing with Kurt, protecting her spa, figuring out what he wanted. And yes, negotiating a truce. Jane almost laughed when she realized she wanted to be friends.

"Talk about hormones messing up your brain," she muttered.

Jane monitored the field through Saturday night, and then a quiet Sunday, waiting for him to test it. She regretted having to stay home, because she had quite enjoyed her first two Sundays at Neighborlee Gospel Church. She changed the energy frequency of the field a few times, in case the Handyman tried to adjust his personal frequency to get through the barrier. If she had learned to do that, to walk through walls and electric fences, then so could he. With time. Jane had no intention of giving him enough time to figure out her tricks and secrets, and work around them.

She had a restless night Sunday, constantly waking from dreams of someone trying to talk to her, someone tapping on the skylight, asking to get into her apartment. It made her cranky and she felt her control over the protective field slipping. Just a little.

To her disappointment, nothing happened all day on Monday, except that all the kittens were adopted by the first woman who came into the spa, in response to the advertisement posted in the library. Jane forgot her offer to let Penny keep one until after the woman left. Would Kurt hold it against her that she couldn't keep her promise to the girl?

Why did it matter to her what he thought? He was the enemy. Even if he wasn't actually on the attack right now. Why wasn't he?

She supposed he had decided to play mind games for a while. Was he giving her the silent treatment, tormenting her with uncertainty, hoping she would crack soon and contact him?

"Don't hold your breath," she muttered, smiled, and went back to filling out an order for nail fashion accessories.

As the Ghost, she had learned the waiting game. She'd always won.

Or were those odd dreams rooted in the Handyman trying to penetrate her defenses while she slept? Did he have some mental Gifts, so he tried to get into her mind, invade her dreams, program her to be open and receptive and invite him inside her shields?

The Handyman had an awful lot to learn about dealing with the Ghost.

Chapter Nine

Tuesday morning, as she came down the back stairs from her apartment, Jane felt a fluctuation in pressure against the outer walls of the spa. The same fluctuation she would feel if she was inside a balloon filled with water, and someone pressed slowly from the outside. She smiled. A snap of her fingers sent a near-invisible flick of power across the room to turn on the lights for the spa. Jane listened, but didn't make a sound in the mental atmosphere. Now to give the Handyman the silent treatment and drive him crazy with waiting for a reaction.

~~~~~

Buried in the bedrock of Neighborlee, something shuddered a few more degrees toward waking. Shadows rippled among lighter shadows among darker shadows. Darkness flicked out its poisonous, acid-tipped tongue and tasted the atmosphere.

It smiled, tasting strength and the tang of antagonism and irritation. The rich brew hovered on the hair-fine balance between creation and destruction. All it needed was a shove in the right—or wrong—direction.

~~~~~

"Do you need a ride home?" Jane asked, as the soft twilight shifted into night.

"No. Thanks." Penny's big eyes sparkled. "Evan's giving me a ride."

"Evan?" She raised an eyebrow in a skeptical look. "Who is this Evan and why haven't I heard about him before?"

"He's just a boy." She caught her breath and glanced out the front window of the spa as an electric green, low-slung sports car slid to a stop in front of the door.

"Rich boy. Good taste in cars. And girlfriends. He's from around here?" Jane added, fishing for information.

When she had been in the orphanage, town boys with their own cars had been bad news. They were usually from surrounding towns, but Neighborlee had its own bad apples who had to be taught a lesson. The Grandstones and their henchmen. Such rich brats considered the orphanage girls to be fair game, put there to be their playthings.

The boy had sun-bleached brown hair (In the winter? That screamed "money.") that hung over his collar, a crimson leather jacket, and four silver studs in one ear. Music belched in an acid stream from the car's sound system. Jane knew nothing had changed. But what could she do?

What did she know, anyway? Evan could be a great guy, captain of the Chess Team, headed for an Ivy League school on full scholarship. Looks were deceiving. She was proof of that.

"Don't do anything I wouldn't do," Jane muttered, as Penny waved at Evan and bent to pick up her purse.

"Is that supposed to be permission, or a warning?" The Handyman halted in the open doorway. He glanced at Evan, then at Penny, and scowled as he watched the girl dash for the car. "You're letting her go out with that kid?"

"All I can do is offer advice. Since I don't know the boy, I'm not going to make the mistake of judging by appearances. If Angela sent her to me, I'm willing to bet Penny has more common sense than most girls her age. Am I right?"

"Yeah, most of the time." He glanced over his shoulder as the car sped past the door. "Still ..."

"Are you here for a manicure, facial mask, or how about a massage? How about some hot stone therapy?" She bared her teeth in a poisonously sweet smile.

Angela swept into the spa before Kurt could do more than glare at her.

Jane froze, stunned. Her protective field hadn't even reacted to Angela's presence, much less kept her out. Did that mean Angela *didn't* have a Gift?

No. Knowing what she knew about Angela, her memories of Divine's Emporium, her theories... It wasn't that Angela wasn't Gifted, but she was something else entirely. Stronger, more mystical and wise. Angela wasn't someone to antagonize, even for the right reasons.

She shouldn't try to get Angela on her side, Jane knew with a crystalline flash of insight, but ensure she was on Angela's side.

"Thank goodness you're still open," the woman said with her usual gracious, slow smile. "Can you match this shade?" She held up a nail polish bottle. The contents swirled metallic and rainbow-hued.

"Let me see what I have." Jane gladly turned away from the Handyman and went to her knees in front of the storage drawers.

"Was that Penny leaving with Evan?" Angela said.

"You know him?" She glanced up and scowled when she saw Kurt come inside. Jane hadn't really expected him to use the door in his next salvo, so she had left a weak point in the field at the doorway. That would be rectified as soon as he left.

"He's just visiting. For how long, well..." She hitched up one hip to lean on the stool in front of the counter and watched her search. "Some folks will be glad when that boy goes home."

"Goes home?" Kurt asked. "He's not a college boy?"

"His great-uncle lives on the border by Darbyville. Evan's not welcome at home. His stepmother thinks he's trying to blow up the house. His uncle offered to get him out of harm's or temptation's way, so he's been exiled to Neighborlee with his credit cards and car. I know a few parents who were relieved when he decided to ignore their daughters."

"But how many worried when he went after Penny?" Jane muttered.

"To tell you the truth, she's been a good influence on him."

Kurt snorted, clearly expressing what he thought of that.

"No, honestly." Angela sighed and her smile broadened when Jane stood up, holding out a bottle that matched the one she had brought in. "If you can order me a bottle every other month, I will be eternally grateful."

"Sounds like you expect Jane to be here for the long haul," Kurt said.

"She's put down roots." Angela turned to face him, a fierce light in her eyes Jane had never seen the woman bestow on anyone before. "This was her home when she lived at NCH. When you stood up for her. As you've conveniently forgotten."

"Angela, don't you—She—" Kurt let out a sound somewhere between a growl and a raspy kind of sigh. Or maybe steam escaping an engine before it reached the critical explosion point. He looked back and forth between Angela and Jane, and his mouth slowly gaped, clearly unsure what to say.

"You big doofus." Angela's scorn was clear, despite her

superior smirk.

The tiles under Jane's feet seemed to ripple for a moment, her sense of reality rocked by the certainty that she not only had Angela's approval, but her protection.

"Heaven help the man who tries to take her away from the home she's made for herself," the woman continued. "Neighborlee needs her, just as much as she needs us. No, I don't want to hear your arguments — or your attempts to apologize for a large dose of caveman prejudice and stupidity. Just think about what I said."

A serene smile replaced her fierce look so rapidly, Jane wondered if she had imagined the other expression. "You might just discover you're very glad she returned to Neighborlee. There are many things far worse that she could do than devote her life and her talents to our town. And not many things that would be better for *you*." She glanced at Jane and her eyes twinkled. "Especially in matters of the heart."

Kurt stayed at his post in the doorway. Jane didn't look at him as she rang up Angela's purchase — she didn't want to look at him — but she thought he looked a little stunned.

To be honest, she felt a little stunned. Where had that come from? Why had Angela said such things, and how long had it taken for her to figure out the Handyman was tormenting Jane, testing her, maybe trying to drive her out of Neighborlee?

Even more strange, why the comment about "matters of the heart"? While Jane acknowledged her hormonal leanings, that didn't mean she had to listen and let them control her decisions. The last thing she needed was to get involved with someone who reminded her of Otis. Just because Kurt had such a useful Gift didn't make up for labeling her a threat to his town.

"You make a good doorman," Angela said, as she turned to leave. "There are all sorts of doors in town that need guarding." She looked back over her shoulder at Jane and winked. "Think about it."

"All of that should have scared you away," the Handyman muttered, when Angela was long gone. He gestured out the door after her.

"Hardly," Jane said. "You should see the place where I grew up, the people who raised me. Neighborlee isn't that unique."

"Baby, you've barely scratched the surface." His smirk returned, but at half the wattage. "What can I do to convince you that I'm not such a bad guy after all?"

"Get yourself run over by a freight train?" Jane flicked her fingers at the door. The latch turned and it swung open, letting another cold gust inside. "We're closed. Please go home."

"Is that any way to treat a potential ally?" He stepped further into the shop instead of turning toward the door.

"If you don't leave now, you won't be able to leave until morning." She swept around the room, turning off lights, pulling shades down over the windows, turning the potted plants so the sun would hit another side in the morning. Her nightly routine took the same amount of time as it always did, but felt like it took three times as long, with him watching. The weight of his gaze made her skin prickle.

"Just a prisoner ... of the heart." He snorted, sounding suspiciously like laughter. "That's a good trick, the protective shield you've been holding up. Got to teach me that one."

"Just because Angela has declared a truce doesn't mean I'd trust you with any more of my secrets than you've picked up already. Out." She pointed at the door.

"How about inviting me upstairs for dinner, and we can talk this out?"

"How about you go back to whatever rock you live under, and I'll go for a long walk to cool off before I do something really ... vicious?" Jane bit her tongue and felt her face heat. She had almost said "stupid."

"We will have to talk. Eventually. Why not do it like two civilized, rational human beings, in comfort, rather than beat up and on our knees in front of Angela, with her scolding us like a couple of snot-nosed brats?"

"My, that's an ugly picture. Do you always end up in front of Angela like that?" Jane hid her sigh of relief when he took several slow, backward steps toward the door. "Besides, who says we're human beings?"

"Good point. Birds of a feather really should stick together, sweetheart." He continued moving, still facing her, until he was over the threshold.

"Not on your life," she muttered, and flicked her fingers so the door slammed and locked. A flash of green-silver sparkles filled her vision for a moment as the protective field solidified inside the spa.

If she wanted, nothing could get inside while she was away. Even air, if necessary.

Jane wouldn't do that to her innocent plants. She satisfied herself with floating up through the second floor and into her apartment. It wasn't enough satisfaction, though. Nothing appealed to her for dinner, so she settled for a fresh bag of microwave popcorn and a movie marathon. Problem was, she couldn't decide on a series of movies to watch.

She dug through her DVD series and settled on *Man from U.N.C.L.E.*, but lost interest halfway through the second episode. She found an *NCIS* marathon on cable, but Ziva was gone, Tony was more irritating than usual, and she really wanted to Gibbs-slap Gibbs. Two-thirds of the way through the second episode, she couldn't take any more.

Jane knew what she needed: fresh air. She grabbed a coat and a blanket to sit on and flew up through the roof.

The night air was almost balmy, compared to the crystallizing air and high winds that had ripped between the buildings the last few days. There was almost a scent, like the promise of spring, though that was still months away. It made Jane think of the most delicate toilet water, in a very expensive, exclusive spa she had visited. That shop had been her inspiration for going into business. Right now, she was heading for the abandoned quarries on the north side of town for some quiet, and room to breathe and think. While it might be the perfect trysting place in the summer, she couldn't imagine anyone going there for privacy and thinking room and quiet in the winter. Which made it perfect for her, now.

Unfortunately, someone else had the same idea. Jane gritted her teeth when she heard the sound of voices just moments after she had found a comfortable spot to sit and look out at the moonlight on the ice-rimmed water. She knew she had been too preoccupied with her private griping about the Handyman, and hadn't adequately scouted the area before settling down.

Then again, she shouldn't need to scout out the territory like someone preparing an attack. Neighborlee was her town, not her patrol territory. It wasn't like her to be so oblivious.

Jane sighed, started to get to her feet, and caught a flash of electric green, then the distinctive slam of a car door. Gut instinct told her Evan and Penny had come here to the quarry on their way back to the orphanage. She remembered what Angela had said.

Jane didn't care if she was retired or not. Right at this moment, gut instinct told her Penny was in trouble, or on the edge of it.

Her hearing sharpened, tightening and tuning in like someone else would adjust the gain on a spy microphone.

"What is your problem?"

Jane smiled, recognizing the distinctive sound of a rich young snot in full sulk. She silently congratulated Penny on standing strong against her boyfriend's blandishments. Jane shifted to Ghost phase and rose up in the air. If Penny needed some help, she would find it close at hand.

"You know the rules," Penny said. She slid out of her side of the car, putting it between her and the erstwhile Romeo who brought her here.

"Good girl," Jane whispered. More problems were caused by the girl staying within reach of the boy who wanted more than she was willing to give. It didn't matter how often she said no, the fact she stayed in the car would cast doubt on her word against Evan's.

Not that Jane would let Evan lay a hand on Penny. While getting out of the car made her vulnerable, especially this far out of town, it was preferable to the vulnerability of staying in the car. Evan could use the electric locks. He could drive fast, taking dangerous turns, frightening her into complying. Hitting the car horn this far from town wouldn't do Penny that much good. Taking his keys wasn't much good for defense, because using them to claw at her attacker would put her within his reach.

Jane sighed. The smartest thing Penny could do to defend herself was the one thing she hadn't done. Avoid Evan.

"Yeah, I know the rules," Evan finally said after another long, loud sigh. In guy speak, it meant, "Can't you see how reasonable and patient I am? Give up and give in." Another sigh, turning into a whine. "But my Dad is letting me transfer in, not just stay until things cool down at home. We should celebrate, you know? I thought we could make it special."

"Special for you," Penny said. "I'll be grounded for the rest of the school year. And what if I got pregnant?"

"Aw, come on, honey, I'd use a condom."

"Condoms break, and there are a lot of diseases that are smaller than the pores in the rubber. Stopping AIDS with a condom is like trying to catch a golf ball with a volleyball net."

"You sound like a freaking science lecture," he snarled.

"And you aren't insulted that I'm afraid of catching some disgusting disease from you," she shot back.

"Good girl. Just yank all the romance wind out of his sails," Jane said, nodding.

"I can't believe I wasted so much time on you."

The next sound to fill the quarry was the rumble of the engine cranking into angry life. Jane smiled and pumped her fist, signaling a score for Penny. She knew the girl was a smart one the moment she met her. It felt more glorious than she could have anticipated, to have her faith in someone pay out in gold for a change.

"Yeah, you could have been spending your money on beer and hookers instead of pretending to be Mr. All-American. Take me home right now, Evan."

"Think again. This taxi just stopped running."

Penny squealed as Evan leaned over, across the car, and reached for the door handle to pull it closed. Jane arched up into the air, ready to dive down. She flinched as her fingertips tingled with energy.

Something flashed gold and white and hit the car with a thud like a small atomic blast.

Evan shouted, sounding like Chekov in a Classic Trek episode. The car leaped up on its rear wheels like an angry stallion.

Penny screamed and stumbled backwards. The car slammed back down onto all four tires and careened up the slope toward the edge of the quarry cliff. Everything happened in the space of two heartbeats, so quickly Jane barely had time to blink and realize what had happened.

"You get the girl. I'll get the car," Kurt bellowed from behind Jane. He swooped past her, arms outstretched, racing the sports car.

Jane almost told him to pull his arms in to cut the wind resistance. She shook her head and dropped down to help Penny, who had rolled away from the car and was struggling to sit up. The teen was covered in snow melt and mud, visibly wobbling, with a cut on her cheek from a sharp rock. Jane cast caution to the wind, became visible and solid, and wrapped her arms around Penny.

"Evan?" Penny twisted around in Jane's arms.

The car stopped with the front wheels hanging in mid-air,

spinning fast enough to blur. The brake lights flashed wildly as Evan fought for control. Out of phase now, Jane couldn't see Kurt, but she imagined him floating three feet out from the cliff edge, holding up the nose of the sports car with one hand, probably smugly pleased with himself.

The car's rear lights flashed white as Evan tried to put it into reverse. Then the engine died. Jane flinched, feeling the flash of energy that had killed all the electrical systems. Silence reverberated through the quarry.

Jane swore she heard a whisper of laughter, chiming in the crystalline cold air. The car groaned as Kurt pushed it backwards, putting all four wheels on solid ground.

Kurt came out of phase with his cell phone already open and pressing buttons. When he said he was calling Evan's uncle to meet them at NCH, Evan went into full-scale spoiled brat mode, daring to give orders. He accused Kurt of sabotaging his car and ordered him to fix it, right then and there.

Kurt didn't bother arguing. He just stepped behind Evan and applied pressure to spots on the back of his neck. Evan yelped, and five seconds later folded like a wet paper doll.

Jane was grateful he knew that technique, but refused to say so, just because he managed to come up with a plan of action faster than she did. What could she do, though? Responding to his hand signals, she distracted Penny while Kurt pushed the car back down to the path through the quarries and got it working again. Short of flying, it was the only way out of there for any of them.

With Penny in the front seat of Evan's car, and the boy still unconscious in the back seat, Kurt drove them back to the orphanage. Jane followed in Ghost phase, to support the story he gave Penny: Kurt had been showing Jane around town, she would follow them to the orphanage in her car and drive him home.

For a few seconds, Jane played with the idea of just ditching him right there, flying back to her apartment, and leaving him to hoof it back home from NCH. When she got far enough out of reach, he couldn't "borrow" her Gift to fly. However, he hadn't told her the limits of his range for borrowing. There was a big difference between fifty feet, fifty yards, and half a mile.

She couldn't do that, though. Angela wanted them to make nice, and he might rat her out if she inconvenienced him. After all, he had a place here. She was still the newcomer. Even though she certainly felt as if she had come home at long last, there was no guarantee Kurt couldn't turn his Gifted friends against her, as well as the rest of the town.

Besides, she had Penny to protect. Jane needed to testify that even though the girl had been at the quarry, it was against her will.

"She'll be just fine," Mrs. Alcott assured Jane and Kurt an hour later. She was the administrator who had replaced Mrs. Silvestri.

The three stood in the front foyer of the main building, watching the tow truck drag away Evan's car, following his uncle's big black vintage Cadillac. The boy was forbidden to drive until the malfunction had been found and fixed.

"Penny's a good girl, and I think she learned a vital lesson without too big a scare. Thank the good Lord you were there."

"Jane's become really protective of this town. Especially Penny," Kurt said. "Even if we hadn't been there, she probably would have sensed something was wrong and gone looking for her." He rested a hand on Jane's shoulder and squeezed. And kept squeezing, giving a miniature massage right in the most painful spot of her tense muscles.

From anyone else, the touch would be soothing. But, of course, this was the Handyman. Her nemesis. Reluctantly, she stepped out of his reach and held out her hand to shake Mrs. Alcott's.

"We're glad to have you back in Neighborlee," the woman said as she shook Jane's hand.

That stopped her cold and Jane stammered, "You know —"

"That you were once one of our students? My, yes." She nodded her silvery-white curly head. "Despite all those records that vanished a few years ago, we do manage to keep track of all our graduates. Besides, Angela let us know of the connection. It's nice to know one of ours is doing so well."

"Vanished?" Jane knew she was starting to sound like a bad echo, but she couldn't help it. If Mrs. Alcott hadn't said "a few years ago," she would have been ready to think there was a conspiracy. As if someone knew her mission to investigate the other Lost Boys and make connections, and they were determined to frustrate her.

"Mrs. Silvestri was quite incensed. We were finally uploading all our paper files a couple years ago, over a century's worth, into a computer, letting other child welfare networks have access. The records were just...gone." She shook her head.

"That's too bad. I would have liked to have looked through those records. Just to see if there was something there that maybe..." Jane shrugged. "Everybody would like answers, you know?"

"There's a lot of that going around," Kurt muttered. Jane shivered, seeing a sparkle of interest in his eyes.

What did he read into her statement?

What were the chances Kurt and his Gifted friends had those missing records?

Finding out would mean more than obeying the truce Angela had decreed. It would mean opening up, sharing information, being honest and trusting him. Could she do it? Yes, that was part of her mission, but Kurt had twisted everything sideways and she didn't want to play nice just yet.

"I really have to get on home," Jane said, to stop the speculations before she did something foolish. Like asking to look through the records that remained.

"That's right," Kurt said. "You have a business to run. A very successful one, too."

"Yes, and Penny just loves working for you," Mrs. Alcott said. "Thank you again for watching out for her."

Kurt explained that she had left her car around the corner, so the lights wouldn't disturb the children any more than they already had been, with the excitement of Penny coming back after hours. They walked down the curving driveway and out of sight beyond the trees in silence. Jane didn't even look at him as she went into Ghost phase and leaped up into the air. He followed. She felt his presence, a sense of warmth through the icy air. It might have been amusing to leave him down on the ground, shouting at her. Or would he just fume in silence and plot revenge?

The flight back to her apartment was silent, giving Jane plenty of time to think further on the incident at the quarry. She had only one conclusion she could draw.

"You caused the accident, didn't you?" she half-snarled when they reached the roof of her building.

"Not me." He held out both hands, palms facing forward, as if to ward off attack. "Somebody else."

"Like who?"

"My guess? Some friend of Penny's." He gestured down at the

alley behind her building, where the lights from other apartments-over-businesses filtered through curtains. "We can argue out here, where some of your neighbors could hear. Or, we can go inside and talk. Your choice. But we are going to talk, one way or another."

"I don't have much choice, do I, Handyman?"

"My name is Kurt," he said.

Jane just gestured for him to follow her and phased out to pass through the ceiling into her apartment.

You're the Handyman, aren't you? She muffled a chuckle. It was ridiculous, arguing like this, him outside and her inside.

When I'm working. I was hoping, after what happened, we could be friends. He paused as he slid down after her.

Jane was pleased to see that he hadn't quite mastered the trick of talking and phasing through solid objects at the same time. She was rather protective of the talents she considered her private territory.

"I doubt it."

"What did I do? Want to tell me that? I'd think after working together to rescue Penny from that juvenile delinquent, you'd be a little friendlier towards me."

"You decided I was a threat and tried to pull the welcome mat out from under my feet the last few days." She almost laughed when he colored and looked away. Was he embarrassed?

What was with some guys? She paused, giving him a chance to apologize, but of course, he just looked at her, his eyes widening a little with discomfort. No, he was one of those guys who couldn't seem to find the words. The question was if he would be one of those guys whose inability to apologize was charming. Some guys weren't able to apologize because they could never admit they were wrong in the first place.

She sighed, pushing those thoughts away. Yes, it angered her, and wearied her, to know the friendship she thought she was developing with Kurt had died under his sudden load of paranoia.

"I would be a little friendlier, maybe," she said, "if you hadn't caused all that trouble, nearly throwing Evan's car over the cliff."

"I already said, that wasn't me." The words came out stiff, almost growled. Gee, did his feelings get hurt because she didn't believe him the first time he denied guilt?

"I didn't notice any other Gifted hanging around the quarry

tonight." She slumped down into the futon, and deliberately neglected to offer him a seat.

"I felt something. Weak. It didn't match what I've sensed from you already. New talent emerging, is my guess. Maybe somebody who likes Penny and hates Evan-the-snot." He settled down on the floor, his back against the hassock.

"Someone you missed, just like the Old Poops missed you and your friends," she murmured.

"Oh, that makes everything really clear." He snorted, but grinned wearily at her, and she found herself grinning back. "How about we start off with some explanations?"

"Such as?"

"Who are the Old Poops? I'm assuming they're the ones who yanked you out of here as soon as you started going invisible, when we were kids."

"That about sums it up. How come they didn't notice you?"

"Me and Lanie, we found each other when we were rug rats. I'm guessing we developed our talents a lot sooner than most kids, and it came on us slow enough we figured out what we could do, what we shouldn't do." He unzipped his leather jacket and looked around her apartment, just a few casual glances that somehow didn't make her feel invaded. Points for him. "Anyway, we read a lot of comic books, and we figured out what we were, or at least made some good guesses, and we learned how to protect ourselves by following the rules in the comic books."

"Different is dangerous," she offered, her voice soft. "Attract as little attention as possible. Never use your Gifts out in the open where the wrong people might see."

"Pretty much. When we discovered Felicity, we helped her hide what she could do. It was kind of fun, us against the world."

"Hiding from the house parents."

"Hmm, pretty much. But we had Angela to encourage us. And then Lanie got adopted out, and her folks..." He chuckled. "They're not your normal grownups. When they realized Lanie could kinda-sorta fly, they didn't freak, didn't send her for testing. They gave us a lot of good advice and accepted us for what we were, through the years. Remind me to tell you some time about the year we decided we were aliens dropped on Earth by accident, and we tried to make contact with the home planet."

"How old were you?"

"Middle school. Those were great times, when we didn't realize how much danger we really were in..." His face seemed to darken and grow weary. "Then you grow up and you realize that the town that has protected you all these years, that let you be as weird as you needed until you could figure out what you were, what you could do, needs as much guarding as it gave you."

He sighed. "Look, I'm trying to say I'm sorry. I just figure anyone who comes from outside, they're not on our side. After what happened at Christmas, with those three kids coming after Lanie ... Maybe coming after all of us. It's kind of hard to trust outsiders." A shrug. "You're not an outsider, though. Even if Angela wasn't vouching for you, it's hard to say you're not one of us, not after tonight."

"About those kids who tried to hurt Lanie—"

"Don't ask."

Chapter Ten

"I'm not asking." Jane fought the urge to squirm when his relaxed, weary expression turned sharp again. "My... The Old Poops took two away for fixing and to keep them safe. They're looking for the one who got snatched before we could move in. We didn't *send* those kids here. Someone else sent them."

"O...kay..." His eyes narrowed and even though he stared into her eyes from across the room, Jane sensed he really didn't see her for a few moments, deep in thought. "We kind of hoped that was you guys who took the boys. The truth is … you were checking out your building the Friday after Christmas, weren't you?"

"Yeah. Why?" Jane shivered, remembering that moment when she felt like someone was watching her.

"Lanie dreamed about you. She followed you, in her dream. You rescued the Colonel, didn't you?" His face relaxed into a weary smile when Jane could only nod. "Lanie recognized you when she ran into you that first day, and we checked you out. They've been ready to pound me for going heavy-handed, but I had to test you. Make sure you weren't working with the rivals and playing mind games with us. Not after that whole ugly mess at New Year's."

"Rivals? How did you know that's what we call them?"

"The Colonel nearly got snatched, when another Lost Kid almost got taken, back when they were kids. Two old men rescued them and let the Colonel go home, and they called the enemy their rivals, so that's how he thinks of them." He shrugged. "Kind of hard to plot strategy when you don't even know your enemy's name, you know?"

"Yeah. I know exactly what you mean." She thought her smile matched his for weariness. Beneath that, something bubbled up inside her. Relief. Maybe giddy with weariness. Now they could move forward, forging that alliance Beau and Demetrius wanted.

"By the way …" His eyes brightened with mischief. "We have access to copies of all those records you were asking about. Mrs. Silvestri made copies of everything. It's taking a long time, but we're gathering up information, everything we can find, on the kids who got taken away and just vanished. There are a lot of Lost Kids who never got taken, though. We think we need to pay attention to them, not just the mutants with superhero powers."

"That's exactly what Beau was thinking." Jane shook her head. "I just don't get it."

"What?"

"How did the Old Poops miss you and Lanie and Felicity? They missed you three, but they got me. My Gift is going invisible, so that's kind of ironic they found me but not you."

"Going invisible is kind of flashy." His expression warmed more. Jane laughed softly.

Her stomach woke up, and let her know the popcorn she had eaten wasn't enough dinner. "Hungry?"

"You could hear my stomach all the way over there?" He grinned crookedly.

Jane bit back a response that no, she hadn't. That felt a little too intimate. She snapped her fingers, focused the Ghost field across the room, and held out both hands. The surfer cookie jar came floating over to her. She waved one hand and sent it spinning gently over to Kurt, first.

"Nice. I can manage the bigger, flashier details, but not something this delicate." He lifted the lid of the cookie jar and the roar of a wave elicited a bark of laughter. He bit into the first cookie he took out, heavy with peanut butter chips, gum drops, chocolate swirls, and sprinkles, sandwiched together with cream filling. A groan escaped him, muffled. "Cookies to die for. Marry me?" He took two more cookies, put the lid back on and sent the jar floating over to her.

"Puh-lease." She rolled her eyes and slouched a little further in the futon. She wasn't about to admit that she got creative and made thousand-calorie-per-bite cookies when she was frustrated.

"What? You have something against perpetuating the species?"

"Figure out what species we are, then we can talk about— Let's concentrate on finding this new Gift, if that's what you were hinting at before. Find all of us, instead of trying to make more of us."

"Picky, picky." He grinned, making her think of an adorable little boy full of mischief, with a thin core of uncertainty and hunger for acceptance. Could he have a few specks of insecurity? Doggone it. She could start liking the guy inside the gorgeous, rough-cut packaging, Jane mused as she took her first nibble. Then something she hadn't considered yet cut through all her other thoughts. She sat up straight, nearly knocking the cookie jar off her lap.

"You sensed something at the quarries. You sense others at work. That's part of how you borrow Gifts, isn't it?"

"I can feel vibrations," he said with a shrug. "Kind of like people would go around with divining rods, looking for water and oil. I can feel when we're under attack. It helps us set up defenses."

"Against others like us?"

"You better hope whatever it is isn't like us. No, Neighborlee kind of ... it's kind of like a plug. Kind of like a patch on weak spots. There's something nasty out there, other realities, trying to get in, and it has to get through Neighborlee. We can use more people to keep watch. Fight it when it comes back. Each time is different. We call it Big Ugly, but sometimes, like at New Year's, there are others involved. We aren't sure if they're more enemies from other dimensions, or the Rivals are working with them, trying to help them come through."

"How can you tell? I mean, tell the difference. How do you know different enemies are attacking?"

"Like an antique TV set when it warms up. You know how you think you hear something, but you're not sure?"

"Yeah. That humming that isn't quite in your ears and not quite in your fingertips." Jane's fingers twitched, remembering that momentary tingle of energy. She wished she hadn't been so busy and could have followed up on it. They might have answers right now, instead of just speculations.

"The sounds that aren't sounds — real clear, right? — they vary, like people's voices vary. Even if everybody is an alto, they all sound different. Kind of like that. Some talents sound, feel different."

"How do I sound?"

"Chiming."

"Chiming?" Jane laughed.

"Yeah, that's how you sound to me, when we're both using your talent. Like wind chimes. Soft and shimmery, like in a dream. But when you're ticked and when you're using your talent — whoo, baby!" He winked again. "Like tonight. You went from a few chimes about two octaves above Middle C, when you were just sitting and thinking, to the entire string section of the Cincinnati Pops, with a couple dozen harps thrown in, when we were trying to keep Evan from doing Evel Knieval on a bad day."

"If I wasn't fighting you all the time, I wouldn't be making a sound. Would I?" She made her tone belligerent, to fight a wave of uncertainty. Jane didn't like the idea of being a noisy talent. High volume, even if Kurt thought it was pretty, didn't exactly fit the image of the Ghost.

"Come to think of it, you were practically silent, until I showed up," Kurt admitted. "Just this nice, soft, kind of hypnotic sound. Relaxing. Kind of like how all those candles you sell would sound if they turned into music."

"Either you've done a lot of drugs in your time, or you're a man who slips through dimensions and sees through other senses without going wonky." Jane slouched back a little more and smiled at him. Maybe she did like Kurt Hanson after all.

"Haven't you turned your brain inside out, trying to figure out what you are, why you are, and why you ended up here?" He sat forward, his smile flattening. "Or do your Old Poops have an answer? Care to share?"

"We don't have an answer," she admitted. "Just a purpose."

"And that is?" he prompted. "It seems to me, if you know your purpose for being on Earth, you know why you were sent, and who sent you."

"Not that kind of purpose."

"What is it? Steal all the Lost Kids, so we're defenseless when the interdimensional monsters finally break through?"

"Please, it's been too long a day, and too high on the weirdness meter to get nasty." She slouched down on the cushions and rubbed at her temples.

"Sorry. Put yourself in my shoes—"

"Too big, and they probably smell. Most guys built like you are sweaty and smelly."

"Built like me?" He snorted and gave her the widest, most natural smile she had seen from him yet.

"Our purpose is to gather all of the Gifted together, give them shelter, let them grow up as normally as possible, and train them to use their Gifts for good. You had friends, people who supported you and gave you guidance and didn't make you feel like a freak every time you turned around. That's what the Old Poops did for us. It's hard to feel like you fit in if you're afraid of getting noticed by the wrong kind of people."

"Yeah, well, the magic of Neighborlee helps a lot. People just ignore the weirdness quotient, or if they can't take it, something about the town drives them away before they go crazy."

"You're lucky," she said, her voice dropping nearly to a whisper.

"Maybe. Okay, your Old Poops gave you a family."

"And they sent me here to make contact with the guardians."

"How do you know that's what we call ... yeah, right. You probably got something from the Colonel when you snatched him and the boys."

"We rescued them from the Rivals." Jane braced for Kurt to argue with her.

"You're right." He cocked his head to one side, studying her for a few seconds. "Okay, we need to compare notes. Get you together with Lanie and Felicity."

"And Angela."

"Oh, definitely. People like us, we have to stick together." He frowned, staring into space for a few seconds. Jane thought she could hear fizzing coming from inside his head, from the intensity of his thoughts. "Priority right now, though ... we have to find this new talent that showed up tonight."

"Before he or she does something really dangerous."

"Agreed. Now, if we could just figure out who was there at the quarry. Any chance it's Penny? It seems to me, Angela might have matched the two of you together, maybe expecting you to have some influence on her, give her guidance. That's the way she works a lot of the time, no clear instructions, just lots of hints."

"No." Jane rubbed her fingers together and held her hand up when Kurt gave her an odd look. "I would have felt something, after all the time we've spent together. I help Beau and Demetrius sometimes, trying to find a new Gift. I can feel power at work, itching in my fingertips. Sometimes the itch is more like a tickle. And sometimes... It's like a really good deep tissue massage that digs out all the poisons from your muscles. It's good for you, but it hurts like bloody murder while it's being done. You know?"

Jane wondered if she sounded as much like a blithering idiot to Kurt as she sounded to herself.

"So where do I fit into all that?" He offered her one of those lopsided grins that made her think he laughed at himself, rather than her. And made her melt a little inside.

She held up her hand, stopping him from continuing, when a new thought suddenly flashed through her mind. "It's a different buzz when someone is just learning. For everybody," she emphasized. "Why can't it be a different *sound* for everybody, too? If you can learn to differentiate... Maybe you can track people down?"

"Yeah. I don't even notice when Lanie and Felicity use their talent. Well, Felicity was pretty flashy, until recently. When we fought Big Ugly at New Year's, she did something that kind of yanked her into synch or something." He grinned wider. "I'll explain later, or maybe let her explain to you when you meet her. But yeah, with enough exposure, I can tune people out when I want to hunt." Kurt nodded. "So... We're hunting together?"

"I guess."

"Gee, don't sound so excited."

"You are a goof." She yanked the lid off the cookie jar and tossed him two more cookies. Kurt snagged them out of mid-air and flipped them between his fingers, like the Harlem Globetrotters did with basketballs. Jane laughed.

~~~~~

Feel anything down there? Kurt drifted beside Jane over the long building behind the orphanage recreation center.

No. She rolled over onto her back and stared up at the clouds. *You have no idea how many times I wanted to do exactly this when I lived here. I had just figured out that I could fly, it wasn't just a dream, and the thought of dive-bombing those bullies...*

You wanted to get away from all the jerks, and prove you were special in a good way.

We all go through that, don't we? She sighed and drifted upright and sat with her legs crossed. *The problem was that I didn't figure out how to stay invisible, how to turn it on and off, until I got out of here. I didn't dare go flying where my Ghost field might fluctuate and people might see me. Even at night. Even this high. I knew it wasn't safe.*

Adolescent boys are notorious for going and looking where you don't expect or want – Hah! Kurt did a front roll and pointed down. Four shadows climbed out onto the flat roof of the sixties-style gym building.

Why do you think it's boys in particular?

I spend a lot of time here as a big brother, and there are three times as many boys as girls here, right now. Besides, who would be more likely to zap Evan for putting pressure on Penny? Kurt floated over closer to her. With them both in phase, she could see him, with moonlight passing through him like a holographic projection.

A jealous boy. Jane sighed. *It'd be nice if there were more girls among us.*

How many are there of you? What was it like, going to school with other kids like you? Growing up, it was just Lanie, Felicity and me.

You had Angela, and Lanie's folks, right? Sounds like you had a lot of support and advice.

We still felt like freaks. He grinned. *But it was fun being a freak. So, what was it like for you?*

Actually... She floated closer to him. *I was the only student. Everybody else was six years older than me. And more. But I had lots of big brothers and sisters, aunts and uncles. It was nice, knowing I could ask questions and practice out in the open, without being afraid some government agency would swoop down and drag me away.*

What do you think those troublemakers down there are up to? Let's follow them and find out. Kurt laughed and did a nosedive, pulling up at the last moment to climb up to rejoin her.

The boys climbing around on the gym roof paused to look up, faces pale in the moonlight. Jane almost felt sorry for them, startled by the sound of laughter above their heads, but those boys had no business being up there on the roof at this time of night.

Shouldn't we be waiting for them to do something? Aren't we looking for a newly awakened Gifted?

You're no fun. He stuck his tongue out at her and drifted back a few yards.

They passed the next hour comparing adventures they had gone on, growing up, or the differences in their training. Jane was amused to realize that much of what Kurt and his friends picked up from reading comic books to apply to their lives, to create the rules they lived by, Beau and Demetrius had taught their decades of students. When she said so, Kurt laughed.

They followed the boys, staying high enough to avoid being

overheard. The boys seemed to be up to the usual mischief of boys who lived here for generations. Nothing happened to make Jane's fingers itch, or generate the hum that Kurt heard when a Gift was being used.

What if it wasn't a Lost Kid at the quarries tonight? Jane mused after several long moments of silence.

Huh? What else would it be? I can't imagine Big Ugly helping Penny. Although yeah, I can imagine him causing trouble just to cause trouble. But we wore him out pretty bad in that fight.

Jane shared the theory Beau had come up with, about the children or grandchildren of Lost Kids who hadn't developed any Gifts, developing gifts of their own.

Yeah, we were talking about something like that a while ago. Honestly, that's already happening. The Longfellow girls are doing some pretty interesting stuff. But later. Ask Angela. After we get other things settled. He pointed down at the boys, who were retracing their steps back through orphanage grounds. *Those aren't our targets. Whoever we ran into earlier, whatever they can do, they're asleep.*

Or maybe the Gift only appears when they're angry or worried or afraid, she offered. *I'm inclined to agree that our new talent is a boy.*

Why?

Penny works for me, remember? All her friends have come into the spa to try out jewelry and makeup samples at least once. I never felt a single blip or itch or tickle. Sometimes Gifts activate at that age just when they get excited, when they're in big groups, maybe vying for attention, or they get mad at someone. She waggled her fingers for explanation. *Not a bit.*

How excited do girls get over all that goop in your store? He grinned at her, and she thought, hoped, he was only teasing.

Hormones. Rivalries. Bullies. Believe me, girls can get absolutely catty over a shade of nail polish they don't want anyone else to use. Or they want to all be exactly alike, and there isn't enough to go around. And we've spent enough time out here. Whoever it is, you're right, they're asleep. Good night. She turned to float back to her side of town.

How fast can you fly? Kurt pulled up next to her.

I don't know. As fast as I need to.

You never timed yourself? No pals who can fly, to race?

Not really. I never really thought about timing myself... I have an idea, though.

~~~~~

Kurt was duly impressed the next evening, when Katie zapped up the stairs to Jane's apartment. Katie let out a yelp that nearly shattered Jane's cookie jar when she saw the stranger step out of the bathroom.

"So you're the Handyman, huh?" Katie calmed once Jane made the hurried introductions. She settled down with her usual cup of chamomile tea, triple strength, that Jane had ready for her.

"My friends call me Kurt," he said with a shrug. He leaned back against the kitchen counter.

Jane was relieved by that pose. It made Katie's usual sport of bun watching and judging nearly impossible. She didn't want to think why she considered Kurt's hindquarters her domain right that moment. She wouldn't let herself think about her conflicting and ever-changing feelings and the reasons behind them.

"Friend of my friend," Kurt added with a grin directed at Jane.

"Uh, if you're rewriting that old saying, it doesn't work. Otherwise, a friend of my friend is my enemy?" She traded grins with him. "So, to what do I owe the honor of meeting the infamous Handyman?" Katie drawled.

"Infamous? How much have you been griping about me?"

"Not nearly as much as you deserve," Jane retorted. Why did it irritate her that Kurt and Katie were so comfortable together, so fast? "We need your help."

She was intrigued when Jane explained the timing question and Kurt explained his confusion why they needed Katie's help specifically.

"I can handle a stopwatch as well as anyone," he said.

"Katie doesn't need a stopwatch at all." Jane summoned a king-size bar of dark chocolate from inside the top cupboard. "She can tell you down to the hundredth of a second and the centimeter how fast and how far you flew, or ran, or swam or dug. Besides —" She tore the wrapper off and paused to study the bar full of nuts and raisins. Maybe she should have chosen the chocolate-covered espresso bean bar instead. "You got me wondering if I can keep up with her. Or maybe beat her."

"Nobody can fly faster than I can run." Katie jabbed herself in the breastbone with both thumbs. She winced, earning grins from Jane and Kurt.

"Nobody who's tried, at least."

"So, where are we going to race?" Kurt hurried to say, forestalling the rebuttal visibly ready to spill off Katie's lips.

"I figure, after the debacle with Evan, nobody is going near the quarries for a while." Jane held out her hands. "Need a lift?"

"I'll beat you there," Katie retorted, and left a momentary blur behind as she flew out the door and down the stairs, before the sound of displaced air crackled through the room.

"I like her." Kurt slid into phase and arched up through the ceiling.

Jane grinned and let him take the lead. She knew better than to waste energy before a race. Battling with words and wit was definitely a waste of energy.

~~~~~

During the third race, around several piles of fragments and through a tunnel dug under a stand of trees, the tingle of energy in Jane's fingertips changed frequency, as if another note had entered the chord of resonance from her, Kurt and Katie all using their Gifts. Ever since her discussion with Kurt, she had thought hard about the differences in the buzz in her fingertips and the back of her neck, the stirring of frequencies and differences in temperature that signaled the use of power. She could tune out most of the energy they expended in their racing. This new buzz had a chill, rather than the pleasant tickle of the three of them going at full strength and having fun.

Despite all her second thoughts and rethinking what she thought she knew, this did not feel like the wavering hum of an adolescent just coming into his or her Gift.

"I didn't hear anything," Kurt said, when she reported the sensation, after they retreated to the sheer drop-off on the edge of town, to sit and talk.

"Maybe we were too loud?" Katie suggested. "I mean, we were going pretty fast. All that wind in our ears, y'know?"

"I think we should go back and see what's there," Jane said. "Whoever we sensed at work last night was protecting Penny. That makes it kind of personal for me. I don't want some off-balance, untrained kid running around zapping anybody who makes him mad. With our luck, this emerging Gift will be powerful, violent, and have a temper." She shook her head, fighting a sudden shiver that had nothing to do with the chill of mid-winter.

"It feels wrong. Kids don't have any business hanging around out there," Kurt said. He shrugged. "Granted, Lanie and Felicity and I came out here a lot, to practice. But still …"

Come out, come out, wherever you are, Jane called, and concentrated on sending her thoughts as deeply and intensely as she could as she rose into the sky and flew out over the quarries. Up to the northernmost edge of the quarries, then south into the portion taken over by the park, then a few degrees west and back north again.

She nearly tumbled out of the sky when she felt the tingling in her left hand fingertips, but not the right. Her left arm hung down while her right hand reached up toward the moonlight. That was a clear directional indicator if she was ever going to get one.

Hello! She sent her thoughts downward and reduced altitude. The buzzing tickle and sense of chill grew in her left hand.

"You want to come out where the rest of us can see you?" Katie called in a stage whisper.

Jane looked down and saw Katie and Kurt standing on the lip of the deepest water-filled pit of the old quarry. She landed and slid out of phase.

"Feel it?"

"I don't hear anything." Kurt spoke softly and didn't look at either of them. "That doesn't mean anything."

"Oh, thanks for that bit of good news," Katie joked. She stepped back from the rock lip. "You know, I used to love skinny-dipping when I was a kid, but that stuff makes me think of those really corny horror movies, where there were always ugly, lumpy, shadowy things hiding in the water. Know what I mean?"

"Creatures from other worlds, that found a crack between dimensions and came looking for a snack," Jane murmured. She shivered, but it wasn't the fun shiver she always got from watching those movies. That dark water looked unbearably cold and unfathomably black. How come it wasn't covered with a skin of ice, like some of the other water-filled holes in the quarry?

"I think we all pushed ourselves a little too hard tonight," she said. "Let's get out of here."

Jane stayed looking down into the water when the other two started to walk away. She rubbed the fingers of her left hand against her thumb, feeling a phantom of the chill, itching vibrations. An echo of what had been there before.

"You still feel something?" Katie asked.

"I don't know." She gestured down, as if she could go through the rock.

"Maybe the kid we're looking for is a frogman."

"Amphibian?" Kurt took a step closer to the edge of the water again. "That would be new. Don't know how useful it would be."

"Useful how?" Katie said.

"In the coming battle of something nasty trying to punch through the dimensions to invade earth." Jane cocked an eyebrow, amused when Kurt seemed a little surprised by her words. "Did I get the gist of it right?"

"Oh, yeah."

Jane thought about asking him to update Katie on what he had taught her, but suddenly, more than anything else, she wanted to just get out of there and go to bed.

Yeah, sleep sounded wonderful. Dreams. Rest. Escape from the disappointment of this evening.

"Whoever he is, we're not going to recruit the kid tonight." She stepped away from the edge of the water. "I'm wiped. You have a delivery to make, I have a business to run, and you..." She flicked her gaze at Kurt, who walked a little too close to her as they followed the gravel trail away from the water. "I assume you're going to meet with Lanie and Felicity. Something tells me you haven't been reporting to them about me. Otherwise we would have had the big meeting Lanie was talking about before. I assume she mentioned my meeting Felicity because she suspected things, and was testing me?"

"Yeah. Pretty much. We've been recovering from the mess with Big Ugly, other stuff going on. Taking things slow." He shrugged, and still didn't look at her. That was a danger sign, in Jane's past experience. "What about the kid we've found?"

Chapter Eleven

"How do you know we've found anybody?"

"Jane—"

"Look, could you two get a little louder, so the whole town hears?" Katie broke in, after turning her head back and forth like a spectator at a tennis match.

"Everything we think we heard or felt tonight could just be an echo, you know?" Jane stopped and glared, trying to convince him with the sparks inside before it blew up into anger.

How she knew she was going to get blazing furious in a couple more minutes, she had no idea. A small, quiet corner of her mind sat back in amazement, just watching. This wasn't her usual reaction to things.

Tired. She was just tired. And cold. It had been a rough, draining, exhilarating, surprising, and yet in some ways disappointing week.

"If there really is a kid," she said, turning to Katie, "no one reports to the Old Poops. No more yanking kids away from the only home they know. Did you ever think they might not know best?"

"Jane!" Katie stared at her.

Looking at her wide-eyed friend, Jane relented. She felt some amusement at the sense of shock rippling through herself. As if she had split into several different people and couldn't believe what was coming out of her mouth. Or the feelings churning inside.

"Suits me," Kurt said, nodding slowly. "Although, if it were me, I might not mind getting taken away and having things explained to me. If we hadn't found each other, Lanie and Felicity and me, we might have gone crazy like the Parker kid. Of course, he had help, but..." He shook his head. "Need some time to think and decompress. Mind if I hitch a ride with you, Jane? I'm used to flying. No offense, Katie, but running isn't my thing."

"None taken." She grinned at him and tipped two fingers off her left eyebrow in salute.

"No problem." Jane lifted her arms to the sky and slid into phase. She waited just long enough for Kurt to phase, and then put on speed, aiming toward her apartment. "See you there, Katie?"

"I don't think so," her friend called. "I have work to do. Thanks for reminding me."

What's her problem? Jane wondered. She looked back in time to see Katie vanish in a flash of blue-white light, heading in the opposite direction.

She's not going to tattle on us about the kid, is she? Kurt asked.

What kid? We haven't found anything yet.

~~~~~

Jane slept badly. Or she thought she did.

As far as she could tell, she totally lost consciousness the moment her head hit the pillow. The next thing she knew, the sun was shining through her window and into her eyes, the radio was blasting downstairs, and she smelled the raspberry white chocolate cappuccino she wanted to taste-test for the spa. Who was down there?

Jane stumbled across her room and found some clean clothes that matched. At least, she hoped they did, because she didn't get her eyes completely open even after she washed her face and brushed her teeth. Then she stumbled downstairs and staggered into the spa.

Penny was in the little kitchen area in the back, where Jane made samples of herbal teas and instant coffee drinks for customers to taste. Apple fritters and cappuccino waited on the little table just inside the display area. The teen looked none the worse for wear. She managed a nearly normal smile for Jane, and settled down on the tall stool used for makeup consultations on the fly.

Jane almost demanded an explanation for why Penny was there, in the morning, on a school day. Then she remembered today was an in-service day for teachers, so no classes.

"How are you feeling?" Jane wasn't about to tell the girl she hadn't needed to come in today. The aromas of fresh-baked fritters and cappuccino made her stomach rumble and melted away that cobwebby, gluey feeling in her head. She wasn't about to discourage Penny from looking after her.

It was nice to have someone looking after her.

Then how come, that quiet voice at the back of her mind asked, *you were so prickly when Kurt started to get protective?*

There's looking after, and there's smothering, another voice snapped from the front of her brain.

That part wanted those fritters and cappuccino but was too proud to whimper or get down on her knees and pay homage to the thoughtful girl who brought them.

"Fine." Penny couldn't possibly know about the war between her mind and stomach. "Evan is heading for military school. His uncle hired some professional shopper. A limousine showed up at the cottage when I got home from school yesterday. Three big boxes of clothes and makeup and other stuff. Totally not me." She rolled her eyes and grinned. "I gave away most of it. It doesn't matter, I figure, because Evan won't be coming back here, so I won't see his uncle ever again, so he won't know."

"Good for you. Bad taste in clothes?" Jane gave up on her pride and picked up a cappuccino with both hands. She whimpered and didn't care if Penny heard her.

"Great taste. If you can't decide whether you want to be the town slut or a Catholic school girl."

"The shopper was hedging her bets, going the whole spectrum, is my guess."

"How do you know so much?" Penny said with a sigh and a lopsided grin. She leaned forward, elbows on the counter.

"I saw how the town jerks thought all orphans were fair game, before I got adopted out. You know who the Grandstones are?" Jane managed a chuckle when Penny gave an exaggerated shudder. "I was just out of their age range, but I watched what happened to other girls. Not much changes, if you really think about it. Although, I do hope they changed that horrid jungle wallpaper in the counselor's office."

"Nope. Still there." Then her mouth dropped open. "I forgot — you said you used to live here."

"Same cottage, too. But that's not why I hired you. Angela said you were good, and that's why I took you. I don't believe in charity when it comes to my business." Jane nodded for emphasis.

"So why did you come back, once you got away?"

"It's not that great out there in the big, real world." She sighed. "The guys are better, at least."

"Let me remind you that Evan came from out of town."

"Oh. Yeah." Penny shrugged and grinned. "So, how are you doing with Kurt?"

"Not. Nothing. Never." Jane sighed. "There are two kinds of guys in the world, Penny. The ones looking for babysitters or mommies or live-in maids with bedroom privileges. The other ones want to suck your brains out and do all your thinking for you."

"Sounds like the guys in the other cottages, all right. But Kurt isn't like that."

"Let's hope so."

The conversation stayed with her through the morning. She zoned out several times, trying to follow the misty, fleeting glimpses of her dream the night before, which had been awakened by what Penny said.

Funny, but she thought she hadn't dreamed at all.

Usually, she remembered all the details of her dreams. Everybody dreamed, everybody remembered what they had dreamed.

Except for her, last night.

Why was that?

Why did she get a shivery, slightly twisting, slightly sick feeling in the pit of her stomach when she tried to hold onto the misty fragment of what she thought had been a dream?

We do have a problem, don't we, darling?

"Who—" Jane caught herself and barely managed not to look all around the spa. Penny had just left to get their lunch. The lunch hour visitors hadn't shown up yet. She was alone.

So why did she have that feeling that if she was careful and moved slowly, she would finally catch a glimpse of the shadow that always hovered at the corner of her eye?

Who are you? She focused her thoughts, aimed in the direction of where the voice seemed to originate.

Ah, lovely. You can hear me when you're awake. My dear lady, how distressed I was last night, when I couldn't contact you during your dreaming time. I was so dreadfully afraid we would never be able to meet.

Jane resisted the impulse to snatch up the decorative throw lying across the couch in the footbath corner of the spa. She felt cold and damp for a moment. The feeling passed when she realized she couldn't discern if the speaker was male or female. There was no "sound" to the voice speaking inside her head. Just a sensation of power, of age, of immensity.

We're meeting now, aren't we? she responded after a moment of hesitation. Exhilaration mixed with the sensation she had been knocked off her feet and couldn't find the floor. It was probably just residue from her late night, all the emotional ups and downs Kurt had put her through, plus racing with him and Katie. It was hard to believe she had done so much, thought so hard, in one night.

Indeed, we are meeting now. I am delighted. As I was delighted yesterday – your time, not my time. How much I managed to learn from your dreams even though we couldn't converse! Yes, my lovely, clever new friend, I was delighted to feel the flow of power and intelligence between you and your two friends. Why is it you have never thought to work together before? Think of all the amazing things you could have accomplished before this, if you had worked in concert instead of in solo missions, as it were.

The voice paused. Jane flinched from a sensation of that great age suddenly weighing down, pressing like tons of darkness and stone and cold. A sensation of loneliness.

It is a wonderful thing to find companionship. And even more wonderful to finally find someone to cross the great gap between worlds.

Worlds? Jane flinched. She hated sounding like a brainless parrot.

Yes, of course. How bright and clever your mind is. Like a light in the darkness of the void separating the worlds. There is more than one world. There are many layers of reality, one on top of another, all occupying the same space, but each unaware of the other. Except for those clever and sensitive enough to feel the crowded conditions of reality, to hear the voices and the tingle of energy that slips through the ephemeral veil of time and space. Of course, you yourself were able to slide through from one world to another, so that likely enhanced your sensitivity.

Slide through? I don't think so.

Part of her was fascinated, and the other part felt like a child told she had to recite for visitors she didn't know were coming. She didn't know if she wanted to hear more, or if she wanted to slam the metaphorical door shut and hide. Another part of her wanted to shriek for Kurt, even for Beau and Demetrius, to come stand with her and explain things.

Realizing that need, that fear, hit her like a slap of icy, filthy slush thrown up from the wheel of a speeding car. Jane sat very still, praying no one noticed, while she seethed inside, hating this feeling of being unprepared, incompetent.

Afraid to look around and realize everyone else had known the car was coming, but they let her stay within range and get soaked.

Afraid to ask questions and learn everybody else already knew about the cracks or crevices or gaps between the worlds.

Or maybe nobody else did. If they knew, they should have told her about them, to look for them, right? If anybody knew about them, they should know the warning signs of that ability in other people, just like the Old Poops knew how to identify Gifted children as they awakened to their abilities. They had a responsibility to find and train those people, didn't they? Just like Demetrius and Beau kept preaching that those with unique talents had the responsibility to find others with unique talents, train them, and use those talents for the good of the world.

Right?

So, in those few seconds of uncomfortable, rapid thought, Jane realized something.

Kurt had talked about someone trying to break through from another dimension. Big Ugly, he had called it. Just how powerful was this interdimensional invader if it couldn't find the cracks and gaps? Why didn't Kurt know about the gaps? Maybe he was lying to her? Testing her? He still didn't trust her, and had only been playing, pretending to obey Angela's orders and make nice?

Yet … what if he didn't know? If nobody had told her about the gaps and cracks or whatever they were between worlds, the multiple layers of reality... Maybe nobody else knew.

Maybe she was the first one, at least in her world, who could hear through to the other side?

That meant she had a responsibility to find out what she could do, what the dangers were, and use the talent properly.

Right?

For two seconds, Jane hung on the knife's edge of shoving away this strange, unanticipated contact and knowledge because she was afraid. Because she was angry. Because Beau and Demetrius and the rest of the older generation would expect her to do her duty. She was sick and tired of doing her duty all alone.

Of course you slid through, the voice continued. He, it, sounded slightly offended. *How else did you get from your world to this one? You don't think you were sent, do you? If you were, why were you separated from your companions? I dare any civilized society or people to allow their children to venture into alien worlds and dimensions without some sort of protection or guidance. Or at least instructions for how to return home. No, my dear, you and others like you were precocious, clever, curious. And you found the cracks, the weak places in the fabric of reality, and slid through to this world.*

Of course... Jane nearly laughed aloud. It made so much sense. It made sense even though it felt like a comic book plot.

What other explanation could there be?

For half a second, she wanted to find Kurt and tell him all about her discovery. Then she thought about his secretiveness, his attempt to drive her away, his decision to consider her a threat to Neighborlee, despite Angela's very evident approval.

He probably knows all this already. Or he's guessed it. Do you think?

Unfortunately, that is very likely. The voice sounded wounded on her behalf. *My dear, new friend, I fear you have been kept in the dark.*

Yeah, tell me about it.

The voice laughed. Jane froze, hearing ice in the sound, and echoes from vast, dark, cavernous spaces. Then the sound changed to nothing but rolling, ringing, bright humor.

Oh, my dear, how refreshing you are! Yes, we have both been kept in the dark. I, because that is the only way I am able to survive, with my mind reaching to all dimensions. And you, because ignorance keeps you safe. But together...ah, together, what wonders we will accomplish.

That's the answer, isn't it?

Answer to what?

Why we are the way we are. Why we don't know who we belong to. Why all of us are abandoned. Jane shuddered, hating the images that doubts put into her mind. *We weren't abandoned, were we? We just got lost and fell through the cracks, right?*

Undoubtedly. Why would anyone throw away precious life? Especially life with so much talent, so much potential and strength? It's barbaric.

So, where do we come from?

I have several ideas. But we need to be together. Physically in one place, one dimension.

How do I get to you? Jane heard the door creak open and muffled a groan as Penny came back, grinning, holding aloft a cardboard tray with their lunch. Her stomach rumbled, pinching suddenly as if she had gone for days without food.

Ah, now, that is the question. You will be a hero, you know. A wonder. Someone everyone will admire for generations to come, if you accomplish this miracle and bring home the lost children. *But you must rest now, my dear. You need your strength. This conversing across the dimensions takes too much of your energy, and mine. Imagine how much energy it will take to cross the barrier?* The voice sighed, sounding centuries-weary and regretful. *I am afraid you will need to bring many others of your kind to help you, to lend their strength. But can it be accomplished? Do any of you know how to work together?*

Not like this. We've never come up against a puzzle like this. Jane mustered up a smile for Penny and cleared off the little table behind her, so the teen could put down their lunch. A mental image of Kurt flicked through her mind.

Be careful, my dear. There is partnership, and there is slavery. I wouldn't want you hurt, ever. Especially not by one who pretends interest in you, and yet indicates so little trust in you.

Then the sensation of vastness, darkness, and emptiness faded from her mind. Jane was glad she was sitting down, because suddenly she couldn't tell up from down, and all the lights seemed to dim. She clutched at the counter where she had been sitting and took a few deep breaths until everything straightened out.

"You okay?" Penny snatched up the raspberry smoothie and slid it into Jane's faintly shaking hand.

Jane shook her head and sucked hard on the straw. The cold of the fruit, ice and cream hit her stomach hard and made her head ache, but she couldn't get enough. The emptiness inside her clamored for more. Finally, she had to stop to take a breath.

"Wow. You must have been hungry. Mrs. Kendle gets kind of woozy when she doesn't eat right, too." The girl shrugged and turned back to spread out the rest of their lunch.

Jane nodded, glad to take the teen's ready explanation. Really, what other explanation was there? This mental communication across dimensions was draining—and the way she felt provided solid proof that it had happened. She hadn't hallucinated. Mental communication with other Gifted people never drained her this way, even the time she had needed to shout across three states.

She would be a hero, the voice had said. Jane grinned as she took a big bite of her veggie wrap. This was the kind of hero work she could get used to, doing important things for people who, despite all their talents and training and experience, couldn't do it for themselves. Finally finding the answer to where she and the others had come from. The answer to why they were the way they were. This wasn't babysitting lazy incompetents. This was something important, something truly epic and heroic.

~~~~~

Deep below Neighborlee, the darkness laughed and stretched luxuriously. Rock melted away in advance of its expanding boundaries. Eyes opened and stared through the layers of rock and soil that lay between the darkness and the lives going innocently through their days.

Hunger rumbled hot and painful through the darkness. The energy it had siphoned so slowly, so easily from Jane, had only served to whet its appetite. Soon, it would need to feed in earnest.

~~~~~

Hello?

Jane felt incredibly foolish, sitting in her living room at 1am, trying to contact a voice that might not actually exist. She had been peeved at Kurt, although she couldn't exactly remember why, and wanting something, anything to give her some answers, an escape, maybe even a little revenge. Hadn't she devised imaginary friends when she lived in the orphanage? They visited her in her dreams and she sometimes believed they were real.

What if she had made up her friend this morning?

A day of thinking, mundane business, silence from the voice, had started the doubts and questions spinning through her mind.

Are you there? Can you hear me?

Yes, my dear. How wonderful to hear you again. You sound rather weary. Have you been occupied fighting the forces of evil?

I've been occupied fighting with my stock room. Jane relaxed into her couch and smiled up at the ceiling. There was just something about the vibrations when the voice spoke. They soothed her.

Oh. I had the impression you were a vigilante of sorts, patrolling the darkness and finding evil and danger to thwart, so innocents could sleep in peace.

Yeah, I wish. Actually, I'm retired, Jane hurried to say, to stave off what she suspected would be a flood of guilt-inducing questions from the voice. She had a flood of her own to hurl back at him. Or her. Or it. For all she knew, the voice could be a "them."

You said before that we had come through gaps or cracks in the fabric of time and space, sliding from one dimension to another. How could we do that when we were kids, without any powers, and we can't sense those gaps now, when we're stronger and more experienced and a whole heck of a lot more sensitive?

Your innocence and untrained potential for power, for talent, let you slip through the gaps. The voice sounded rich with amusement.

Usually, Jane's hackles would have raised at that sound. She had always equated it with the evil, oily chuckle of a master criminal, just before he pulled the lever on the trap door that dumped the hero into a vat of piranhas or sharks or acid or boiling oil. Or into a dark pit that went on forever.

Now, oddly, she smiled, infected with the amusement that seeped through her from her new friend. She wanted to know what the joke was.

So it was all by accident, then, our coming to Earth's dimension?

Accident. Or fate. Or perhaps your parents sent their innocent children away to protect them from unspeakable horrors. Now that you are older, wiser, trained and experienced, perhaps you should try to go home, to help them.

How could we go back, if we can't find the cracks?

Jane fought down an image of an invasion force, trickling through the cracks in the dimensions for generations, from a world that wanted to take over Earth. That wasn't possible. Was it?

Together, perhaps you can do it. Perhaps...ah, but no, that would be asking too much.

Asking what? She sat up straight, trembling slightly, positive she hovered on the edge of something life-changing.

You need a guide, my dear. And you need to gather your friends and harness all their talents, their power, the unity of their minds. That's the only way to return home, in force, to find your parents and learn the truth of your heritage, your potential. The reason why you were sent away from your homes.

Sent away. Jane shuddered. The idea of deliberately being sent away from her family made her ache more deeply than the suspicion she had carried all her life: she had been abandoned, no one noticed, no one cared when she wandered away and lost herself. *I don't understand. How can needing a guide be —*

If you and your friends could find me, first, my dear, then I could act as a guide across the dimensions and help you find your true home. I am quite talented myself in tracking the pathways, even when they are decades old. Alas, I am trapped here, alone, in the dark, so cold.

Why don't you go home?

As I said, this requires energy. Teamwork. And I am alone. So dreadfully alone, he added, his warmth and strength dropping away to a chill whisper.

That impression of vast darkness and emptiness and cold washed over Jane. For an instant, all her training, Beau's lectures and her own nightmares rose up, demanding that this needed to be fought and if not destroyed, then harnessed.

Please, my dear, I know it will cost you greatly in strength, but once I am free... The voice sounded so drained and weary.

As drained and weary as Jane felt. She imagined how she would feel, lost and alone, cold and in the dark, with no one for company but voices that came from other dimensions.

I don't know if I can help you, but I'll try.

Not you alone, my dear. It would be too much for you. It might harm you. Drain you permanently. I don't want that on my conscience.

The thing is, I really don't have that many friends.

Tosh. I find that hard to believe. Someone as warm and alive and intelligent as you, with no friends?

Jane bristled at the slight emphasis the voice put on "no" friends. She had friends. Not many, but those she kept in contact with were gems. Still, she supposed she could have put a little more effort into keeping in contact with the Sanctum family, even if they were all so much older than her. Hadn't she hated feeling like she was always left behind? It was a two-way street, after all. She should have made an effort to keep in contact. She certainly wouldn't be in danger of failing her new friend now, if she had more friends to call on.

They are at fault for abandoning you, my dear. You owe them nothing. You have always been loyal and dutiful. Perhaps too much. Were you born to live in subjugation to the stupidity of others?

Jane caught her breath, torn and pulled between the scorn in the voice as he echoed the lingering resentment toward Fendersburg, and the sympathy that warmed and filled her. She was so tired. The day had been too long, too draining, and even though she had escaped the stupidity in Fendersburg, there were stupid people everywhere.

What's it like in the other dimensions?

Intelligence, compassion, warmth. Minds and souls as high above the people of the world of your exile, as you are above a common beetle.

I feel like a common beetle right now, she retorted, and slouched down on the couch again. Quiet, drained laughter spilled out of her. Jane felt rather punchy. Odd, how the more she thought about it, the more tired she felt.

No, my dear. Yours is a fine and bright spirit. Full of energy. Full of warmth. You have brought change to my dark, cold prison, just in the short time we have conversed. If you and your friends could find and free me...ah, what wonders I could show you. I would lead you to the world, the dimension, where you belong. I could almost believe my exile and suffering well worth it, if we could be together, face-to-face, one day.

~~~~~

Jane dreamed of falling and cold, of fire that ate through her bones and darkness that suffocated. She woke gasping, chilled almost to the point of numbness. Her head ached, as if she had strained herself with a full night of heroic maneuvers. She huddled under her blankets and pulled more out of the closets with a mental effort that frightened her, but the physical work of getting out of bed was too much. She shivered and wrapped blanket after blanket around herself, until the weight alone was enough to comfort her. When she fell asleep, she finally began to feel warm.

Morning came, with a residual chill clinging to her flesh. A hot shower didn't drive it away. Penny gave her an odd look when she came in after school and found Jane with a sweater over a sweatshirt.

"I think I'm coming down with something," Jane explained.

"Keep it away from me." The teen grinned and made a cross with her index fingers. "There's no way I'm going to miss school this week."

"The world is coming to an end. A kid who actually wants to go to school." She felt better instantly, as if the lame teasing had punctured a barrier, a film that made the day seem gray and damp, instead of brilliantly crystalline white.

Penny filled up the silence between customers, talking about the field trip her journalism class was taking to visit the offices and then the printing plant of the *Plain Dealer*. By dinnertime, Jane felt completely herself again. She ordered a huge meal delivered for her and Penny, with extras of everything and desserts, and gobbled it all as if she hadn't eaten since the day before. Which, when she slowed down enough to think about it, was rather strange. She had eaten an enormous breakfast, too. A whole grapefruit, three eggs, four slices of toast and half the jar of apricot preserves. Lunch had been two Godzilla burritos from Hunky & Dory's. Usually she could only eat two-thirds of one, and saved the rest for a snack.

"Are you pregnant?" Penny asked.

Jane nearly spat her mouthful of apricot smoothie across the counter.

"Why would you ask that?" she demanded, once she got the spatters cleaned up.

"You're packing it away like you're starving. And you were dragging when I first got here. And that sweatshirt..." Penny shrugged.

"What about it?"

"Could cover a lot."

"I am not pregnant. Not in a million years. Nothing in the world could convince me —" Jane sighed and carefully put down her jumbo-size paper cup.

Otis and all his lame pickup lines. His insinuations that she had no choice, eventually she would give in and give herself to him. Penny's words revived all the frustration of being chased by Mr. Wrong and fear she would never find Mr. Right. Feelings she thought she had exorcised and escaped by coming here to Neighborlee. What in the world was wrong with her?

"Did you see me coming?" Kurt asked as he strode through the door.

"What?" Jane just gaped stupidly at him. Had she missed out on part of a conversation?

"You look pretty furious. I thought maybe you saw me coming." He shrugged and settled on the stool next to the counter Penny had vacated when Jane started spattering smoothie.

"You wish." Her face burned seconds before she realized how juvenile that retort sounded. But somehow, she couldn't be angry when he grinned at her like that. Jane sighed. "Any progress on those...questions we had?"

"Nada." He glanced at Penny. "Total frustration. Thank goodness I never could resist a challenge or a mystery."

"Oh. A mystery."

His smile certainly was infectious. What was it about him that made her feel warm, as if the sun had come out?

"Interested in going on patrol tonight?" He held out his hand. "Just for kicks?"

"Your kicks, or mine? Seems to me I'm the one who's going to do the driving."

"You need a navigator." That hand waited, not wavering a bit.

Jane studied it for a moment. Long enough to feel Penny watching them intently, with that knowing grin of hers growing. She resisted the urge to clasp his hand and sat back, crossing her arms at her waist. "What's in it for me?"

"How about we talk about it over dinner?"

"Better bring your credit card," Penny muttered. "She's eating for three right now."

The teen turned bright red and hurried into the storage room, muttering something about checking inventory, when both Jane and Kurt turned and stared at her. Then he glanced past the counter, at the table that held the remains of their dinner.

"Oh. Sorry. Guess I'm kind of late, asking you to dinner."

"We ate early." Jane gathered up wrappers and cardboard trays and didn't bother looking around before heaving all the trash into the barrel by the storage room door with a mental shove.

He shook his head. "Sorry. I don't have any right to ask, but if something weird is going on—" Despite his visible attempt at nonchalance, Jane saw his gaze drop down to her stomach.

"Penny has a really warped sense of humor, that's all. I'm low on energy and extra-hungry. End of story."

Funny, but now that Kurt had come back into the spa, she didn't feel like she had a black hole in her stomach.

"So, any more contact with your mysterious power source?" He lowered his voice so Penny couldn't have heard four feet away.

Chapter Twelve

Jane opened her mouth to answer, but then stopped. Should she tell him about the Voice, and what it, he or she said? Should she keep it a secret? It bothered her that she was undecided. This was something important, beyond her personal feelings. It affected all the Gifted, not just her. Especially if this was the answer to the questions that had plagued her, all of them, for decades.

Something cold dropped heavy and hard in her stomach. Jane wanted to keep the Voice all to herself. The secret to her identity, her heritage, her home.

What was wrong with her?

She could almost hear Demetrius lecturing her on thinking beyond her own needs and hurts and desires. That would have firmed her longing into a resolve to keep the Voice to herself. But along with echoes of Demetrius' voice, Jane had a memory glimpse of Beau giving her that sorrowful, disappointed look, and slowly shaking his head. He always expected high things of her, continuously saying she was special, talented and wonderful. Beau concentrated on what she owed herself, rather than on what she owed the rest of the world.

For Beau, then.

"Jane?" Kurt reached across the counter to clasp her shoulder. "You okay?"

"Uh...thinking." Her face felt hot enough to melt candles. "Yes, I've had some contact."

"Contact? As in?" His eyes brightened and he leaned closer, resting his elbows on the display case.

"Maybe we should save that for dinner. Well, dessert, for me. Where we won't be overheard." She tipped her head in the direction of the storage room, and Penny. Jane had to hand it to the teen, staying in there and giving them plenty of time to talk. But she was only a kid and curious, and it would be unfair to tax her patience.

"Yeah, she's pretty observant, isn't she?" He straightened up and turned toward the open doorway. "Hey, Penny? Can I ask you a few questions?"

"What are you up to?" Jane stage-whispered.

"Research. We have a new talent to hunt down, remember? If it's not the same person as you sensed, we might have trouble."

"He'd never hurt anyone!" She slapped her hand over her mouth, but it was too late.

"He?" One eyebrow quirked up in question. And challenge.

"What's up?" Penny asked, emerging from the storage room.

Kurt gave her another look, promising an intense evening, no matter where they went.

"You're a pretty sharp kid, right?" He doused her in a knee-wobbling smile. "Do you see anything ... I don't know ... anything weird, going on at NCH?"

"Everything's weird. Boys between five and fourteen should be put in the basement and not allowed out until they learn to bathe regularly and how to pull up their zippers and use a fork." Penny rolled her eyes in disgust. "My friends at school complain about their brothers and sisters. I've got it twenty times worse!"

Jane barely paid attention to the next few things Kurt and Penny said. The revelation that had slapped her in the face dominated her thoughts.

What kind of an idiot was she, to consider herself alone all this time, when she had a huge family at the Sanctum? Just like any family, she had her feuds and her favorites, her mortal enemies and her soulmates. But Jane knew everyone who ever studied with the Old Poops would lay down their lives to help her, if she needed it. That was just the way they had been raised, what they believed in.

"A secret admirer?" Penny laughed. "Yeah, right, as if some guy out there is so in love with me, he doesn't have the guts to tell me."

"Most guys never learn to communicate," Kurt said with a shrug and a grin. "Are there any guys you can think of, a little smarter than everybody else, maybe who get picked on but never seem to get hurt? You know. Someone sets up an ambush to get back at him, and he walks right past it. Or around it. Or isn't there when you expect him."

Penny frowned, but it wasn't the "you're crazy" frown Jane expected.

Just what the heck do you think you're doing? Her head ached as she sent her mental demand to Kurt. Standing only a few feet away from him, it should have been as easy as breathing. What was wrong with her?

He didn't even blink. Was he that good at ignoring her, or didn't her words reach him?

"I've never really noticed," the girl said slowly. "There's so much going on. Everybody's always doing something or coming back from somewhere. We have chores and meetings and ... just normal life, I guess. Weird things? I'd have to think about it."

"Do that for me, would you?"

"Why? Are you working for the *Tattler* now?" She grinned at him and glanced at Jane. "What's up?"

"I haven't the foggiest," Jane said slowly.

She would have an earful for Kurt when he showed up after she closed up the spa for the night. If she bothered sticking around to wait for him. Maybe she should just go for a solo flight. Maybe his presence interfered with her reception and tracking abilities. Wouldn't that steam him, if she said so?

~~~~~

What's wrong, dear?

Jane muffled a shriek and nearly knocked the sugar bowl across the room. She hadn't felt that subtle tingle in her fingertips to warn her the Voice was about to make contact. Why hadn't she? Could she blame it on the fog that had wrapped around her brain most of the day?

I'm just tired, that's all. Didn't sleep well last night, and the day was more draining than usual. Maybe it's the weather.

You must be more careful of your strength. Stop frittering it away on inconsequential things.

Making a decent living is not inconsequential. She winced at the ache that reverberated through her head. Had she really *yelled* at the Voice? Why did she feel so ... guilty?

Why do you worry about such useless things? When you are home, in your proper place, others will concern themselves with your needs. You will be surrounded in luxury, revered and admired for all you have accomplished.

Until we figure out how to open up the cracks between dimensions, I'm going to need a place to stay and to pay the electric and buy food.

Hmm. True.

Jane nearly laughed. The Voice sounded extremely disgruntled. She imagined her inter-dimensional friend hunched in his chair, scowling, looking and sounding just like Demetrius had looked and sounded when she countered his arguments.

Come to think of it, she actually missed those days of frustration and arguments, chafing against rules and aching for a chance to stretch her wings.

We need to plan how you'll convince your friends to give you their strength for this endeavor. You can't do this alone, you know.

I haven't even tried yet, Jane snapped back. She closed her eyes and sighed, and reached blindly for the jumbo mug of coffee, double sugar and triple cream, that she had fixed the moment she stumbled out of the elevator. She needed something to chase the cobwebs from her head, and the bad taste from her mouth.

Odd. She hadn't even realized she had taken the elevator, instead of phasing out and floating up through the levels to her apartment. Maybe it was an unconscious move to save her energy, but shouldn't she at least have been aware she did it?

True. How wonderful it would be if you could open the doorway by yourself, with no help from anyone. You would certainly prove what I have believed about you since the moment we made contact: You are powerful and talented and worthy to rule. A true heroine and friend.

Jane opened her eyes and stared down into the swirling, creamy depths of her mug. What was it about the Voice's words that bothered her, even while they made her feel like a cat being stroked? She wanted to stretch luxuriously and purr, soaking in the sensation of approval and admiration she certainly had never received in Fendersburg. And yet...

The buzz from the intercom at the back door startled her, so she nearly dropped her mug. Again.

"Anybody home?" Kurt's voice was full of static, like something was interfering with the connection.

Gotta go. Sorry. Problems to deal with. Jane nearly stumbled as she stepped away from the counter. She reached back for the mug and guzzled it as she went to the intercom panel to open the door.

She walked there and pressed the button when she should have stayed at the counter and used the Ghost field to open the door for Kurt. Was she that depleted that she did physical things without thinking, and didn't use her Ghost power automatically, the way she was used to?

Maybe she was coming down with something that sapped all

her strength. It had to be something powerful, to overcome her immunities, after all.

"Hey, you okay?" Kurt blurted when he pushed the door open and saw her, still standing by the intercom. He reached out a hand to grab hold of her arm, and then Jane realized she was listing to the left far enough to threaten her balance.

"Yeah. Fine. Just tired."

"Something was going on in here, just a minute ago. I could feel you using your talent, but the tones were going sour and sounded muffled." He guided her over to the closest futon and settled her with a gentleness that brought tears to her eyes.

How long had it been since someone treated her like she was made of glass?

Then his words cut through the haze, like heavy cotton candy, trying to spin around her thoughts.

"You finally felt it?"

"Felt what? I knew you were doing something." He stroked a few sweaty hairs out of her eyes. "Whatever you were doing, it took a big bite out of you."

Jane shook her head, trying to clear her mind just a little more. She moaned as a throbbing moved from her temples inward, and from the base of her skull up, until the three points banged into each other and tumbled down into her stomach. It was a good thing her stomach had felt like an empty cavern for the last hour, or she might be emptying it onto his shoes right about now.

Maybe it was just low blood sugar giving her the woozies. Where had she left her coffee? Oh, yeah. It was in her hand. Funny, she had emptied it, but her insides still felt empty. The caffeine and sugar sure weren't doing her any good.

"Jane? Hey, Earth to Jane." He snapped his fingers in front of her nose. "Where did you go?"

She resisted an urge to bite his fingers.

"It's nearly ten, I'm wiped out and starving. You didn't hear anything when you came up?"

"Nothing but the chords going sour. You chime when you use your talent, but something is making it clang." He held onto her hand. Jane decided she liked that. "Maybe I should get you back to your school and have one of your teachers or doctors or whoever knows what's up take a look at you."

"Thanks, but I've had enough of Dr. Frankenstein's theories and exams for two lifetimes."

"Something is wrong. You were wiped out when I came in before, weren't you? And eating for three..."

Jane felt another surge of nausea race through her, accompanied by panic. She tugged to free her hand, feeling trapped.

An image from her nightmares shot through her mind, reverberating through her senses so that for a moment, she was truly there. In the deep, blacker-than-black, echoing cavern. Colder than cold. Beyond temperature, chilling the mind and soul. Darkness that sucked at her mind and heart and congealed the breath in her lungs.

"Snap out of it," he growled, and shook her hard, both hands gripping her shoulders tightly enough, she thought she might have bruises in the morning. "What's going on? You were fading away on me. What were you doing that I should have sensed when I came up here, but didn't?"

She stared into his eyes, caught between lunging at him with her fingers curved into claws, or collapsing in his arms in a weeping fit. What was going on? What was wrong with her?

"We're on the same side, remember? We're the good guys. We're here to help people, and that includes each other." He tried to smile. "Tell your old buddy Kurt what's been eating at you, and maybe we can do something about it, okay?" The fear darkening his eyes convinced her.

"Help people," she whispered. "Yes, we have to help him." She swallowed hard and grimaced at the foul taste in her mouth. "If I don't eat something, first, I'm going to be flat on the floor."

"Kind of hard to talk to that way." Kurt nodded and glanced around the room. "Okay, you sit tight and let me figure out what's what." He didn't wait for her response, but strode into the kitchen.

Kurt Hanson was more of a Handyman than he ever could have guessed. Jane sighed in delight when he came back after a minimum of rummaging and slamming of doors. The tray he carried proved she had found a sympathetic soul.

Nuts. Chocolate-dipped biscotti. Ice cream. Fudge sauce. Peanut butter sauce. Two frosty bottles of ginseng green tea. Chicken salad sandwiches piled high with pickles, lettuce, tomato and cheese slices. Her stomach growled loudly enough to echo when he set the tray down on the steamer trunk coffee table. She laughed, no time for embarrassment, when he handed her the ice cream first, instead of the sandwich.

"My kind of guy," she mumbled through her first mouthful.

Then the ice cream hit her taste buds, and a moment later her stomach, and she had no time or energy to concentrate on anything else. She inhaled her food, and felt only a little sheepish when she raised her head, looking for more, and found him just starting on his sandwich. He had eaten the ice cream first, also.

He swallowed, wiped mayonnaise from the corner of his mouth, and tore his sandwich in half, offering her the untouched portion. "You need it more than me," he said, when Jane stared. He grinned when she nearly snatched the sandwich from his fingers and devoured it.

"Okay," he said, when there was nothing left to eat but the last two biscotti and a few mouthfuls of tea left in the bottles. "What happened?"

Feeling energized, without that gaping hole in her middle that drained her thoughts and good humor, Jane nodded. She owed him that much. Hadn't he been right when he pointed out that they were indeed on the same side? They were here to help people, and the Voice — whoever or whatever he was — needed help. She took a few seconds to gather her thoughts, then gave him a step-by-step recounting of every encounter with the Voice. Jane couldn't repeat most of their conversations, and that worried her. Usually her memory was so good with details. She could only give him her impressions of what she had discussed with the Voice.

"We're from another dimension," Kurt said slowly. He nodded and tipped back the bottle for his last mouthful of tea. "Makes sense. And this guy is trapped in some other dimension and needs our help to get home. That's the gist of it?"

"Basically."

"I'm a little worried. Whoever this guy is, he's not like us. Or different enough that you can feel his presence and talk with him, but nobody else can hear him. And I can't feel his talent at work. Whatever it is." He captured Jane in an intense frown. She couldn't move for several seconds while he stared into her eyes. Maybe that was another talent he had? Mesmerizing his prey.

No, she wasn't his prey. He was her friend. He would help the Voice break free of his prison. Wouldn't he?

"Did you notice that you're wiped out every time you talk with this guy?"

Jane opened her mouth to say no, but stopped with the words caught at the back of her tongue.

"I told you we fought Big Ugly at New Year's. It attacked during the New Year's Eve party, draining people, sending them down time loops, doing things to our brains. The thing is, I could sense when it was about to attack, but I can't really sense what's going on with you now."

"But if you felt the enemy working before, then that means the Voice isn't it. Big Ugly. Right?"

"Yeah, I guess. What I'm snagging my brain on is that this thing is draining you. Trying to suck energy out of you. Just like the oil slick monster."

She snorted, muffling a giggle. One side of his mouth quirked up.

"Well, that's what it looked like, how it manifested when it was feeding on people at New Year's. The thing is, every time we beat it back, it changes its tactics. Maybe it can change its signature, it's energy patterns, so it's not familiar. Maybe it has learned enough from coming up against us, it can hide from how we always sensed it before. It's trying for subtlety now, and making contact." His eyes narrowed and he stared at a point in the air just above the trunk while he slowly shook his head. "The question is, why you?"

"Maybe because I'm new. I haven't encountered it before. It isn't familiar, but I don't automatically assume it's evil. *If* it's an enemy. The Old Poops taught us 'different is dangerous,' so because we're different, we must never be dangerous. While other people shoot first, we're the ones who need to raise our shields, and ask a lot of questions before we even warm up the photon torpedoes, you know? We're always supposed to try to blend into the crowd and observe, instead of assuming someone from another planet is out to steal all our air and water."

"So even though this thing stays in the darkness and doesn't show its face and drains you whenever the two of you talk, you automatically assume it's *friendly*?" Kurt's eyebrow raised high enough in skepticism to threaten to shoot off his forehead.

"Don't you go the other extreme, when something unusual shows up? Didn't you approach me as an enemy?"

"That was a mistake."

"Duh!"

For a second, a spark of anger touched his eyes, then turned to amusement, and he blushed. Nice to know a guy could feel embarrassment. She was relieved he saw humor in his stupidity.

"Here's the thing. Maybe because I'm new, it isn't afraid I'll attack it like you guys do whenever it shows up. How friendly would you be," she hurried on, when Kurt opened his mouth to respond, "if every time you tried to make contact, people attacked you and shoved you back through whatever doorway you're trying to get through?"

"For one thing, we don't attack. We don't go looking for it. It finds us. Most of what we do is defensive."

"Yeah, from your viewpoint."

Kurt grinned. "The best defense is a good offense."

"I need to learn more about the last encounter with this thing. Consider that the Voice *isn't* the oil slick monster or Big Ugly or any other things you've fought. All that activity, all the psionic energy or whatever you want to call it, disturbances of the walls between universes at New Year's, it woke up the Voice."

No negative reaction from Kurt.

"What if this is something or someone entirely new? You said you sensed me when you came upstairs, but not anything or anyone else, right? So it's *not* the same vibrations as the oil slick New Year's monster. Right?"

"Right," he said, his voice a soft rasp. "But consider this. You're exhausted after talking with it. Would a friend suck you dry?"

"Not dry yet." She felt slightly nauseous, or maybe the correct sensation was dizzy, from the combination of guilt and irritation and a faint undercurrent of fear. Kurt was right to point out that snag, and she wondered why she didn't see it as a danger sign. If anything, she was irritated that he had to point it out.

"This thing isn't like us—"

"Duh!"

"Let me finish. It's not like us, to the point that I *can't* feel its power signature, whatever vibrations it gives off when it uses its talents. You can't mix us and them—it's not like those movies where the brilliant human scientist cobbles together an interface between his laptop and the alien tech using nothing but duct tape and baling wire." A crooked grin cracked his face for a moment. "Granted, that's what I do, but that's *me*. Fact is stranger than fiction. The thing is, this isn't gizmos and machines. It's our kind of mutants or aliens or whatever, *not* mixing with what's out there."

Jane grinned, pleased that such logic holes irritated him just like they irritated her. A wave of exhaustion surged through her, making her wonder if she was just so wiped out that her mind went off on tangents.

"Okay, you've got a point. What do we do about it?"

"You..." He looked around her apartment, and then hooked his thumb toward her bedroom door. "Get some rest. You need to build yourself up again, and if you can, ignore him when this Voice guy comes calling again. First, I need to do some research. Check some things. People I need to talk to. Then I'm going to talk to Lanie and Felicity, compare notes, and we'll finally have that meeting we should have had the day you got here."

Jane shivered, feeling as if he wasn't really there in the room anymore—not mentally or emotionally. He was already out somewhere, lining up the people he needed to talk with, the things he needed to check out. His body was there, but the parts of him that mattered were already gone, working. She shuddered, feeling a little nauseous again, when she wondered if he was worried about her at all, or all his concern was focused only on Neighborlee.

"It might be a while." Kurt took a step toward her, and Jane imagined, just for a moment, he would hug her.

That was ridiculous. They had barely shifted from antagonists to allies. She was just tired. Exhausted to the point of hallucinating. And starving again.

~~~~~

The next day brought an irritating mix of ice and slush and fierce winds, to the point Jane could convince herself the weather was a sentient being having a hissy fit. Business was slow, and that suited her just fine. She didn't have to deal with many customers, or many questions that taxed her brain. She made a big pot of her favorite restorative herbal tea and sipped it all day. In between snacks. Slow traffic and few customers made it easier for her to munch her way through the day. This further evidence of the drain on her energies made her more inclined to really think about what Kurt said and accept his theories.

That still irritated her. At the same time, she found some humor in the whole situation. Maybe that was a sign she was recovering.

Jane amused and distracted herself, playing with the wording for the report she would eventually have to write up for Demetrius and Beau and the Council. After rush hour dwindled down to nothing on the street outside, she played with the idea of closing up early. The people in Neighborlee had a lot of common sense, and that included staying home on a night like this. She was grateful she only had to go upstairs, not outside, to go home.

That settled it. She was closing up early and spending the evening goofing off. Maybe she would be fully recovered by the time Kurt showed up with some information, some decisions, some more solid theories.

Her hand shook as she reached for the sign in the window, to turn *Closed* to face the street. What if, now that she was totally alone, with no people popping in on the spur of the moment, the Voice returned? What if it drained her even worse than before? What if the draining was entirely unintentional, unconscious on its part, a result of being in such entirely different universes or dimensions or realities?

Don't borrow trouble. Jane clenched her fist to stop the trembling, opened her hand and resumed reaching for the sign.

In the few seconds she was distracted, a Jeep had pulled into the parking spot directly in front of her door. She looked through the sleety snow blowing at about a thirty-degree angle and saw a woman in a hooded cloak get out of the passenger side. Stepping into the light from above the door, Angela smiled at Jane from the depths of the hood. Jane hurried to the door, shuddering in her eagerness to talk with Angela. She mentally punched herself. Why hadn't she gone to Angela before? If Kurt was busy trying to track down answers, wouldn't he have gone to Angela for counseling? Maybe Angela was here with information from Kurt?

Then Jane saw a young woman with long amber hair scramble out of the back seat and yank up the hatch of the Jeep. The driver got out and it looked like she held onto the door while her passenger hauled a wheelchair out of the back of the Jeep.

Wheelchair equaled Lanie. Logic said the woman with the amber hair was the third member of Kurt's trio, Felicity.

"And here I thought this storm would drive away all my customers," Jane greeted them as she pushed the door open, "and I could close up early, have a movie and a big bowl of popcorn."

Her fingers tingled, just for a second, as Lanie's wheelchair popped a wheelie and came up the curb onto the sidewalk without Lanie visibly pushing it. Well, at least she could still feel other Gifts at work. During a few low spots while gnawing on questions throughout the day, she had worried that she had somehow been burned out by her contact with the Voice. Jane exchanged a grin with Lanie and watched as her wheelchair bumped over the threshold and down the into the spa.

"Sorry. Purely social call," Felicity said, after all three of them were inside the shop. She shut the door. "Just slide the latch?"

"Sure. If this is social, then come on up. Have you had dinner yet? I have lots of pizza and salad in the fridge." Jane laughed at herself. This could not be a social call. Not after all she and Kurt had discussed and argued about over the last few days. The rest of Neighborlee's guardians had come to see her. While they might enjoy getting to know each other, this evening would be full of seriousness and work.

At least she wouldn't be alone, vulnerable if the Voice decided to make contact again. The presence of others seemed to be protection against contact. She shuddered as she realized she had turned a corner, albeit a small one, subconsciously admitting she might just need protection.

"Maybe you should hear us out before you let us into your sanctum," Lanie said.

"Ooookay." She stepped around behind the big glass display case and hooked the tall stool over, hitching one hip up on it, and sitting down with her elbows on the case. "What's up?"

"We know you're the Ghost," Felicity said.

"Ghost?" For a few seconds, Jane felt lost. Then she grinned. Hadn't Kurt said they had researched her? "I hope the big jerk told you everything from the last few days."

"Including coming at you like you were a spy for the Taliban?" Lanie rolled her eyes. "The guy has never gone so off-balance before. We walloped him, but it looks like we'll need you to help keep him in line from now on."

"It's a deal." Jane sensed more healing in their shared, quiet laughter and affectionate scorn for Kurt than an hour of apologies. "Who hung the moniker of Handyman on him, anyway?"

"The whole town did, seeing as that's what he is."

"What do they call you?"

"You mean my superhero name?" Lanie grinned. "Kurt calls me Snoop, because I can get into people's heads once in a while, if I touch them. I used to be able to fly, until I broke my back."

"Yeah, that. Isn't there anybody out there who can bounce bullets off their chest?"

"You're not invulnerable, either?" Felicity dragged over two more stools for her and Angela.

"When my Ghost field is on, everything passes right through me. Or I pass through them. But when it's off, I get hurt just as easily as everybody else. So, what do you do?"

"Sometimes they get away with calling me Zap. I couldn't control my EM bursts. Until recently."

Jane studied their faces for a few moments. Angela just perched on her stool, her slightly bemused smile blessing them.

"We should make ourselves comfortable." She gestured upstairs. "I can see this taking a while, and I'm going to need a lot of chocolate before we're through."

Once they were upstairs, Jane threw together some refreshments, whatever was handy. Felicity and Lanie jumped in immediately, relating how Lanie and Kurt had met as children in the Neighborlee Children's Home, discovered their slowly blooming talents, and then met up with Felicity as she was discovering what she could do. They developed their ground rules from comic books and learned early to hide what they could do from grownups or anyone who might try to separate them and put them in a lab.

Jane covered her trunk coffee table with cups and plates, cookies, hot chocolate and hot cider, cheese and crackers, and listened. Kurt, Lanie and Felicity had had to figure things out by trial-and-error. They didn't have the theories and lessons and rules Demetrius and Beau had developed over the decades. At the same time, they had Angela as an advisor and confidante. Jane suspected Angela was worth the entire Council, cubed.

About the time she decided they were going to be there all night, she excused herself and put two big gourmet self-rising pizzas in her oven.

Irritation mixed into her fascination with the story she was hearing. Her teachers should have made a move to ally with Neighborlee's guardians years ago. They should have caught on decades ago that someone was defending the town against the Rivals. If they had been working together all this time, they could have at least kept the Rivals from taking Gifted children.

If Demetrius and Beau had stopped being so secretive and defensive, Jane would never have left Neighborlee. She could have grown up under Angela's guidance. She could have been part of Lanie and Felicity and Kurt's team. Like brother and sisters.

"The Old Poops have a lot to answer for," she said.

"That would be the owners or managers or whatever you want to call them at Hoax?" Felicity said.

Through all the talking and comparing notes and theories, Angela just sat there, quietly sipping her milk with a dollop of gingerbread flavored syrup in it, watching them with that serene, slightly amused, bemused, thoughtful smile Jane decided was her standard expression. She would have to live here in Neighborlee a long time and spend more time working with Angela before she could even approach a theory of what the woman's talents and duties were. The guardians protected the magic and general weirdness of Neighborlee. Angela was in the middle of it all, the reason and the grand protector.

"Okay, here's the scoop from my angle." Jane stopped short and grinned when the timer went off on her oven. "Hold that thought," she said, getting up to answer the summons.

Chapter Thirteen

"What thought?" Felicity leaped up to follow her. She snatched more dishes off shelves, and utensils and the pizza cutter wheel. She brought over a second coffee table to where they were sitting, as Jane slid the pans of pizza from the oven and sliced them.

"Okay, where were we?" Jane deposited the pizzas onto the low round table within everyone's easy reach. She watched Lanie lift two pieces onto a plate without touching them. What really intrigued her were the little streaks of light swirling out from Lanie's forehead and temples and fingertips, wrapping around the plate and sliding under the slices of pizza.

"What do you see when she does that?" Felicity asked. "Do you see any energy at work? When we fought the oil slick after New Year's, with all the warping of fields and dimensions and whatever, Gordon could see the power going out of Lanie when she slammed a bunch of chairs into it."

"Yeah, streamers of energy going out from her head, and ghost arms reaching and lifting the pizza and the dish," Jane said, her thoughts spinning. "And I definitely need more details than the little Kurt told me, about New Year's and the fight right afterward. Not that I'm going to tell Demetrius and Beau squat until I get some more answers from them." She nodded decisively.

"Okay, as I was starting to say before." She took a tiny bite of pizza, chewed three times, and swallowed. "The Old Poops have a pattern they rely on to help them figure out what kids to watch, to wait for powers to start developing. You three fell through the cracks somehow."

"Four. Jay is one of us," Lanie said.

"Yeah, but the Rivals didn't catch him until he went into the military, after your accident kind of shocked his Gift into activating."

"Is that what you really call the creeps?" Felicity said. Her expression wavered between amused and disgusted. "Since you left that note on the Colonel, and he told us how he got snatched and released, that's what we've been calling them."

"But for you it's a name, right? Capitalized?" Lanie added.

"Pretty much," Jane said. "What's scary is realizing how big their operation has to be, how many ties they have into authentic power, if they could take those three boys from the military and start training and brainwashing them."

"Are the boys all right?" Angela asked.

"The two we rescued are getting back to normal. Un-brainwashed, I guess you'd say. Our healers are cleansing their bodies of all the drugs they've been subjected to. We're learning a lot about how the Rivals operate, but we haven't been able to track down their permanent headquarters. All these years, we've only been able to locate what are essentially mobile operation centers."

"I need to call Franklin and arrange a meeting with your teachers. The short version of the story is that another boy these Rivals took and tried to turn into a weapon ... fell into our hands during the whole ugly mess at New Year's. Franklin got him away into protective custody, and he's been learning a great deal of unpleasant information about our mutual enemy."

"We've liberated a few people, always the ones who are unwilling soldiers," Jane said. "Never the ones who joined up willingly, or got brainwashed or whatever."

"These creepazoids have a lot to answer for," Felicity said, her voice quiet and tight. Jane was fascinated to see streamers of sparks swirling around her clenched fists.

She had said she got her EM bursts under control, hadn't she?

Lanie reached over and rested one hand on Felicity's, and the sparks slowed and faded. "What exactly brings you here? Besides getting away from those lazy idiots in Fendersburg?" Delighted malice sparkled in her eyes. "It's been fun, digging into the stories in the Fendersburg paper, following the career of the Ghost, and all the scolding you've done over the years, basically telling them to take some responsibility for their own lives."

"Didn't do any good, did it? Not until I sat back and let them take their lumps ..." Jane sighed and slumped a little in her chair. "I went to Fendersburg to make noise, to catch the attention of the Rivals. Bait in a trap. My Gifts let me have two lives, two identities, so I was safe when I was plain Jane who ran the spa."

"So why did you dismantle the trap?" Angela said.

"Besides the collective IQ of the town dropping in half because they didn't bother to think for themselves anymore?" She shook her head. "The Rivals weren't watching anymore. Either they figured the Ghost was bait and they weren't biting, or they turned their focus elsewhere." She spread her hands. "Here?"

"That makes too much sense," Lanie said quietly. "With all the ruckus at New Year's, sending in Sylvia, trying to make contact with Big Ugly, break through the dimensional gate, yeah, they're focusing on Neighborlee. Both our enemies have pulled back and are licking their wounds, gathering their strength for the next attempt. We're a long way from winning."

"Consider that this alliance Jane's teachers are offering could be the turning point in the war," Angela said.

"Which brings us to this new guy or thing or whatever you met," Felicity said. "New player, or new tactic?"

"What if the Voice is telling the truth?" Jane blurted. Something ached inside her, almost like panic. She was stunned at how much she wanted the Voice to be friend and not foe.

"It's a tricky combination. Asking you to help him, and sucking you dry worse than all of Buffy's vampires," Lanie said. "Kurt thinks it's Big Ugly trying a new tactic, but it's too soon to tell. I do agree that we shouldn't make the mistake of taking him at his word, that he's friendly."

"I need to know more about your previous encounters with Big Ugly." Jane took a big bite of her pizza.

Lanie and Felicity filled in all the gaps in the things Kurt had mentioned or glossed over, starting with the power fluctuations at Eden, items and then people vanishing and reappearing, and the temporary amnesia that essentially made people shrug off what should have been frightening incidents. Jane shivered and agreed with their suspicion that the disappearance of Lanie's parents near the Bermuda Triangle might be tied into the stepped up activities of the Rivals, the attack on Lanie before Christmas, and especially the attempt to either contact Big Ugly or open the barrier between dimensions.

"What are the chances Big Ugly or the doorway it's fixated on is located specifically underneath Eden? I can analyze better with my Ghost field turned on, but you can't exactly go invisible in the middle of a crowd."

Lanie glanced at her watch. "Maybe we should see how well

we work together, and do something about the vortex or event horizon... Are we ever going to come up with a name for that thing?"

"Probably when it's closed up for good or we can get control of it," Jane said. She put her now-empty plate down on the table and jumped to her feet. "How late is Eden open?"

Felicity and Lanie exchanged satisfied looks. Angela just laughed. To save time using the little elevator, Jane grabbed hold of Lanie's wheelchair and turned on the Ghost field, leaving Felicity and Angela to come down the stairs. She and Lanie were laughing about the sensation of energy wrapped around her, and waiting in the Jeep by the time the other two caught up with them. Felicity reported that she had called Kurt and he would meet them at Eden. Angela wouldn't come with them, saying her work was done. Lanie could drop her off back at Divine's before going out to Eden.

Kurt caught up with them when they were a block away from Eden. Jane was surprised to see any cars in the parking lot, considering how lousy the weather was, and less than an hour left until the center closed down. Normal people should be using common sense and staying home in this weather.

Gina was in the office and waved to them as the four came inside. The sounds of running feet and scattered cheers and the thuds of a basketball came from the main gym and indicated where most of the people in the building were. That left the four free to move unnoticed. Lanie led the way as they walked Jane through the building, giving her the behind-the-scenes tour. They explored the smaller gym, where a game called Murder had been set up, the locker rooms and bathrooms where various people had been found, even going into the furnace room, so Kurt could point out the HVAC control panel that had vanished and reappeared.

"Yeah, some echoes of warping," Jane said. She gestured at the HVAC unit.

"Got it. It's like the molecules haven't quite shifted back to where they were before, and they don't like it. They're disturbed because they can't finish settling back where they belong." Kurt caught Lanie and Felicity staring at him. "Oh, sorry. The Ghost field. I'm riding the slipstream, so to speak."

"Uh huh." Felicity raised an eyebrow at Lanie. Jane could read that look enough to know the two of them were going to get together later and compare notes.

"Hey, do you guys get uniforms?" Felicity said, when they had returned to the lobby and Jane found spots in the floor where the duel with the oil slick had left residue of molecular disturbance. "You know, like the X-Men movie uniforms?"

"No." Jane made a face. "What good is a fancy costume when your power means going invisible every time you use it?"

"Hey, guys," Gina sang out as she scurried from her office. "Need anything? I'll be right back," she added, before hurrying through the doors into the gym.

"Whatever we do..." Jane turned up her Ghost field, sensing something, before she saw ripples of black light sweeping through the walls and floor. "Uh oh, here it comes," she said, her voice softening.

"Can you enclose all of us in your field, make us all invisible, and let us see what you're doing?" Lanie asked.

"Yeah, I think... Oh. Sure." Jane looked around the lobby. "It would make it easier if nobody saw us stand here and stare at something nobody else can see or feel, wouldn't it?"

"Can you still fight it, covering us?" Felicity said.

"I'll cover us." Kurt stepped around so he stood on Felicity's right, while Jane automatically moved to the left to put Lanie and Felicity between them. "That should leave you free to do whatever you have to."

Jane focused, mentally drawing a bubble around all of them. The air surrounding them turned hazy. Gina hurried through the lobby, looked around, and clearly didn't see them. She walked right through Kurt's side and didn't react. Lanie flinched. Kurt gave Jane a queasy grin. It was kind of reassuring to know he wasn't quite used to all the aspects of borrowing her power.

Two seconds after Gina went into her office, a swirling whirlpool of energy appeared in the center of the lobby, right where Lanie and Felicity had described the fight taking place New Year's day. The maelstrom of colors made Jane feel nauseous and on the verge of falling off her feet. She yanked her gaze off it and regained her sense of equilibrium. So, it was a mental attack. She strengthened the Ghost field.

"Hit it right between the eyes," Felicity said.

Her EM energy built up in a sizzling electric blue cocoon

spinning around her. Her eyes became openings into her skull, showing a spinning, blinding bright core of the same electric blue power. Then bolts of energy shot out of her eyes and mouth and fingertips and hit the phenomenon dead center.

"And stay out," Kurt said between gritted teeth, as the maelstrom flared, then collapsed in on itself and vanished. A squealing sound made them all flinch and clamp their hands over their ears.

Felicity staggered sideways. Lanie grabbed hold of her, holding her up.

"I'm okay," Felicity insisted, as they hurried outside, through the closed doors.

Jane kept the Ghost field up, so nobody passing through at the wrong moment saw them suddenly materialize from nowhere.

"I just... I'm just getting used to having control, and that was about the strongest burst I've ever used. It took something out of me." She giggled and sank into the passenger seat of Lanie's Jeep, guided by Kurt. "That was incredible! Kind of dizzy, but good."

"As long as you didn't burn yourself out," Jane said.

They ended up at Lanie's house. Her brothers were both busy elsewhere, so they had the house to themselves. Along with the biggest junk food feast Jane could have wished for, Lanie had a stash of dark chocolate to re-energize them. Dark chocolate-dipped cookies and triple chocolate hot cocoa mix. Jane, Lanie and Felicity laughed almost in unison when Kurt grumbled about just not understanding what it was with girls and chocolate.

"It's just another proof that men are a completely different species, that's all," Jane said, cradling the big, clunky, cobalt blue mug filled with hot chocolate and whipped cream.

"An inferior species. Yeah, yeah, I've heard all that before," Kurt grumbled. He winked at her.

Her face burned, and stayed hot when she saw the grins and raised eyebrows Lanie and Felicity exchanged.

Once they had all regained their equilibrium, Felicity ran next door to her garage apartment and brought out a photo album. Jane was stunned to see photos of children from Neighborlee Children's Home. Lanie admitted they had filled the photo album from NCH records, provided by the former orphanage director, Mrs. Silvestri, who was just as interested as they were in finding out what happened to the children who had been spirited away. It took a few moments to get to the page Felicity wanted. The photos were arranged in order of dates when the children arrived at NCH.

Jane shivered a little when she saw the candid photos someone had taken of her, on the playground and laughing with some girls in her cottage. Her throat closed, and for a few seconds she was almost overwhelmed by the flood of good memories of her years at the orphanage. The four of them could have grown up together and been friends, if Demetrius and Beau hadn't snatched her away.

"You were nice to me when I was feeling like such a freak, like I was the only one going through what I was going through," Jane said, tracing a fingertip over the picture of herself at age eleven.

"What? Puberty?" Felicity nodded. "I bet you were scared, but then you got rescued and landed with a lot of people who knew what was going on. So that was good. I could be jealous, but I'm glad we got left behind, y'know?"

"Neighborlee is our home." Lanie shrugged. "It's your home now, too." They exchanged smiles.

They broke up some time after Lanie's younger brother, Pete, got home from some activities at church. By then, they had come to several agreements. First, Jane would give only an abbreviated report of what happened that night to Demetrius and Beauregard. They weren't going to ask anyone's advice or share information with outsiders until they got a better handle on what they were facing. Felicity had given the oil slick a stronger jolt than she had given it at New Year's. If it wasn't permanently disabled, it would stay shut down longer. If the Voice didn't make contact again with Jane, that would be confirmation that it was indeed Big Ugly.

~~~~~

Jane told Katie what had happened. She didn't consider her an outsider. After all, her friend had met Kurt and had Angela's approval, and she knew about the guardians. Katie would be alarmed if Jane suddenly stopped reporting on her progress in unearthing Neighborlee's secrets. Alarm would lead to reporting to Demetrius and Beau.

"So..." Katie said, two days later, after Jane filled her in on what had been happening. Her somber mask of concentration cracked into a curiously sheepish grin and she flopped back in Jane's couch.

"So what?" Jane finally asked, knowing she was being set up.

"So do you think, if the Voice guy is not the enemy, if he's for real, and if he knows where we come from and we can go home..." Katie took a deep breath and her grin went even more crooked. "If we do go home, do we hold onto our superhero powers?

"What if," she hurried on, when Jane hesitated, trying to find an answer, "it's like when Superman returns to Krypton? What if our world makes us ordinary people? No more Ghost field for you, no more supersonic speeds for me. And on and on."

"Ever consider that the old joke is true, and we're the rejects? Maybe we aren't strong enough to survive back where home is. No immunity to native diseases. We could get infected within five seconds and just curl up and die. Real nice homecoming."

"You know what the Old Poops say. Don't borrow trouble. We'll deal with those complications when we run into them. Who says we'll ever get home? For all we know, the doorway to wherever we came from is one-way. Maybe that's why the Voice seems stuck. He's trying to go in through the out doorway."

"And maybe he's a liar and the enemy, or a worse enemy than the oil slick monster." Jane shivered a little, remembering that encounter at Eden.

"What if it is?" Katie said. "What are you going to do about it?"

"I don't know."

"Then concentrate on something you *can* do something about."

"Such as?" Jane wavered between amusement at the smug little smirk Katie didn't make any effort to hide, and irritation.

"The kid. Whoever swiped at the spoiled rich snot to rescue Penny. *Someone* at the orphanage is a developing Gifted, just learning his or her powers. Concentrate on finding that kid instead of worrying about the oil slick."

"Easier said than done," she grumbled.

"Since when do any of us choose the easy way?"

"True." Jane decided to be amused by Katie's constantly up attitude and outlook.

She related the conversation to Lanie the next day, when she stopped in on her lunch break. Her new friend was suitably chagrined.

"We're so used to not having anybody like us around," she admitted. "We should have learned our lesson when the trouble triplets showed up. We need to change our mindset. There is more weirdness in the rest of the world and like attracts like, so we should *expect* trouble in Neighborlee. We do watch NCH for kids like us showing up." Lanie shrugged. "That's why we do the mentoring thing. Obviously, we haven't been doing enough. Someone is developing powers and we didn't notice."

"What do we do?"

"You seem to be even more sensitive to powers at work than Kurt. Maybe the two of you together can kind of boost each other with the Geiger counter routine."

"What exactly do you have in mind?" Jane fought down a little shiver when Lanie's eyes lit up and she grinned and sat back in her wheelchair, looking her over twice.

"Well, we can get you into the cottages easily enough. Just introduce you as Kurt's new girlfriend. The kids will flip."

"Is that a good thing, or bad?"

"Oh, definitely good. The kids love Kurt. He's kind of like Santa Claus, always fixing things for them, helping them with their science projects, making gizmos for them to play with."

"What about any little girls who plan on marrying big brother Kurt when they grow up?"

"Hmm, none that I know of." Lanie snorted. "Just our luck, the jealous one will be the one with the superpower and she'll try to zap her new rival."

"Well, if it brings her out of hiding, that might be good."

"How good will it be for you and Kurt?"

"I don't—" Jane swallowed, stunned by a fluttery feeling.

"The guy is interested. He's never been interested in us, but we know each other too well. No mystery. Kurt has been looking for someone like you for a long time. Of course, we always figured he wanted a top-heavy, single-digit IQ type of girl. Not someone smart and able to kick his butt when he needs it. If some jealous kid attacks, well, that'll wake him up, get him moving faster to strengthen whatever it is building between the two of you."

"That's a little too fast. Considering I loathed him up until a few days ago. Considering he was trying to drive me out of town up until a few days ago."

"Maybe the guy was scared."

Jane decided to laugh. Better than admitting she felt a little scared, too.

You wanted a normal, ordinary guy, remember?

"Of course, if the new superhero is a boy, he could have a crush on Penny, which makes him protective of her, which explains him attacking that rich kid." Lanie shrugged. "All we can do is introduce you to the kids and see what happens."

~~~~~

The night before Jane was to go to the orphanage and be introduced as Kurt's new girlfriend, she dreamed she was walking through a dark, chill, damp place. The details were too hazy to give her a sense of location. Tunnels or vaulted ceilings? Underground? A massive ruined building? Alone? Or surrounded by malevolent, quietly breathing, massive, cold-blooded entities that watched and hated her? She walked, stretching out her senses, trying to find a way out, trying to discern if anyone was nearby. Trying not to bolt and run until she was exhausted. No matter how far she walked, she never reached a doorway or a turning place or a source of light. No matter how hard she shivered, she couldn't get warm.

She woke three times from the dream, shivering and sweating and hovering at least two feet above her bed. She changed her sweaty pajamas twice, and the third time took a long, hot shower before putting on her last pair of clean pajamas. It didn't help.

The fourth time the dream caught her, Jane ran. The floor was uneven and she stepped into holes and tripped over obstructions constantly. Each time she stumbled and started to fall, she called up the Ghost field to protect her. It lasted long enough to get her steady on her feet again, but she couldn't maintain it. She thought about flying, trying to rise up and out of the darkness of her prison. What if the Ghost field failed her when she was high enough in the air to fall hard and fast and break all her bones? What if it failed her while she was in the middle of solid rock?

Jane woke up to the cold silver light before dawn streaming through her skylight, shivering and drenched yet again, and sick to her stomach. She stumbled into the shower and stayed there until all the hot water was gone, her bathroom was filled with steam, and her fingers looked like prunes. She made breakfast only because she knew she needed to eat for energy. Nothing appealed to her, and she had to close her eyes and pinch her nose before she could bring the first spoonful of oatmeal to her mouth. Her throat closed and convulsed, like she would vomit.

Once the taste of the oatmeal hit her tongue, heavy with butter and brown sugar and raisins, her stomach turned into a raging fire-filled cavern. She had half the bowl of oatmeal down her throat before she took a breath. As she stumbled to the refrigerator, she shoveled the rest of the oatmeal into her mouth, then licked the bowl clean while she scanned the shelves for what to eat next. Leftover buttered noodles followed, with slightly questionable ham loaf after that. She caught herself grumbling about the stupidity of natural peanut butter that required mixing before it could be eaten, and stepped back from the ransacked refrigerator.

What was happening here?

She hadn't been talking with the Voice, so why was she drained and eating for three?

Get help, stupid.

The lights were on in Divine's Emporium and the front sidewalk was swept clean despite the three inches of snow that had fallen overnight, when Jane arrived less than ten minutes later. She swallowed down a sob of relief and flew through the front door.

Tried to fly through the front door. She hit it, with the Ghost field at full strength. Something caught hold of the edges of the bubble surrounding her and set her down on the front porch. Sighing into a sob of frustration, Jane turned off the Ghost field and lifted her hand to bang on the door. It opened before her hand touched it. Angela caught hold of her wrist and drew her inside.

"Protective fields," Angela explained, slipping an arm around Jane's waist and leading her through the house, to the stairs up to her private quarters. "The house knows you're a friend, but the energy you generate to be the Ghost...well, it's *tainted*. That's the best explanation I can come up with. I had the oddest dream of you running down long, dark, wet tunnels, with leaches reaching down from the ceiling and taking little sips from you as you passed."

"That about sums up how I feel," Jane admitted, as Angela ushered her through the door into her apartment. "You were there in my dream? How come I didn't see you or even sense you? I was completely alone."

"You belong to Neighborlee," she said, her stern expression somehow warm and comforting. "You are never alone. Especially when you are involved in protecting our home. Sit." She pointed at one of the chairs pulled up to the table, set for three, and stepped through an open doorway. Glimpsing a white, old-fashioned stove and matching refrigerator, Jane guessed it was her kitchen.

A shiver of something somehow familiar and warm passed over her as Angela came out with an enormous teapot covered in unicorns and maidens in Renaissance gowns in one hand, and a basket of steaming muffins in the other hand. Jane's stomach woke up, aching from emptiness again.

"Drink first," Angela ordered, tipping the teapot to fill the dark green mug large enough to hold four cups, sitting in the middle of Jane's plate. She went back into the kitchen while Jane obeyed, and returned with butter and a tripod holding small bowls of jewel-toned jellies.

"What happened?" Kurt demanded, barreling through the door.

Jane guessed that shiver she felt a few seconds ago was the house reacting to him coming through the door. She wondered if he had had the same dream, or if Angela had called him. Angela gestured for her to keep drinking, so she emptied the mug, though it seemed to take forever. Whatever was in the tea, fruity yet salty, pungent with herbs she didn't recognize, streamed directly into her bloodstream and out to her extremities, relaxing the muscle-cracking tension and dousing the fire in her belly.

Angela explained about her dream, her suspicions that Jane had been visited by the Voice and drained again. Kurt leaned close enough to sniff the tea. Then he snatched up a muffin, broke it open, slapped butter on it, and handed it to Jane as she swallowed the last mouthful and put the mug down.

"Eat first." He patted her shoulder. "Should have thought you'd get attacked. My mistake. Sorry."

Jane took a big bite, mostly to keep from blurting the first thought in her mind: Kurt was acting like they really were boyfriend-girlfriend.

Maybe... Maybe he'd agreed so easily to Lanie's plan because he *liked* the idea?

Chapter Fourteen

Between mouthfuls, she related her dream, including how many times she woke up and couldn't stop returning to it. Halfway through, she realized the muffin had been as big as both her fists put together, chocolate batter studded with chocolate chips and chocolate sugar crystals crusting the top. Angela certainly knew what would give the most comfort.

"You know what stands out?" Kurt said, in between slow bites of his own muffin. "He seems to know Jane isn't going to listen. He didn't even try more of his con job."

"How did he know?" Angela said.

"I have the feeling that I...leak," Jane ventured. She tapped her temple with her free hand, and then popped the last mouthful of muffin into her mouth.

"You mentioned having some dreams you couldn't remember," Kurt said, nodding. "Maybe it was talking to you then. Preparing the way. It had to get a foothold in your head before you could hear it. Just like when the Longfellow girls had their near-miss. They were overhearing what Big Ugly was planning."

"Yes, but as far as we could tell, it didn't know they were eavesdropping. You notice this time around, the girls didn't hear it building up to attack the New Year's party," Angela said.

They could only come up with theories, but agreed that the Voice was able to tap into Jane's thoughts and knew she didn't trust it. Why carry on the pretense of friendship when it knew she wouldn't cooperate?

"The thing is, if it can tap into Jane and drain her, maybe she isn't safe. During the day, when she's conscious and can resist, hold up shields, no problem." Kurt reached over and caught hold of Jane's free hand.

She almost laughed, but the sound just caught in her throat, as she realized she didn't feel that zing she had always hoped for when a man held her hand. Granted, this wasn't what she considered a romantic setting, but Kurt was being protective. That was romantic, wasn't it? She liked the warmth of his hand, the strength—compared to the chill still lingering in her bones, the weakness in her muscles, a sense of fading away. If she didn't concentrate on being solid, would she fall through the chair, the floor, to the floor below, to the basement? Would she keep falling down through the ground underneath the town?

Not a good mental picture. Not when she envisioned the Voice in some big, cold, dark, damp hole somewhere below her feet.

"During the day, Jane will never be alone," Angela said. "At night... Well, the situation is different, and we have learned something since the last attack, so she should be safe if she sleeps over here."

"I was thinking about camping out on her sofa," Kurt muttered.

"None of my sofas are long enough to take you comfortably," Jane said. Her face felt slightly warm. She imagined she was so drained she couldn't even blush hot red. "But thanks."

Felicity and her fiancé, Jake, were waiting when Jane returned to her shop. They would run the spa while Jane went to the orphanage with Kurt, after the children got home from school. The morning went quickly, and Felicity was a quick study. Jane watched the interaction between her and Jake and had to fight down more than her share of sighs. Somehow, the two of them were going to make marriage work, even though Jake wasn't Gifted. Felicity had revealed what she could do during the New Year's crisis, and Jake hadn't freaked out. How many non-Gifted could take the revelation of a suddenly expanded, suddenly much stranger and more wonderful and threatening universe? Maybe having grown up in Neighborlee helped Jake accept it all. Jane hoped that love, real love, had a lot to do with it.

She felt a little guilt leaving the spa in Felicity's hands, because Iris, the new nail technician, was due to start with her first appointment that afternoon. Iris knew what she was doing, and she had come in yesterday to set up her station. Still, Jane didn't like leaving things in other people's hands. She had to remind herself this was Neighborlee, where people who could think for themselves were the rule, not the exception.

"Everything's gonna be fine," Kurt said, as Jane slid into the passenger seat of his truck and glanced back at the spa.

"What do we do if we rile up Penny's defender and he or she attacks? What if when I'm wiped out like this, you can't borrow my

Gift to defend us?"

"Uh huh." He concentrated on navigating down the street for a few seconds, then gave her a sideways glance and smile. "You've been thinking about this a lot."

"And you haven't?"

"There is so much going on, and like Lanie says, we're sitting dead center of the weirdness capital of the whole USA. It's kind of hard not to have it in the back of your mind all the time." He sighed and let up on the gas when the stoplight ahead of them turned yellow. "The thing is, we've always had an 'us against the world' mentality. Especially when other kids with powers vanished. Were they taken back home, wherever home is, or were they snatched up by the evil mutants? It's nice knowing your Old Poops—" Kurt snorted and they shared a genuine grin. "— your Old Poops were trying to do the right thing, safety in numbers and all that. Still ... we might be touching the outer edges of the answers. Something beyond this world."

Someone tapped a horn behind them. Kurt glanced in the rearview mirror, and then crossed the intersection.

"Anyway," he continued, "there's so much going on, it's kind of like—what do you call it—exposure reducing your sensitivity."

"Desensitization therapy?"

"Yeah. You don't exactly get numb, but the adrenalin doesn't shoot through you when more weird things on top of weird things hit you. It's just an ordinary day in Neighborlee, Ohio."

"Is that good, or bad?"

"Depends on who you're spending the day with." He winked. "Let's concentrate on today's problem, forget about the Voice trying to make like a vampire."

"Today's problem." She took a deep breath, let out it slowly. Took another. "Right. Trying to identify the kid who's about to burst into a Gift."

"Someone who thinks he or she is a defender."

"What if it's a boy who's jealous of anyone Penny likes?"

"I'd prefer being an optimist. We're looking for someone who was defending his orphanage sister against that leach."

Jane thought about it a moment, and decided Kurt was right. She would much rather come up against an emerging Gifted who wanted to be a hero.

Penny was waiting when they arrived at NCH. From the grin on the girl's face, the way she bounced up and down on her toes, she was excited.

"Is that relief I see?" Kurt pulled into the visitor parking slot nearest the front door of the administration building.

"I was worried she might resent having to stay home today, not go to work. You know how girls her age love makeup and having spending money," Jane retorted.

He snorted, but at least he didn't tease her anymore.

Twin girls, maybe ten years old, followed on Penny's heels as she scampered down the sidewalk to meet them. As soon as she came to a stop, the twins separated and each caught hold of one of her hands. Penny rolled her eyes, but Jane noticed she didn't tug her hands free as she introduced the girls, Kelly and Kory. The twins were either ambidextrous or determined to keep their grip on Penny, because neither one let go when Jane held out her hand to shake theirs.

"Hey, octokittens, how about some help here?" Kurt said, with a heavy whine in his voice. That got giggles from all three girls.

"Octokittens?" Jane murmured, when the trio had filled their arms full of the boxes and bags for this afternoon's project. She watched them scurry back down the sidewalk to the main building of the orphanage, where parties took place and the children gathered when the weather was too miserable to play outside.

Kurt was giving one of his junior mechanics classes, teaching how to build small engines and then figure out what to do with them. Jane had brought makeup and manicure equipment and beads to make jewelry.

"Too small and cute to be octopuses--octopi?" He nodded, gesturing at the girls with his chin, since his arms were full of the largest crate of equipment. "They're always hanging on Penny. Needing contact. Gotta be a lot of hurt, scared under all the cuteness. If it were me, I'd be going nuts, but Penny's a good kid with a good heart, and she puts up with it. I think she snatched the job when Angela mentioned it just to have some time away from this place."

"Now I feel guilty, taking away one of her escape days."

"Nah, she likes the kids. She just needs someone to come between them and her once in a while." He frowned as they approached the big double doors at the front of the building. Penny and the twins had already gotten inside and vanished from sight. "Gotta wonder now if she fell for Evan's lines just as an excuse to go somewhere without them."

"I don't suppose Angela has something cooking to keep them busy when they're not at school? Penny needs some time for herself, no matter how good a girl she is."

"Never know. Maybe she's just waiting for someone to ask. You know how she is about expecting us to think for ourselves."

"I'm getting the picture." Then they were at the front doors, and she hurried to shift the straps of three bags into one hand, so she could pull the door open for Kurt, since his hands were full.

The afternoon and evening passed quickly, and there were times when Jane forgot that she had ever left. The children who laughed and teased each other over their piles of gears and wires or argued about matching nail polish colors and beads could have been her family when she lived here.

Kurt managed to put them back-to-back at the long craft tables, and from time to time leaned back far enough to fall off his bench, to make comments to her. The first few times, Jane was startled to feel the warmth of him brushing against her arm and turn her head to see him looking up at her with a patently false look of innocence. The mischief sparkling in his eyes always made a lie of the rest of his expression. After the third time, she decided he liked startling her. Two could play that game. After he sat up again, she scooted over on her bench, into the spot where he would land.

The next time Kurt leaned back, he pressed against her back. That earned peals of laughter from her girls, and hoots and chuckles and comments from the older boys and girls at his table. Kurt sat up for a few seconds, then leaned back, pressing her against the table.

"Do you mind?" she growled, finding it hard not to laugh, and winked at the girls sitting directly across from her.

"Yeah, I mind. Something's in my way!"

"No, you're putting your big backside where it doesn't belong." She wriggled a little, put down the string of beads she had been tying off, braced her hands on the side of the table and prepared to push. In that pause, she called up the Ghost field, to give Kurt a nudge he couldn't resist. If she had to, she would adjust the solidity of the bench so he fell through it.

Jane's fingertips tingled on her right hand. She slowly turned her head to the right, and in those few seconds of pause, she caught a rainbow-tinged flicker of light swirl once around the clasped hands of the twins. Then the light was gone, the same moment their little frowns vanished and they let go of each other's hand and picked up their bead projects.

Did you feel that? Kurt asked, still pressing against her back. This time it was all for communication, not for teasing.

Yeah, and I saw it.

Your table, not mine?

Answers a lot of questions.

Save it. Take notes.

Duh, this isn't my first rodeo.

Kurt burst out laughing, and let up on the pressure against her back.

When they took a break for dinner, Kurt asked her to help him take his supplies out to his truck. Jane decided to do the same with her few supplies that hadn't been used up. The evening would shift to homework help, with some other alumni of the orphanage scheduled to come in, so craft time was over.

"Little kids," Kurt said as soon as they were outside.

"What did it sound like?"

"You know those cheesy triangles they gave us for music time in elementary school? Two of those tapping and clunking a few times, like they were being hit against each other. Which one of the kids at your table?"

"Two." She waited and was pleased to see understanding widen his eyes. He paused a few steps away from the front doors, and she could almost hear the fizzing of the circuits of his brain.

"Just one question. If it's the twins, how did they zap Evan without leaving their cottage and going to the quarries that night?" He started down the sidewalk again, but taking slower steps.

"Maybe they don't need to be physically there." Jane told him what she had seen when she felt the pulse of power, before the twins visibly decided not to do anything about Kurt's teasing.

"Sounds like they've latched onto you, too," he said as they reached the truck.

"I'd like to see what they could try against the Voice, if he tries to zap me for wising up to him." She shuddered and paused, two steps behind him.

"What?"

"They know an awful lot about the spa, the specialized creams and mud packs and all the nail polish colors I didn't bring with me."

"Penny told them." He put his box down in the bed of his truck and tugged the tarp up to cover it.

"Maybe not." Jane barely registered as he took her bags from her and put them in the cab of the truck behind the passenger seat. Her mind spun through all the things the twins had said, analyzing Penny's reactions to them and seeing everything in a different intensity of light. "There were a few things she said she never told them about, like that muumuu ensemble she wants to get for this summer."

"Hey, you're chiming," Kurt murmured, and reached out to catch hold of both her hands. Jane gasped at the contact, yanking her out of the memory loop.

"They asked me about the raffia sandals that came in *today*. I unpacked and priced them just before you picked me up. Penny *didn't* see them. She didn't see the catalog, and I usually place orders in the morning, before the first customers come in."

"They tapped into you." He gave an exaggerated shudder. "Strong little monsters, then. Aren't they too young for their superpowers to be waking up?"

"Being twins, they might have enough energy between them already, they don't need it to build up to the point of overflowing, or the hormonal burst that the rest of us did."

"Okay, so how do you want to handle this? You've got more experience telling kids they're joining the Avengers." He hooked his arm through hers and turned them both around to head back to the building. Then he paused and glanced at a car that had just pulled into the parking lot. "Mayor Wellington."

"One of us?"

"Lost Boy, but not a superhero." A horn blared behind them and he flinched, muttering as he glanced over his shoulder. Then Jane felt him relax. "Lanie."

"Conference?"

He bared his teeth in a fierce grin that made her very glad they were on the same side. A moment later, Jane's knees went a little wobbly. Yes, they were on the same side, weren't they? She wondered why she had doubted him before. Maybe that was the Voice's bad influence?

Several more NCH alumni came in, driving past them to look for parking spots, while they followed Lanie to the handicapped parking spot and Kurt took her chair out of the back seat of the Jeep.

"Oh, you're going to have tongues wagging all over town," Lanie said as she dropped into her chair. "Holding hands already?"

"Um—we—it's our cover, remember?" Jane sighed. She remembered a day when such teasing never would have flustered her. Maybe because it wasn't entirely teasing? She liked Kurt. What was wrong with that?

"Target sighted," Kurt said, and linked their arms again.

"That was fast. Who?" Lanie asked.

"Kelly and Kory."

Lanie whistled, nodding slowly. They couldn't talk for a few minutes, as other alumni joined them, heading for the front doors. Jane was almost grateful for the interruptions, even though she caught several people giving second wide-eyed, sometimes grinning glances to her arm linked with Kurt's. Obviously, no one was used to him being paired with anyone. They seemed glad. So, Kurt was well liked.

Why wouldn't he be? He was a great guy. A little too defensive of his town, but was that a bad thing?

Jane pushed those thoughts aside for later. She had to deal with people who were trying to remember her, if they had been in NCH at the same time. Some had vague memories, and her cheeks warmed several times as various people welcomed her and made a point of telling anyone else they ran into, "Have you met Jane Wilson? Do you remember her? She was here when..."

She and Kurt and Lanie didn't have a chance to speak privately, but later on she looked up a few times to see the two of them with their heads close together, talking. She was relieved. Kurt and Lanie knew the twins much better than she did. They would have a better idea how to approach the girls and explain their emerging Gifts.

When the evening ended, Jane kept watch on the twins and Penny. She was relieved to see the older girl really did like the twins. As if they were her younger sisters in truth. She smiled, feeling a little teary, as Penny guided the twins through polite thank-yous and farewells with the adults who had come for dinner and homework help, and made sure they put their coats and gloves and boots on for the short walk to their cottage.

"So, you think she'll be relieved or she'll miss them when they're gone?" Lanie said quietly. She and Jane watched the three walk around the far side of the administration building.

"Gone?"

"They need teaching, and we're not set up to teach them. Not twins. Not smart ones who already figured out how to use what they've got." She tugged her coat closer around herself.

"You want me to call Demetrius and Beau to come get them?" Jane wasn't quite sure how she felt about the idea. Granted, the twins would probably love being the sole students of the Sanctum. Everyone would spoil them. The question was if her teachers, who had been ancient when she became their student, were up to handling mischievous twins.

"That's the idea so far. We should take this up with Angela, first. And get into the records, to see if they're Lost Kids, or something else." Lanie glanced over her shoulder as headlights touched her.

~~~~~

Jane and Kurt went to Divine's Emporium in Lanie's Jeep. They could just fly back to get his truck when they were done. This gave them time to talk before conferring with Angela.

They spent the drive over to Divine's discussing what Jane had seen and Kurt had heard, and speculating why Lanie and Kurt and Felicity hadn't noticed anything unusual when they were around the twins before. The girls' ability to tap into Jane's recent memories could be worrying, and indicated their potential strength. Lanie agreed with Kurt's assessment that the twins weren't vindictive and would see the fun side of their powers rather than their chance to take revenge on people who didn't give them their way.

"I'll ask Athena to hack into the records," Angela said, when they had settled down in her quarters. "She can determine if the twins were found, or they came to Neighborlee some other way."

"What if the girls aren't lost like us?" Jane asked.

"Stanzer." Lanie grinned when Jane gave her a confused frown. "Local P.I. He has some otherworldly background of his own. Cuts down on the need to explain things and worry we'll blow his mind."

In the end, Angela agreed that no matter what they learned about the twins' background before the orphanage, the Sanctum would have to be contacted. Demetrius and Beau were experienced in training Gifted children, with good results. She did stipulate that she wanted to talk to the two elderly men before they got to work pulling strings to get custody of the twins.

"Oh, boy, I would love to be a fly on the wall when that clash of the titans takes place," Kurt muttered, as he and Jane and Lanie left Divine's Emporium shortly after eleven.

"The Old Poops are nothing compared to Angela," Jane said, stifling a need to giggle. "She's going to scold them for being too oblivious to sense that Neighborlee could take care of its own. They won't be able to get a word in edgewise."

"So, you're going with her?" Lanie glanced at her Jeep and the door swung open.

"Going?" Jane said.

Lanie's keys lifted from her pocket and shot through the air to take a sharp turn around the windshield and into the car.

"I guess we just assumed you're going to see your teachers tonight, get things rolling." Kurt shrugged and jammed his fists into his pocket. They both flinched when Lanie's Jeep started up. "Maybe you want some moral support."

"You can't fool me," she said with a snort and a grin. "You just want to see the Sanctum."

"Heck, yeah." He bowed and stepped off the sidewalk, letting Lanie slide her wheelchair past him, to head for her car.

"You two have fun," Lanie called over her shoulder as a flicker of rainbow-tinted light spun around her wheels and she slid down from the sidewalk to the street without a bump. "Just not too much fun. We've already got people speculating on how soon Kurt sticks a crowbar in his wallet and buys you a ring."

"We do — they are?" Jane's face felt hot enough to steam in the icy night air. Despite the shadows, the bluish tint the moonlight gave everything, Kurt's face definitely looked as red as hers felt. She shifted into Ghost phase and shot up into the air.

Kurt caught up with her before it occurred to her that she should slow down and stay within his range. He pulled ahead of her and gestured toward the orphanage. She nodded and they flew in silence to get his truck. After she called and talked to Beau, to let him know they were coming, they rode in silence to the parking lot behind her building.

"Look," he said with a sigh as they got out of the truck. "I've never really had a girlfriend. Nobody ever stuck around long enough for people to start talking—"

"That's probably why people *are* talking."

"The thing is... I don't want to mess things up, okay? I like you. Maybe you like me, despite how I did mess up. So can we go slow?"

"I think..." She slid partially into Ghost phase, so she could rise up a few feet but he could still see her. "I think we're going to be busy for a while, straightening out everything with the twins and the Voice. Time to think, figure it all out. Slow enough?"

"Oh, yeah." He grinned, and Jane felt the momentary buzz in her fingertips from him accessing the Ghost field.

They raced each other, as much as they could race without getting too far apart for him to borrow her Ghost abilities. Going so fast, it took all Jane's concentration to point out landmarks below them. She did most of the talking, painting a picture of Beau and Demetrius to introduce him to the old men who had been her fathers and teachers and role models.

When she led Kurt down the hallway into the library, Demetrius and Beauregard were waiting with a roaring fire and a tray of sandwiches and hot cider on one end of the long meeting table. Jane introduced Kurt and braced for comments from her teachers, either defensive or teasing or an avalanche of questions.

The silence was worse than anything she could have imagined.

Kurt must have imagined something much worse, because after a few moments he just took a step back, jammed his fingers into his pockets, and grinned. A few more moments of silence, he glanced at the tray of food, glanced at the empty seats on the other side of the table, picked up two plates, borrowed Jane's Gift just long enough to lift food onto the plates—earning stares from Beau and Demetrius—and sat down. Jane felt decidedly awkward as she slid into the chair next to his.

"So you're the Old Poops," he said, voice thoughtful.

"Old Poops." Beau's shoulders shook, silent laughter making a lie of the brow-lowered glare he aimed at Kurt. "Keep it up. You might just prove you're good enough for our gal."

"Beau—" Jane blurted.

"It's all right, Cookie." Demetrius slouched down to his trademark comfortable listening posture. "So, I'm guessing you have an offer of alliance from the powers-that-be in Neighborlee?"

"No time for that. We have a set of twins whose powers are starting to wake up, way too early, and we're dealing with a chronic problem that we don't want them to experience."

"Chronic problem?" He raised one eyebrow so far it vanished into his shaggy hairline, and glanced at Jane.

"All that weirdness at New Year's was from the Rivals attempting contact with an interdimensional threat that tries periodically to break through into Neighborlee. It might be the same disembodied voice trying to pull an us-against-the-universe scam on me." Jane clasped the mug of hot cider in both hands and held it close enough the steam bathed her face. "And trying a psionic vampire routine at the same time."

"Do tell," Beau murmured. "We might need something far stronger for this meeting."

Kurt tipped his head and frowned at Jane. She just grinned, remembering his earlier comment about "girls and chocolate." Her teachers had some long, convoluted, pseudo-scientific explanation for why chocolate seemed to be a tonic and mental booster. When they wanted something "stronger," they tapped their stockpile of chocolate. The seriousness of the situation could be measured by the ratio of chocolate to whatever it accompanied. Jars of hot fudge topping, eaten straight from the jar, rather than spooned on ice cream or used to dip Oreos, hinted at a world-threatening crisis.

"Janie, do the honors?" Demetrius said. "And send a Gamma-level message to the residence halls, in case anyone who's home cares to participate?"

Amelia and Theo were the only members of Hoax currently in residence. Both had hurried downstairs by the time Jane came up from the larder with a tea cart piled with chocolate provisions. Amelia brushed a kiss on Jane's forehead as she passed her in the hall and hurried into the kitchen. The seventy-three-year-old wisp of a woman preferred her chocolate mixed with coffee as black as her skin and eyes, and had a special blend kept under lock and key that she preferred to prepare for herself.

"Bless you," Theo said, reaching around Jane to snatch the two bottles of Tabasco sauce from the cart.

When the TV show *Roswell* had played, he had been intrigued by the alien teens' penchant for spicy-sweet combinations, such as drenching chocolate cake with hot sauce. Then he had tried it, became addicted, and regularly went through four bottles a month.

Kurt, Beau and Demetrius seemed to have come to some sort of consensus, or maybe just a truce, by the time Jane and the others joined them. She wasn't at all comforted by Beau's grin and wink and the exaggerated tip of his head toward Kurt. There was no time to indulge in personal panic attacks. She made quick introductions as the six of them settled around one end of the long table.

~~~~~

"People are gonna talk," Kurt said, as he and Jane landed in her living room at eight the next morning.

The war council had lasted until 2am, then she had settled Kurt in a guest room while she took her old room. They slept until six, had a hurried breakfast, and flew back to Neighborlee. Demetrius and Beau planned to spend the day digging up information on Kelly and Kory before assembling the paperwork and false histories they would need to take custody of the twins. If all went well, they would arrive in Neighborlee by the weekend.

"Talk about what?" Jane thought about taking a long, hot soak in her tub. Some aromatherapy to help clear her mind and prepare for the strain of the next few days of waiting would be helpful. She couldn't exactly dive into the tub while Kurt was there, though.

Then her brain latched onto the present situation, and that crooked, slightly sheepish, slightly mischievous twist to his mouth.

"If you leave in the next five minutes, we should be safe. Most of the businesses around here, people don't start arriving to open up until around nine."

"Yeah, that's true." He hitched one hip up onto the stool at the breakfast bar he had built for her. "Would it be so bad if people ...talked?"

"About us, you mean?" Jane shrugged. "I guess it depends on what you want to have happen from all that talking."

"Laying my claim, mostly. Before other guys figure out you're here." He focused on his interlaced fingers, his hands tight-pressed together on the counter.

Jane knew she hadn't spent enough time with Kurt to interpret all his little mannerisms, but she guessed his inability to look her in the eyes was significant. That had her heart racing for a few seconds.

Funny, but she felt more clear-headed than she had in a long while. Maybe since before the Voice started touching her dreams.

"I had the best night's sleep last night," she said, testing the idea aloud. That got a confused frown from Kurt. "No intruder, no weird dreams."

"Uh huh. That's good. Look, about what I was saying—"

"Kurt, I'm flattered that you're interested, but I think we need to figure out *why* you're interested and I'm flattered."

That got another confused frown, which earned a bubble of laughter. She shook her head and stepped over to the refrigerator. Definitely, he wasn't going to be leaving before anyone saw and recognized his truck behind the building. She decided they might as well be comfortable and have a second breakfast while they worked things out.

"All that talk about studying the next generation, the children and grandchildren born to Lost Kids who didn't develop powers. The Old Poops speculating on what Gifts the children of two Gifted parents would inherit, or if they'd come up with something new."

"You think I'm latching onto you because you're the first female of the species that I don't see as a sister." Kurt nodded. "Maybe. But maybe it's a lot of hormones, and feeling like I've been waiting for someone like you for a long time."

"Hormones, huh?" Jane grinned into the refrigerator as she pulled out milk, juice, and butter.

"Along the lines of, 'Mama, get me one of those,' just about the first time I laid eyes on you."

"Hormones... That's better than feeling like the continuation of the species rests on us."

She had been hoping for an ordinary guy. One who would want her for the girl he saw and not her potential to give birth to an even better, second generation model of superhero.

"Jane?" Kurt reached from far across the room and caught hold of her wrists. His voice sounded stretched and distant.

Chapter Fifteen

Jane took a breath and wondered why the room spun around her. A buzzing-tingling sensation began in her fingers, raced up her arms, turning into red-hot pinpricks before twisting around in her gut and flashing all along her left side. Two little girls shrieked inside her head.

She clung to the school bus seat in front of her, digging her fingers in so hard she felt the old metal bending and the paint flaking away. Children screamed all around her as her stomach twisted and the world spun.

"Jane!" Kurt shook her, pulling her out of the bus, away from the children.

She still heard Kelly and Kory shrieking in her head, but the terror and shock had turned to fury and Jane could deal with that much better. Fury pushed her into action, while fear paralyzed.

"It's got the girls," she spat, and twisted her hands around in his grip to hold onto him before the sensation pulled her down into the school bus again.

A school bus that fell through a sudden oily black hole in the pavement, down and down, twisting in darkness that was thick, cold, smothering, like dirty, frozen motor oil.

Kurt growled and light flashed all over him as he pulled her close to his chest and shot up through the roof of her apartment.

He held onto her even after she regained her breath. They flew to Divine's. She regained her equilibrium enough to be disgruntled that the protective shields around the house didn't even slow him down as he flew them both through the front wall. They landed in the main room and he set Jane down in a chair.

"The children," Angela gasped, and stumbled into the room, so pale her hair looked dirty brown against her skin.

"What happened?" Kurt demanded as he caught hold of her hand and guided her down into a chair next to Jane.

"A whole school bus full of kids." Jane shuddered, feeling a cold so deep inside she thought it might never be warmed away. "My impression was of a deep hole. The bus just kept falling."

"It's after the twins," he said. "That's the only explanation."

"My fault."

"No."

"Why do you think that?" Angela asked, her voice almost normal again, but for a whispery rasp, as if she had screamed and strained her vocal cords before they arrived.

"I was just thinking that I slept really well, undisturbed sleep last night. We were at the Sanctum, far enough away the Voice couldn't get at me. It's been focusing on me, so it didn't feel the girls. I'm a stronger, hotter, maybe a louder power source. Maybe they weren't generating enough energy for it to be interested, or even notice them. With me gone, it felt them, probably got inside their heads, decided they were just starting to settle into their Gifts, no defenses, now is the time to take them." Jane's stomach twisted around the remains of the breakfast she had eaten in the Sanctum.

"If it couldn't feel the girls until you were gone..." Kurt pressed his fists against his temples. "Any chance it might be so busy with them, it doesn't know we're back?" He turned to Angela.

"Let's hope so." She had regained a little of her color. Reaching for Jane's hands, she caught hold of them, interweaving their fingers so they were palm-to-palm. "You have a strong enough link to the twins that you felt and saw what happened to them. Maybe they reached out to you, unknowing."

"Or maybe Big Ugly sent the impression to Jane, to set a trap." Kurt stepped back, fists jammed into his hips, frowning as he looked back and forth between them.

"What did you see?" Angela said. "Think hard. Focus on the smallest detail. I can feel all the ground shaking underneath Neighborlee. The power fluctuations make it hard to find what's hidden inside the churning."

Jane closed her eyes and concentrated, taking deep, loud breaths through her nose to fight the nausea. Angela's hands gave her an anchor to resist the sensation of simultaneously falling and spinning up through the air. Halting, feeling as if she pulled the words out with pliers, she described the cavern, the damp and cold and thick, filthy slickness.

When she finished, Jane cautiously opened her eyes. Angela still held onto her hands and she sat with head bowed, eyes closed, gnawing on her bottom lip. Slowly, she shook her head.

"What's wrong?" Kurt said, his voice gentle enough to make

Jane shiver. Again, it struck her that she didn't know him well enough to read all the subtleties of his face and body and his reactions, but she sensed he was afraid.

"I'm sorry." Angela slowly raised her head and opened her eyes. "You have a link with the girls. But Divine's shields me, perhaps blocks the link. I don't want to ask you—"

"To go outside and see what comes to me." Jane managed to smile and tugged her hands free. "For the girls. For all the kids. That's what we were born for, if you really think about it."

Kurt caught hold of her hand and she was grateful, though she really didn't need any support or his guidance to walk to the front door. Jane took a deep breath and braced for the first onslaught of terror, a return to the feeling of darkness, cold, filth, and falling.

It didn't come. She glanced back once as she stepped down from the porch. Angela stood in the doorway, watching them.

"You might need to get entirely off the property," she said. "I have an idea. We might need something to help us get to the children, and your description reminds me of something I read once ..." She frowned, her gaze going distant for a few moments. "Go on, and I will join you as soon as I can."

"I'm gonna call for reinforcements," Kurt said as they walked down the path to the fence across the front of the yard. He grimaced and looked up as an icy wind full of snow swirled down around them. "Well, duh. We left so fast we didn't get our coats. Here." He pulled out his phone, then let go of Jane's hand and wrapped his arm around her.

"I can do better." She activated the Ghost field enough to ward off the wind.

"Nice. Now—" His phone rang and he turned it so she could see Lanie's name on the display. "What's the word?" he said as he opened the connection.

"We just heard about a school bus vanishing. Any chance Jane got anything?" Lanie asked. "Any link with the twins?"

"And then some," he said. "We're at Divine's. Meet us in the park."

"I'll fly us," Jane said. "You talk."

"Marry me," he muttered, pressed a kiss against her forehead, stunning her thoughtless for a precious five seconds, and got to work filling Lanie in.

Jane felt the tingling of Lanie's Gift at work as she brought them in for a landing inside a stand of trees in the park in the center of town. As she made them visible again, Lanie's chair came sliding up the sidewalk faster than she had ever seen a wheelchair move, but her hands weren't on the wheels.

"What has she got— That's why Lanie is our fearless leader." Kurt had kept his arm around Jane until that moment. He stepped away, out of the field she used to shield them from the wind and snow, and went to meet Lanie.

Now Jane could see that she seemed to be bent over, holding something dark on her lap. A few more yards closer, and she guessed it was a thick bundle of material. Lanie tossed part of it to Kurt, and it unfolded, turning into a long coat.

"I borrowed some things from the Goodwill collection box behind our building, on the way out," Lanie explained. "No need for you two to freeze while we're looking for the kids."

"Thanks." Jane released the Ghost field and caught the coat Lanie threw at her. It was a pea coat and she muffled choked laughter. She had always wanted a pea coat. Then the sensation of thick, oily, filthy cold and damp wrapped around her. "Getting the signal." She went to her knees on the sidewalk and gagged, feeling as if the thick, dirty, icy oil tried to flow down her throat. "Duh. My field cut off the connection."

"It talked to you before, when you were flying," Kurt said. He dropped his coat and helped Jane put on hers. "Maybe it's distracted."

"The girls are probably putting up a good fight," Lanie said. "What do you see? What do you feel?"

Hello, darling, the Voice said. The elegance and humor had vanished. Jane hoped part of the snarl in the tones were from strain, that yes, Kelly and Kory were fighting the creature that kept them captive. *It's about time you were polite enough to listen when you're called.*

Polite? What do you call someone who takes what isn't offered? You've been draining me, all the while you were talking about sharing and working together. Don't go throwing stones when you're more guilty than anyone. What do you want?

You, of course. The children are delicious, but not what I need. Too much time and effort and waiting until they'd be useful. I'm tired of waiting. Come join them?

Jane gagged as the oily cold sensation overwhelmed her. She found herself clinging to the bar behind the driver's seat on the old school bus, peering through darkness. The sound of weeping came to her, barely able to penetrate the thick, oily cold that filled her senses. The longer and harder she concentrated, more details emerged. The children were slumped in their seats, on the floor, drenched and coated with darkness, all unconscious, just like the bus driver who lay in the doorstep well where she had fallen. All except for the source of the snuffling, weeping and gasping sounds. Jane pushed against the cold that solidified the air. It was like wading through lard. She sensed warmth up ahead, where the sounds came from.

A faint, rainbow-tinted flicker of light guided her, until she reached the seats two-thirds of the way to the back of the bus. Kelly and Kory clung to each other, huddling on the floor in front of their seat. Jane called their names, but they didn't seem to hear her.

I'll get you out, she promised, and stood up, looking around, trying to find something, anything, to give her a clue where the bus was trapped.

The darkness swirled around outside the bus, as if it was immersed in exactly what the air felt like — thick, cold, dirty oil. Jane focused on glimpses of movement that went counter to the swirls in the oily substance, straining her eyes until the ache in her temples and the back of her head grew strong enough to threaten to burst outward. What was that? Long lines, fading into darkness. Blunt ends, disturbing the swirling of the oily darkness. They stretched overhead, going from jagged-edged darkness, through the gap where the bus sat, to more darkness. They looked like...broken pipes?

She didn't want to leave the school bus, to go outside into that greater darkness, but she had to do it. She needed to find something that would tell her where the school bus had landed. Besides, she wasn't physically there. She wasn't there, so nothing could really hurt her. She wasn't —

"Jane?" Kurt wrapped his arm around her and lifted her to her feet. "Are you okay?"

She choked and spat, but it didn't take the filthy, oily feel and taste out of her mouth. "How long was I gone?"

"Gone where?" Lanie said. "You fell and Kurt picked you up."

"It felt like I was there, in the bus with the kids, for...twenty minutes maybe?"

"Where are they?" Kurt demanded. "Did you see anything?"

"I think so." Jane shared the details she could make out as he led her over to a park bench only a dozen or so feet away. Lanie glided over the snowy grass to join them.

"Does that do you any good?" she said, when Jane stumbled to a halt.

"Maybe. There's a legend, rumor, whatever you want to call it. Back when the town was still growing, while the quarry was still a quarry." Kurt turned and gestured out the western side of town, past the city hall and the slopes down into the park, toward the quarry. "There's an old sewer system. It got abandoned when they rebuilt the town." His expression grew grim. "When sinkholes opened up in the middle of streets."

"Previous attempts by Big Ugly to get through?" Lanie mused.

"Who knows? The thing is, they covered up a lot of it, threw reinforcing material across the holes. Ford Longfellow knows all about the town history, and he has schematics and blueprints and old surveys. Some parts of town never should have been built on again, but people did, because a lot of records were lost in a fire around the turn of the century."

"Big Ugly just yanked the school bus down through the street, into a cavern that's already there," Jane said. "You have an idea where that cavern might be?"

"I'll have to check with Ford," he said.

"We'll check the school bus route," Lanie said. "Go on." She pulled out her cell phone without waiting to see if Kurt would go.

"Are you gonna—" he began.

"I'll be fine when the kids are safe," Jane said. "Go."

She wished he would have kissed her again, even if it was just on the forehead, but she was glad when he hurried down the sidewalk. He pulled out his cell phone as he hurried. Fortunately, her spa wasn't too far away. He could probably get to his truck before he finished his phone call.

Lanie got the information she wanted from a friend in the school administration building before Jane felt fully recovered from her first visit to the cavern. Despite feeling a little queasy, she stood up when Lanie closed her cell phone and tucked it in her coat pocket. They shared a grim, determined nod and Lanie turned her chair around and led the way out of the park.

The transportation department of the Neighborlee School System had its routes down to a science, knowing where each bus should be at any moment during the morning and afternoon pickup and drop-off routine. This gave Lanie enough data to approximate where the bus had vanished, based on what Jane and Kurt had experienced, and when. It also helped that when the bus was five minutes late, the next family on the route called to find out if there was a problem. The disappearance occurred on a stretch of non-residential road running north of town, parallel with the quarries.

"Should have guessed," Lanie said, gesturing at Eden, seeming to crouch on the horizon ahead of them.

It took a moment for Jane to connect the pieces and confirmed her theory that the weak spot where Big Ugly tried to break through was physically underneath Eden. Close to the spot where the bus had vanished.

"This has to be it," she agreed, looking across the stretch of too-quiet road, to the snow-covered strip of park ground with a tall fence between it and the drop-off into the quarries. There was something menacing about the playground equipment sitting there with nothing behind it but open sky. She shivered despite the warmth of the pea coat, remembering riding the bus to school along this very route. She had always tried to sit on the side of the bus that wouldn't face the drop-off. Her imagination had been too strong back then. She had envisioned the ground crumbling away, devouring the park, and the bus tumbling over and over, down the steep slope to the quarries a few hundred feet below.

Ready to talk, darling?

I'm not your darling, Jane snarled. She shook her head when Lanie reached out to her, concern creasing her face. She refused to be weak and shaky any longer.

Oh, but you are. For all eternity. You and I shall have such fun. All you need to do is relax and enjoy what comes next. It's all up to you. I don't much care either way how quickly you decide, since I know I will win in the end. However, since you find something endearing about the children, you might want to hurry.

What are you going to do to them?

It's not what I'm going to do. It's what I'm **not** *going to do. And what you won't do unless you come down here and decide.*

Not going to do what? Jane growled.

Come down. Straight down.

The gleeful satisfaction in the Voice made her shudder while fury heat shot through her.

"This is the place," she told Lanie. "I don't know how you'll break through, if I can't get back out with the kids, but..."

"Jane?"

What **aren't** *you going to do?*

They're such filthy little things, they really do need a bath. The Voice chuckled, and an image filled her mind of all the leaking pipes suddenly gushing, shattering, spilling down water that washed away the thick, icy, dirty oily substance.

That wasn't oil. It was time, slowed so a few seconds lasted what felt like hours. The Voice had slowed time, but any moment now it would resume its normal pace, the pipes would burst and fill the cavern and flood it, drowning the children.

Jane blurted what she feared to Lanie, called up the Ghost field, and dropped. Down through pavement. Through solid ground. Down through a tangled net of old steel girders and rebar and concrete and rusting iron pipes.

Her first impression was that there was no room. When she had been inside the bus and cavern before, in her vision, the impression was vastness. Now that she was physically here, pushing through air that was like gritty, icy syrup, even inside the Ghost field, she saw pipes and concrete and dirt and rock pressed up tight against the bus. There was literally no room to turn around. The Voice had managed to pull the bus down into the hole, maybe move the hole around to accommodate the bus.

She heard creaking, felt the trembling through the fabric of the bus, the scraping of metal and stone fighting to occupy the same space. Jane shuddered, envisioning the stone and rebar and girders pushing back into the spot where they belonged, where the bus didn't belong. She could almost see the carnage of compression, the shattering and bursting as flesh and bone and blood lost the battle.

That wasn't water about to burst out of those pipes. That was reality flowing back into the shape and space where it belonged.

Why couldn't the Voice pull itself into Earth's dimension and reality, if it had the power to do this? Jane shuddered again. Did all this power come from what it had sucked out of her?

Come now, darling, don't be arrogant. Though for such magnificent creatures as us, destined to rule, arrogance is necessary. Healthy. No, this isn't from your power. I used that up in moments as soon as I drained it out of you. This is fresh, untapped, untrained. Untamed power.

The twins. Jane leaped forward, down the aisle of the bus to reach the twins.

She *tried* to.

The air thickened around her. The rippling light flared. She heard one girl whimper. She understood. The Voice drained the girls to fuel what it was doing. They had no understanding of their power, no training to help them resist. She remembered how they had clung together, light swirling around them. They defended themselves the only way they knew how, totally unconscious.

The energy they expended fed the Voice and kept her away.

Come, darling. Time to get smart. You'll quite enjoy being queen of the universe. All the universes. Just let go.

You let go, Jane snarled. She snatched up two girls in the curve of one arm, a boy from the other side of the school bus aisle in the other, and shot up, through stone and iron and dirt.

She gagged and collapsed to her knees as she emerged aboveground. Hands pulled the children from her arms and she rolled onto her back, struggling to breathe. The sun was so bright, piercing her body with heat and light.

Eleven children and the driver remained on the bus, according to the information from Lanie's friend at the school board office. She had to go back. Where was Kurt? He could take children too.

"He's on his way," Angela said. When had she gotten there? She helped Jane sit up and wiped damp hair out of her face. "We can't go down with you, but we can help get the children up."

"No, you can't. I can barely hold up the field around myself." Jane staggered to her feet. Time raced by belowground. Any moment now, the Voice might let the crushing begin, just to be nasty. To punish her for not giving in.

"Don't ask how." Angela guided Jane away from the edge of the road. "Just believe that it will work. Look up for help."

She pointed at what looked like a frame from a painting lying in the snow and grit a few steps off the side of the road. Dark water with rainbow streaks swirled around in the frame, rippling in waves, back and forth. It reminded Jane of the material that made up the Wishing Ball, but liquid.

"We could see you in it," Lanie said. She was on her knees in the snow, both hands pressing hard on the frame. "Maybe if you can see us, you can hand the kids up to us through it. I'll pull, and you push. There's no maybe about it working. It has to."

Yeah, it has to. Jane took a few more deep breaths, then stepped back from Angela's support.

The crunching of tires on the gravel at the side of the road startled her and she turned, praying it was Kurt coming to join them. Her heart sank when she saw the black-and-white SUV. The biggest policeman she had ever seen climbed out.

"Came as soon as I heard," the officer said.

"Gordon, this is Jane Wilson. She owns the new spa. Gordon belongs to my Star Trek club," Lanie said with a crooked grin. "That means totally freaky won't blow his circuits."

"Uh huh, thought so," Gordon said. He nodded to Jane. "Okay, Captain, what do you need me to do?"

"Start thinking of a good story to explain whatever happens next," Angela said. "Jane?"

Jane shook her head. She would wait for later to ask for all the explanations, the subtexts of said and unsaid. She was just grateful one of the local cops would be there to support them and cover up something so huge, even all her Ghost powers couldn't handle it.

If she had any Ghost powers left when this rescue was done.

She saluted them, took a deep breath, and descended.

Stop fighting, the Voice said. The raspy undertones were stronger. At the same time...was it possible it sounded weaker? *Give in and give yourself to me, and all this will stop. Stop wasting your energy.*

Stop wasting what you want to use for yourself, you mean. Jane focused on the bus driver. The woman was thin, with elfin features, elegantly long legs, narrow hips — and felt like she weighed about a thousand pounds as Jane tried to pull her up out of the stair step well where she had fallen.

She couldn't breathe. The pressure against the Ghost field made her feel as if she would be crushed in another moment. It contracted around her, tightening. All she had to do was release the field and she would be able to breathe.

"Whatever feels right, whatever feels easy when you're in crisis moments," Beau had said multiple times, *"is probably the worst thing you could do. If you think you're going to drown, that's when you take the deep breath. Anyone strong enough, Gifted enough to fight your Gifts, probably has the talent to make you believe the opposite of what is real."*

Letting down her Ghost field would let the Voice take over.

Of course.

Jane almost laughed, but she had no breath to spare as she pulled harder on the bus driver. The Ghost field protected her, kept the Voice from taking over.

Why was she pulling on this woman? Why did she seem to have pointy ears? What was she doing down here?

She couldn't breathe. If she could get some air, she could think more clearly. She could remember.

"No," Jane said, and inhaled as deeply as she could. She turned her head away from the woman and threw herself backwards.

They came out of the stair step well like a cork sliding from the neck of a bottle. Jane laughed as she staggered back. She wrapped one arm around the bus driver and turned to look for a child to lift up to safety.

Look up. Someone had told her to look up. She couldn't remember who, but...

Her neck hurt as she tipped her head back. Like something didn't want her to look up. So that meant she *should* look up.

"Freaky," she muttered, seeing black rainbow ripples in the ceiling of the bus. She was pretty sure school buses didn't have reflecting pools in them. Especially not in the roofs.

It wasn't a reflecting pool, was it, if she couldn't see herself? Come to think of it, she could see someone, maybe two someones.

Angela and Lanie. Jane shuddered at the realization that she was forgetting what she was supposed to be doing. She took a deep breath, just because someone had told her to do the opposite, so if she thought she couldn't breathe, that meant...

Yeah, her lungs filled with air and the thudding in her head softened and she could think.

"Upsy daisy," she muttered, and caught the bus driver by her belt, lifting her up. Jane shuddered as the woman's head vanished into the rainbow swirls of glistening black, then her shoulders, then suddenly it sucked her upwards and she vanished.

What are you doing!?!

The thick, oily substance of halted time rippled and swirled around her. Jane had an impression of a giant child shaking a snow globe before hurling it to the ground to smash it and send all the glitter water and plastic figures spilling out.

She took a deep breath and snatched up the closest child. Lifted her into the darkness and rainbows. Suction took the child from her hands before she got to the end of her reach. Jane let go and turned, looking for the next. A boy holding a Yoda doll. Breathe deep. Pick up. Lift. Shove into the rainbows. Breathe deep. Turn. Find another child.

The shaking grew stronger. The ripples knocked her off her feet, but the suction pulled up on the boy she had shoved blindly toward the rainbows in the ceiling. Darkness spun around her. She felt tingling in her fingers and toes and the Ghost field contracted so it pressed against her skin. She couldn't breathe. There was no air around her. She had been shrink-wrapped and couldn't breathe.

Shrink-wrapped. A giggle escaped her. Probably she was going brain-dead from lack of oxygen.

Stop! The Voice roared the word over and over.

The bus creaked. Support struts rippled, bending inward like modeling clay falling under its own weight.

"Jane. Come on, Jane. Just a few more."

She didn't know the source of the voice, somewhere behind her, but the man sounded nice. He sounded warm. Strong.

Another hallucination. Another trick of the Voice. She had to fight. She had to concentrate on what she knew was real: she was alone in this bus about to be shredded by reality smashing back into the space where it belonged. All the children were unconscious, frozen in time, and it was up to her to get them out.

Chapter Sixteen

"Jane, come on! It's okay!" Hands burned her skin. They reached through the Ghost field, warmth shocking her with the realization of how bitterly cold she was. Her blood had turned to syrup. "Breathe. Come on, baby, breathe! It's okay."

Breathe? She inhaled, despite knowing she would just inhale the plastic bag that clung to her like a second... No, that was air.

"Kurt?"

"Yeah, it's me." He shook her. "Come on. Four more. Get that one."

Jane blinked hard as the blackness faded. Kurt lifted a little girl, thrust her with ease into the black rainbows. He held another in his other arm. As the first was sucked up, he shifted the other.

Jane took another deep breath—why had she forgotten to breathe?—and bent to pick up another child, a girl. She staggered backwards, as something hazy gathered around her head again.

Right. She'd forgotten to breathe.

Breathe.

Bend.

Lift. Breathe.

Hand the child to Kurt. Breathe.

"I can't find any more." She choked on the sudden need to burst into tears.

"Where are the twins?" Kurt caught hold of her shoulders and shook her.

For a few seconds she just looked at him and blinked. *Twins? What twins?*

Kelly and Kory. Right. They were right over...

"They're gone. I know I didn't lift them." Jane took a deep breath. Her head cleared a little.

"Give them up!" Kurt turned and glared out through the front of the bus.

"I don't have them."

"Not you. Big Ugly."

She shuddered, positive he had gone crazy. Who was he

talking about? It was just them in the bus. She had lost the twins.

How could she have lost the twins? They were right...there?

Jane squinted, focusing on the place under the seat where she knew the twins had been. They were holding onto each other, wrapped in rainbow streaks of light. They should still be there.

"He's hiding them from us," Kurt said.

"Who?"

"The twins."

"No, who's hiding them?"

"Jane!" He grabbed her shoulders, making her Ghost field buzz against her skin where his hands pressed hardest. "Think! The kids are down here, the bus is down here, because Big Ugly dragged them down here. To trap you. To force you to give yourself up to it. Trade you for them. He's hiding them."

"No..." She took deep breaths, fighting to clear her mind, knowing he was right, but he was wrong, too. "They're hiding."

That was it. The twins were hiding. They were afraid. They sensed the power at work here, sensed the power trying to drain them dry.

That was why the Voice sounded weak and strained. It... He... They... Whatever the Voice was, it wasn't getting energy from the twins. They were fighting. They had hidden themselves.

"They're here." She threw herself forward, fighting the syrupy feel in the air that sucked on her, dragging her backwards. That had to be a sign she was going in the right direction — the enemy didn't want her going near them.

The support struts in the ceiling of the bus creaked, the sound rising an octave, turning into a squeal.

"You can't have them!" She lunged into the space between the seats where she had seen the twins. "Kelly! Kory! You have to hear me!"

Jane bounced. A clang resounded in her ears. The energy surrounding her buzzed, prickling, flashing at the corners of her eyes.

"I think they're there," Kurt said.

She grinned, baring her teeth at him, and knelt just short of where she had almost landed. Jane thrust her arms into the empty space and gasped as a sensation of fire and wasp stings raced up and down her arms. It crawled up her arms, higher as she kept pressing, into the bubble of energy.

"Kelly!" Kurt shouted. His voice reverberated in Jane's ears as he pressed his hands into her shoulders. "Kory! You gotta listen."

"Mr. Kurt?" The little girl voice sounded faint, far off and sleepy.

Jane shuddered, knowing that had to be dangerous. What happened if the girls fell asleep?

"Not gonna happen," she growled, and spread her arms, pushing herself face-first into the energy, despite the sensation that her flesh was crisping right off her bones.

Ghostly images of the girls, clinging together, faded in and out through the haze filling her eyes. They turned to her, moving with glacial slowness. Jane wrapped her arms around them, though she was sobbing with the pain.

"Got them!"

"Got you," Kurt grunted, and shoved her up in the air.

Jane nearly screamed with the pressure, as something dragged her down while Kurt lifted her up. She felt squeezed flat. Then the bubble around the girls popped, shattering with a sour chiming that grew louder with every second. She lifted her arms, shoving them into the black swirling rainbow.

A howl rose up from the chiming, filling her ears, bursting her eardrums, shattering her bones to dust. Through it all, she felt Kurt holding onto her.

"Go, go, go!" he shouted.

Go where?

The pressure sucked her down through the crumpling metal floor of the bus. That meant she should go up. Jane pushed off, even as the metal collapsed under her feet. Through the furious howling, she heard the scream of metal and the chiming of glass shattering.

Then suddenly silence, as rock and concrete and antique iron pipes scraped at her fading shield. Cold surrounded her, but it felt as bracing and refreshing and warm as summer sunshine compared to the dank and damp and oily thick freezing that had sucked at her bones and brain.

She fell into a snowbank, gasping. It was like she had to learn to breathe all over again. She shuddered and scrubbed at her arms and chest and face, trying to wipe away the oily residue.

"Move, move, move!" a man shouted, just as the ground

heaved upwards under her.

Hands grabbed her, dragging her farther into the snow. Jane couldn't get the breath to protest. She heard children's voices and then sirens, and a rumbling underneath everything that somehow helped to pull her out of the exhausted, empty, wrung-out feeling.

Breathe. You keep forgetting to breathe.

"Hey." Kurt helped her sit up.

Correction. She was sitting on his lap. Jane snuggled down against him, soaking up the warmth that surged out of him like a furnace. Somehow she got her eyes open.

"Pretty close call, huh?" He pointed, and she followed the direction of his finger.

The road wasn't there anymore. Jagged edges pointed up through the snow and a haze of dirt and debris flung up in the air. She saw the ends of pipes, chunks of concrete, and blackness where there had been asphalt for a good fifty yards of road.

"Well, that kind of makes it easy," a man said. Footsteps came up behind them. Jane recognized the voice as the man who had shouted for them to move.

"Hey, Gordon." Kurt slid Jane off his lap, but only long enough to get to his feet and pull her up against him. "Have you met Jane?"

"Oh, yeah. Welcome to Neighborlee." Officer Gordon Priebe nodded to Jane, grinning.

"Makes what easy?" she said, her thoughts snagging on his inexplicable words.

"Well, explaining what happened to the bus, how you got the kids out. We'll just tell part of the truth. The bus fell into a sinkhole. You and Kurt got yourselves banged up getting the kids out of the bus before it collapsed completely. Kind of convenient everybody was unconscious."

"Convenient nothing," Kurt said.

"That's just how things work out in Neighborlee," Angela said, coming over to join them. She held out both hands to Jane.

The moment her hands touched Angela's, Jane found it easier to breathe. The heavy, oily, dragging, clogged sensation evaporated. She lifted her head and looked around. Emergency trucks were just starting to pull up. The school children sat in huddled bunches, holding onto each other. Many of them were crying, most looking like they had just awakened.

"The twins?" Jane asked, as Angela let go of her. She still felt empty, hollow in her bones, like a breath of wind could blow her away. Funny, but she didn't mind.

"Over here," Lanie said. She had both girls cuddled up on her lap in her wheelchair.

"How are they?"

"Exhausted. The air wasn't very good in the sinkhole," Angela said. "Everybody is suffering from tainted air, probably all sorts of noxious gases. Hallucinations."

"And how about the big bad hallucination that was giving us such a hard time?" Kurt caught up to Jane and wrapped his arm around her waist. He pitched his voice low, including only Angela and Gordon.

"Uh huh. That thing from Eden?" The police officer looked Jane over, head to foot, and let out a low whistle. "Welcome to Neighborlee."

~~~~~

The cleanup seemed to take forever. Jane found it ironic that everyone was bundled up and taken to Eden. Only Gordon showed any hesitation about crossing the threshold. She remembered hearing that Gordon had been let in on the secret of interdimensional invaders lurking under Neighborlee, during the troubles at New Year's.

Gina dug out blankets and then all sorts of odds and ends of clothes that had been lost or discarded in the building, to replace everyone's muddy, wet clothes. Her staff scurried around, making hot chocolate and pulling out cookies. The staff nurse took each child into the infirmary for an examination while they waited for parents and NCH authorities to show up.

Jane was glad that Angela and Gordon had come up with their cover story. It left her free to curl up in two blankets and oversized neon pink sweats (very easy to understand why someone deliberately forgot them in the women's locker room) and pretend to be somewhat in shock, to avoid answering questions.

She wasn't completely pretending. There was a lot to process, figuring out what had happened. She had nearly been trapped. Thank goodness Kurt had been close enough he could tap into her Gift and join her. Jane shuddered as the sound and feel of the bus collapsing in on itself reverberated through her mind and memory.

What if she had been caught in there?

What if the twins had been caught in there?

Would they have been caught in there? The more she thought about it, the more sure she was their twin-bond, their shared powers and concentration had kept the bus from collapsing. It wasn't anything the Voice had done. He might even have been trying to kill the twins, or using the bus incident to trap her.

"What if the twins did it, and not the Voice?" she murmured, when the police officer who was taking the incident report walked away to talk to one of the emergency responders.

"Did what? Pushed them down into the hole?" Kurt grinned and started to shake his head. She saw the exact moment his expression froze, meaning he realized it was possible the twins, with their untrained, awakening Gifts might have pushed the bus into the cavern under the road totally by accident. He swallowed hard. "Those kids need to go to school."

"How are the Old Poops going to get them out of here with so much attention focused on them?"

"Wait a couple days, then have them show up and claim they saw the girls' picture in the paper and think they're the spitting image of a runaway granddaughter and..." He trailed off, eyes narrowing, while Jane fought not to burst out laughing. "They probably have much better stories than that already in their files, I'm guessing."

"Oh, yeah. Airtight. Hard to fight. But we still haven't determined if they're Lost Kids or not."

"Jane Wilson, you are the most interesting girlfriend I've ever had."

"Uh huh." She closed her eyes and leaned back against the wall.

"What's that supposed to mean?"

"So it's official? You and me, boyfriend and girlfriend?"

"Hey, you can't go through what we went through and just walk away. I mean, you know, facing the Old Poops like I did. You owe me."

A giggle escaped her as a snort.

"So...have we had an official date yet?"

"Around here..." Angela stepped up in front of them. Jane opened her eyes to see her holding out a tray of sandwiches. "Considering what we have to face as guardians of this town, what you two went through qualifies as a wonderful date."

"Hate to admit it, but she's right," Kurt said.

"So, did we win?" Jane asked, softening her voice.

"Only time will tell." Angela moved the tray of sandwiches closer. "Eat up. We have a lot of work ahead of us."

"Us." Jane smiled and leaned in closer to Kurt. The brilliant grin that lit his face, even his eyes, put a funny, churning warmth in her middle. "That sounds really good."

END

Neighborlee, Ohio

(Title, Original Title, Release Date)

Confessions of a Lost Kid (Growing Up Neighborlee) 05/20
Semi-Pseudo-Superheroes (Dorm Rats) 07/20
Virtually London (London Holiday) 09/20
Living Proof (that no good deed goes unpunished) (Living Proof) 11/20
Night of the Living Proof, 01/21
Quitting the Hero Biz (Hero Blues) 03/21
Bride of the Living Proof, 05/21
Shrunk: The Exile of Maurice (Divine's Emporium) 07/21
Return of the Living Proof, 09/21
Allergic to Mistletoe (Have Yourself a Faerie Little Christmas) 11/21
Dawn of the Living Proof, 01/22
Angela's Knight (Divine Knight) 03/22
The Living Proof Gets the Blues, 05/22

ABOUT THE AUTHOR

On the road to publication, Michelle fell into fandom in college and has 40+ stories in various SF and fantasy universes. She has a bunch of useless degrees in theater, English, film/communication, and writing. Even worse, she has over 100 books and novellas with multiple small presses, in science fiction and fantasy, YA, suspense, women's fiction, and sub-genres of romance.

Her official launch into publishing came with winning first place in the Writers of the Future contest in 1990. She was a finalist in the EPIC Awards competition multiple times, winning with *Lorien* in 2006 and *The Meruk Episodes, I-V,* in 2010, and was a finalist in the Realm Award competition, in conjunction with the Realm Makers convention.

Her training includes the Institute for Children's Literature; proofreading at an advertising agency; and working at a community newspaper. She is a tea snob and freelance edits for a living (MichelleLevigne@gmail.com for info/rates), but only enough to give her time to write. Her newest crime against the literary world is to be co-managing editor at Mt. Zion Ridge Press and launching the publishing co-op, Ye Olde Dragon Books. Be afraid ... be very afraid.

www.Mlevigne.com
www.MichelleLevigne.blogspot.com
@MichelleLevigne

Also by Michelle L. Levigne

Guardians of the Time Stream: 4-book Steampunk series
The Match Girls: Humorous inspirational romance series starting with **A Match (Not) Made in Heaven**
Sarai's Journey: A 2-book biblical fiction series

Tabor Heights: 20-book inspirational small town romance series.

Quarry Hall: 11-book women's fiction/suspense series

For Sale: Wedding Dress. Never Used: inspirational romance

Crooked Creek: Fun Fables About Critters and Kids: Children's short stories.

Do Yourself a Favor: Tips and Quips on the Writing Life. A book of writing advice.

Killing His Alter-Ego: contemporary romance/suspense, taking place in fandom.

The Commonwealth Universe: SF series, 25 books and growing

The Hunt: 5-book YA fantasy series

Faxinor: Fantasy series, 4 books and growing

Wildvine: Fantasy series, 14 books when all released

Neighborlee: Humorous fantasy series

Zygradon: 5-book Arthurian fantasy series

AFV Defender: SF adventure series, space opera.